If He Wakes

Zoe Lea lives in the Lake District with her husband, their two children, three dogs and peregrine falcons. She has previously worked as a teacher, photographer and freelance journalist and is a writer in the day and a reader by night. *If He Wakes* is her debut novel.

if
he
wakes

ZOE LEA

CANELO

First published in the the United Kingdom in 2018 by Canelo

This edition published in the United Kingdom in 2020 by Canelo

Canelo Digital Publishing Limited
31 Helen Road
Oxford OX2 0DF
United Kingdom

A CIP catalogue record for this book is available from the British Library.

Print ISBN 978 1 78863 404 5
Ebook ISBN 978 1 78863 098 6

Look for more great books at www.canelo.co

Printed and bound in Great Britain by Clays Ltd, Elcograf S.p.A.

To Stephen

Tuesday

Cloudy skies with a cold wind and periods of rain.

1

Rachel

My world fell apart on a cold, rainy Tuesday afternoon in November.

I didn't make a sound when it happened. Sitting outside the cheap hotel I was close enough to see it, but too far away to be involved. I was trying to get a better view of him, craning my neck and cursing the long line of cars in front of me. I'd never followed my husband before and wasn't used to hiding.

I'd lost him when we entered the retail park. Took a right and got caught up in the traffic coming out of the hotel. Queuing for the exit, I'd watched his car go over to the fast food restaurant fifty metres away.

And then the hit and run happened.

It was over in seconds. If I hadn't been stationary and staring so hard I would've missed it.

A car suddenly speeding.

A body flying over a windscreen and landing in a crumpled mess on the ground.

The sound of the engine screeching as it left the carnage and went towards the dual carriageway.

I took in a shocked breath and held it. I'd stared at the figure on the ground, which now looked like a discarded pile of clothes and asked myself if it had really happened. *Did I just see that?*

The windscreen wiper blades scraped against the glass as I watched the aftermath in horror. People in the vicinity dropped their shopping and ran forwards. Someone began to perform first aid, falling to their knees and putting their hands on the body. Figures ran in and out of the restaurant and a growing crowd quickly surrounded the scene and obscured my view. Staff darted about in their red caps and aprons accompanied by screams and shouts as the blades of my wipers grated through the scene. The hot air blowing from the fan heaters was suddenly stifling and I couldn't catch my breath. I needed air.

Those around me began to get out of their cars and I went to get out of mine. I undid my seat-belt and turned toward the door, but I'd forgotten my car was in gear with the engine still running. As my foot released the clutch, my other foot caught the accelerator and the car rushed forward in a shocking way straight into the back of a silver Mini.

My chest hit the steering wheel hard making the horn sound continuously and my head connected with something sharp, but it was my foot that made me scream. The heel of my shoe had broken on one of the pedals, as had something inside my ankle.

A man in a crumpled suit opened the passenger door, his eyes still on the commotion at the opposite side of the retail park.

'Bloody hell,' he said as he eased me off the steering wheel, releasing the horn, 'you alright?'

He pulled on the handbrake and his eyes went to my ankle.

3

'Good God!' he shouted turning around. 'We need an ambulance over here!'

I went to say how that wasn't necessary but was sick all over the passenger seat instead.

–

Because of the hit and run that had happened minutes earlier, everyone treated my minor accident with much more attention than it deserved.

The man in the suit barked instructions to the other drivers who had been queuing for the exit. Cars were moved. The young woman I'd rear ended needed someone to look at her neck. The hotel staff were informed, hot tea and a useless first aid kit was brought out.

There was much discussion about whether I should be moved whilst waiting for the paramedics, but when I started to get out of the car myself, they all jumped into action.

I insisted that I was taken into the hotel. I wanted to be out of my car with its stench of vomit and as far away as possible from the horror of the hit and run and its aftermath. People were watching as if it were a show, shivering in the cold, blatantly rubbernecking.

I was carried in by a man wearing motorbike leathers that creaked heavily as he moved. He placed me down on a wicker chair in the reception area and another one was hastily brought over for my ankle. I screamed loudly as they raised my leg to rest on it.

An elderly couple by the reception desk, in the process of checking out, stared at me. The expression on their faces told me how bad I looked. Vomit on my chin and blouse, make-up running down my face and one leg of my suede trousers hoisted up around my knee, and my damaged ankle, bloody and bruised and an odd shape. I wiped my face, tried to pull at my trousers, hide my bare leg, but it was useless. I was shaking too much to do anything.

A few of the hotel staff insisted they stay with me until the ambulance arrived, an older lady and a teenage boy with a shiny chin. They gave me sympathetic looks and offered me tea, coffee, water. I'd shaken my head. The thought of drinking, of consuming anything was ludicrous. I could barely speak and I was cold; in my rush leaving I'd left my coat at home. But I couldn't tell them that, I couldn't form a single clear thought.

The older lady who had been by my side, left to help with the growing congregation of tourists that were gathering around the reception desk and I was glad. I wanted to be left alone. I prayed the teenage boy would wander off. I listened as she informed everyone that there would be a delay if they needed to get their car. Someone asked if the ambulance had arrived for the person hit over at the fast food restaurant. Someone asked if it was a hit and run. Someone asked if the person hit had been killed and a cold sweat broke out over me, making my shaking pronounced. *Had I just watched someone die?*

'I'm guessing you saw it then,' the teenager asked as the tourists dissipated from the reception area, 'that's what made you go into the back of that car. You saw it all.'

He was looking out of the glass doors, toward the direction of the restaurant where the crowd was. He started to bite his thumbnail as a galloping panic overtook me.

5

'I didn't see anything.' My voice came out in fits and starts, it sounded alien. 'I wasn't looking out of my window.'

He stopped biting and stared at me.

'I was fixing the radio,' I told him. 'I had my head down.'

'You didn't see?' he frowned. 'You didn't know it had happened?'

I tried to turn away from him, to change position, the action sending shooting pains to my ankle. I made a low groan but was glad of the pain, glad of the distraction.

'Didn't know what had happened?'

The woman I'd crashed into was young. Pretty. Her face was impeccably made up, her hair groomed as if she were on her way to a film set when I'd gone into the back of her. Since the accident she'd had a mobile to her ear and she stared down at me with a kind of disgusted pity. I had a fourteen-year-old daughter that looked at me much the same, it was all hair flicking and rolling eyes. The thought of my daughter, Katie, brought a fresh wave of adrenaline that hit my stomach and rolled up through my chest and for a second I thought I might faint.

'The hit and run,' the teenager said as I struggled to gain control, 'she didn't see it.'

She looked down at me and I took a deep breath. My chest shuddered.

'I'm sorry,' I said quietly. 'I'm so, so sorry.'

They stared at me a moment in silence, both of them, then she gave a little shrug.

'I'd have crashed into the back of someone if I'd have seen that,' she said. 'Don't beat yourself up.'

'I didn't see it!' the loudness of my voice surprised us all and I raised my hands slightly in shock. 'I'm sorry,' I said.

'I'm sorry.' I began to cry, losing my battle to stay in charge of my emotions, 'So sorry, but I didn't see anything. I wasn't watching. I just want to go home.'

I tugged at my trouser leg, I wanted to hide my ankle that was changing shape. It had increased in size since I'd been sitting, a large bulge to one side. It looked like somebody else's ankle, it didn't belong to me. I didn't belong in the hotel lobby, I shouldn't have been there. I should be at home in my warm kitchen, listening to the radio and filling the kettle. This was all wrong.

The young girl put her hand on my shoulder and I flinched at her touch.

'It's my sister's car anyway,' she said, her voice soft, 'and she won't care; she's in Tenerife.'

I looked up at her sympathetic face. She gave me a small smile, squeezing her eyes to convey a kind of visual hug, before taking her attention back to her phone. I watched her expertly navigate the screen, swiping and tapping and ran a hand over my wet cheeks.

'Could I use that?' I asked. 'It's just, I need to call home. I've not got my mobile and I need to call them.'

She paused for a moment, her finger hovering over the screen.

'I need to speak with Della, to see if…' I took a breath, swallowed down a lump of panic, 'to tell her what's happened. I don't have my phone and the ambulance will be here soon.'

She paused for a moment, the teenage boy to the side of us shifted his weight and she felt at her neck. She looked out of the window toward the fast food restaurant where the drama was still being played out, and then handed me her phone.

'I'll need your insurance details,' she said as I took it from her, 'and your name and address.' I nodded as I tapped. It was answered on the fourth ring.

'Della?'

'Rachel?'

I closed my eyes at the sound of her voice and took a moment to steady myself.

'Della, I've been in an accident. It's not serious, but I can't drive and they've called an ambulance.' My voice wobbled. 'In fact, I think I may have broken something.'

There was a shocked silence.

'Oh Rachel!' Della's voice was high. 'Are you alright? Where are you?'

'The retail park,' I told her. 'The one near Grosvenor Square.'

'Shall I come?' Della asked. 'I could speak to…'

'No,' I said quickly, stopping her, 'you don't need to. The ambulance will be here soon. It's just,' I paused, rallying myself. 'Della, are you alone? Phil? He didn't come back, did he? He's not…'

There was a moment of silence.

'Phil's in London,' she said and relief flooded through me. *Phil was in London.* 'Do you want me to call him?'

'No!'

The young woman in front of me flinched at the sharpness of my voice, her hand reaching for her neck as she did so.

'Don't bother Phil with this. No, but could you give Jessica a call and tell her what's happened and be there when Katie…' I took a sharp intake of breath as I remembered, 'Katie's coming home early! I wrote her a note this morning, she didn't want to do hockey so I wrote to the school saying she had a dentist appointment. She'll be catching the two thirty bus, could you…'

'You've told me,' Della said. 'Katie's catching the early bus and then dropping in at the library. She's walking from there.'

'I did?' I closed my eyes. A distant memory of hastily made arrangements discussed over breakfast amidst the busy morning rush came back to me. Katie pleading with me to miss games, Jessica running around for her course work, Phil leaving early for London as Suzie phoned to tell me of an exciting meeting. I remembered saying goodbye to him, how he kissed me breezily on the cheek before he left, a piece of buttered toast in his mouth, Katie singing something annoying as he drove away.

'Rachel?'

I opened my eyes.

'You still there?'

'Della.' My voice was thin. I squeezed the phone, took a deep breath, concentrated on what needed to be said. 'Would you call Suzie for me?'

'Suzie?'

'I haven't got my phone. Could you…' I paused, wiped my eyes. The teenage boy produced a tissue and I took it gratefully. 'Could you ask Suzie to meet me at the hospital?'

'Suzie?' I could hear the surprise in Della's voice. 'Of course. I'll call her. You sure you don't want me to call Phil?'

'No. No, don't bother Phil with this, not when he's in London.'

The young woman stepped forward. 'Oh and Della, could you get my insurance details and give them to this woman? I drove into the back of her car and can't

9

remember what company I'm with. They're in the office, in the cabinet by the window.'

I passed the phone back and watched the young woman walk to the reception desk for a pen and paper. I shivered, speaking to Della had made it real, made it harder and I put my arms around myself. A few Spanish tourists had gathered at the side of us, small rucksacks in their hands, staring out of the glass doors, over to the restaurant. Over to where it had happened. They were speaking quickly to each other, rapid little words and I followed their gaze.

From where I was sitting, I couldn't see the fast food restaurant, I could only see people looking at it. Small groups gathered on the car park, shaking their heads, hands in their pockets. Some were in cars, waiting to get on with their day, impatiently moving forward past my broken car that had been moved into the disabled spot by the hotel doors.

'My mate broke her ankle,' the young woman said as she came back toward me. 'It was twelve weeks before she got rid of the crutches. She did it in six inch stilettos.' She looked at the court shoe on my left foot with the small kitten heel.

The glass doors opened sending an icy blast of air over us and a man with a name tag and the same uniform as the teenager walked through.

'Police have arrived,' he said as he approached the reception desk. 'Ambulance should be here any second.' He went over to the Spanish tourists and started to explain something to them, a map was brought out and he pointed to it.

'I heard they were thrown into the air,' the teenager said in almost a whisper and my shaking increased. 'They were caught head on. So either the driver didn't know someone was there, or whatever, but he just like… BAM!'

I lifted my hands and looked at them, my wedding ring catching the light, the tremors apparent in my fingers. I made my hands into fists and put them up to my eyes.

'Who would do that?' the young woman asked, almost absently. 'Who would do something like that and just drive off?'

The image of the body flying over the windscreen played out in my mind. The way it flew up and over. I wasn't anywhere near enough to have heard it, but in the replay I heard a soft crunch as it hit the windscreen. The breaking of bones. My stomach curled in on itself.

'CCTV'll get him,' the teenager said and my shaking threatened to turn into convulsions. I put my arms around myself again, tight. I tensed my muscles against the movement.

'It's all recorded around here,' he pointed vaguely in the air. 'The police will have that driver before the end of the day. They probably already know who it is.'

Saliva filled my mouth, my heart began to speed dangerously. I needed to get home. I needed to get away. I needed them to be quiet, to stop talking, to shut up. To just *shut up*.

A droning sound began and got louder and louder.

'They should throw away the key,' the teenager said, sounding much older than he was, warming to his theme, 'someone who does that.'

'And then just speeds off!' the young woman agreed. 'To just leave. If the police want to talk to me they can, I didn't see it happen but I saw the car as it left. It was a BMW. A black BMW.'

My throat constricted as she said it.

I couldn't breathe. The more I tried, the harder it became and my heart started to beat fast. I screwed my eyes tight against the image but it wouldn't leave my mind.

A black BMW. She'd seen it. He'd seen it. I didn't imagine it. It was real.

I'd been watching him. I expected him to stop. To get out. That was the type of man Phil, my husband, was. He was caring. He did the right thing. He didn't throw bodies over windscreens and drive away.

Except he had.

It was Phil's black BMW.

It was my husband's face behind the wheel.

I expected to see him with another woman. What I saw was so much worse.

2

Suzie

Suzie had been running alongside the River Dee when she got the call from Della. In her tight black pants and fitted fleece, her small muscular frame slowed to a jog as she fiddled with the armband that held her phone. She had reached the favourite part of her route and with the November sun low in the sky, it was beautiful. The Groves, Chester's riverside promenade with its Edwardian bandstand overlooking the water stretched out before her, the shadows of the trees lengthening, the cobbled stones glistening in the pale light.

Suzie ran three times a week and it was this part of the run that motivated her to do it. Lying just below the sandstone wall to the south-east of the city, she'd jog along the steps leading to the Roman gardens, which was where the beauty really began. The sudden change in space and atmosphere always amazed her, it was the thing she liked most about Chester, the fact that she could leave the busy, traffic-filled streets and be alongside history within seconds.

Here she jogged amongst building fragments taken from a Roman fortress. Columns from the bathhouse and ruins from military constructions dotted her path, and as she breathed in great gasps of air, filling her lungs, she admired her surroundings and never felt more alive. It was as if the history of the place somehow energised her.

From the gardens she went to a paved walkway beside the river, and then up toward the Edwardian bandstand that was a magnet for visitors and tourists no matter what the time of year or weather. In summer it was host to concerts and regattas. Local artists would set up shop along the bank and row boats could be hired. There were also pleasure boats that would take out tourists on sightseeing cruises.

Wooden benches flanked the river, and mature trees grew between the thick black iron of the Edwardian lamp-posts. It was where the day-trippers came, where families fed ducks and where, on a winter afternoon, if you looked out and forgot the icy chill, you could remember what summer felt like.

The river cruises had long since finished for the season but shoppers and tourists always made the place busy and Suzie had to dodge several people until she reached one of the empty benches. The loud, energetic, house music set at one hundred and forty beats per minute was interrupted by Della's voice, which seemed to be stopping and starting at a similar speed.

At just five foot, Suzie often got mistaken for a child. It was something she'd had to battle against her entire life, and now, as Della spoke incomprehensibly in her ear, Suzie stretched out her hamstrings and pulled off her hat so the teenagers leering by the neighbouring bench could see she was a grown woman. She had short brown hair cut in a spiky style which, when sprayed, added another two inches to her height. Put this together with her four inch heels and Suzie never felt small in her working day, but with both her hair and feet flat, she felt vulnerable.

Giving one last glare to the group of teenagers, who had long since lost interest, she concentrated on listening. Della always seemed to talk in riddles. In Suzie's mind, she was a very immature girl for her age and she couldn't understand why Rachel employed her. Why Rachel employed anyone, in fact, to do things that she surely could do herself. Rachel was busy, but then, wasn't everyone? Yet Rachel was the only person she knew who employed someone as a kind of, what exactly was Della? Suzie supposed a household help and nanny, although she'd never asked. But that was where Suzie and Rachel differed. Suzie could barely justify the expense of employing a weekly cleaner whereas Rachel employed someone to clean daily, hourly even, as Suzie wasn't entirely sure what else it was that Della did.

'Sorry what?' Suzie asked and listened as Della stuttered over her words. She was talking about the retail park, about Rachel breaking her ankle but Suzie couldn't make any real sense of it. Della was in her early twenties and had the annoying habit of talking fast and not pausing for breath. The easiest way to deal with her was to ask her a series of sharp, short questions where Della could only answer yes or no. After six questions, Suzie ended the conversation and paused for a second to process what Della had just told her.

Rachel had been in an accident and was waiting for her at the hospital.

She had gone to the retail park after all. To catch her husband being unfaithful and now this had happened. Suzie watched an elderly couple take pictures of each other as they posed at the bandstand. Their breath caught like smoke in front of their faces, their gloved hands on the decorative railings as they laughed at each other. A family with a toddler strolled past, the pushchair bouncing over the paving stones as they went.

'She should've called me,' Suzie muttered to herself, thinking of Rachel alone at the hotel, watching her husband meet his mistress and then crashing her car at the sight. 'I would've ripped off his fucking face.'

The mother of the toddler turned abruptly, Suzie's words had been louder than she intended. She flushed and turned back the way she had come, running with purpose.

It didn't enter her head to go home and shower, or to get changed out of her running clothes and trainers. Her mind full of adultery and dishonesty, she was blind to her surroundings and could only feel the dank cold seep out from the river behind her. Her heart pounding as she passed the city walls and ran to the busy roads, to the fumes of cars and the streets swarming with shoppers and buskers. She got into her car, wiped her gloved hand over the inside of the windscreen, too impatient for the heaters to clear the fog, and drove through the juddering traffic straight to the hospital and to Rachel.

–

She was sitting in a wheelchair, just outside of the waiting room. Her leg was propped up on the rest and although she shook her head, making motions as if everything was okay, Suzie knew that her friend was very far from fine. She rushed over to her side, Rachel's elfin face was swollen from crying, her green eyes puffy and red rimmed. Her usually immaculate clothes looked stained and crumpled, her sleek bob was in disarray and there was a stale, ripe smell to her.

In all the years that Suzie had known Rachel, even the disastrous time back at high school when Rachel insisted on camping for her Duke of Edinburgh award in the floods, Suzie had never seen her in such a state. Putting a hand on her shoulder, she looked around the waiting room for someone in authority. Besides the woman at reception there seemed to be no one. Rows of blue padded chairs and walls filled with posters describing alarming symptoms stared back at her. There were two other patients, both at the far side of the room, and opposite them a youngish woman with blonde dreadlocks and fluffy boots over what appeared to be pyjama bottoms. She watched them with narrow eyes, her hands clasped around a colourful satchel. Suzie couldn't tell if she was a patient or visitor but before she had a chance to find out, Rachel grabbed her hand tight. Suzie went to the nearest chair and perched on the edge of it, leaning in close.

'You went there?' Suzie whispered after a moment. 'You went there and saw Phil? Saw him with *her*?' She squeezed Rachel's hand. 'What a bastard.'

Rachel didn't even look up and for a moment, Suzie wasn't sure if she'd heard. 'Why didn't you call me?' she asked in a lower voice. 'I would've come. I would've driven you. You shouldn't have gone there on your own. You shouldn't have seen that alone. No wonder you went into the back of someone.'

Rachel shook her head absently at Suzie's words, 'I thought you were at the bank. I didn't want to…'

'I haven't been to the bank yet,' Suzie interrupted, 'and even if I was, this is much more important.' She took a moment then wrapped both her hands around Rachel's cold one. 'Who was she?' she asked. 'Was she young? Don't tell me she was young. Was he screwing someone younger than us? Someone from work?'

'No,' Rachel said, her voice barely audible. 'She wasn't anything. There was no one. He wasn't there to see anyone.'

Suzie leaned forward as if she hadn't quite heard. 'But...?' she pointed to Rachel's propped up leg and Rachel started to cry again. Silent fat tears rolling down her cheeks.

Suzie dug about in her pocket trying to locate a tissue but found nothing. She glanced about the waiting room, hoping to find a passing nurse or a doctor but only saw the dreadlocked woman. She was staring back at them, enjoying the drama with a smirk, and there was no way Suzie was going to ask her.

'But you did see him?' she asked Rachel in a whisper. 'After what we found this morning, he was there?'

Rachel nodded. Then shook her head.

'No,' she said in a tight voice and covered her face with her hands. 'Oh Suzie, I shouldn't have gone there. I shouldn't have gone. I didn't see anything.'

Suzie watched Rachel cry into her palms and was at a loss. That morning it had been pretty clear what Phil had been up to. After what they'd found, Suzie would've bet her life that Phil was having an affair. It was suddenly so obvious, and she realised that her friend's perfect life wasn't so perfect after all. She'd felt such a rush of emotion then, when it became apparent that Phil was being unfaithful, that she would've done anything for Rachel. She would've gone to the retail park for her, she would've confronted Phil; Rachel shouldn't have been doing that alone.

'No,' Rachel said between sobs from behind her hands. 'It can't have been,' she lifted her face. 'No, not Phil. It wasn't Phil.'

'But earlier…' Suzie began and Rachel shook her head, stopping her.

'What we found this morning was nonsense,' Rachel sniffed noisily and ran a hand over her cheek, her mascara was all down her face giving her a greyish complexion. She swallowed and straightened herself. 'It meant nothing.'

'Rachel,' Suzie said carefully. 'What we found this morning was proof.'

–

They'd just come back from meeting a new client when it happened. They were both high off the success of landing a new job and getting it from right under the noses of rival company, Tailor Made Events. Suzie had heard about it from Mandy in the coffee shop. Between ordering a double espresso, Mandy told Suzie about the party her daughter was going to on Saturday. A twenty-first birthday over towards the Tattenhall area in a reno-vated house overlooking the golf course. Suzie started listening when she heard that address, it was one of the most affluent areas in Chester, offering quaint village life but just fifteen minutes from the city centre.

The birthday girl had tried to organise the party herself. It was to be a nineteen-twenties theme, Great Gatsby style, and her parents had spent a small fortune on three hundred glitzy invites and a jazz band, but, apart from that, she had forgotten everything else. She'd only just realised that she needed extra rooms for her guests and that the band wouldn't play all night and everyone would need feeding. Suzie had listened as Mandy relayed how the father was willing to pay any price at such short notice.

It was the perfect opportunity.

Suzie and Rachel had only been working together for three months, and if Suzie could get this job, it would prove to Rachel that their joint venture hadn't been a mistake. Farrell McFadden Events could work. Rachel could start to wind down her private catering business and Suzie wouldn't have to take on the soulless gigs. No more budget weddings. No more styling and photographing B&B's, restaurants and businesses. She'd be photographing the good life. Glamour and prosperity. She'd be photographing wealth.

So far, they'd worked together on a few smaller jobs, some hotels and modest corporate meetings, but it wasn't enough for Suzie to show Rachel the full extent of her ambition. A twenty-first party in the affluent area of Chester could be just the event to share her vision with Rachel. They would style and manage it together, the catering done by Rachel and Suzie as photographer with images to sell on to the guests afterwards.

Suzie had used all her charm and flattery in getting the name and number of the girl from Mandy and after a short conversation with her, Suzie had arranged a meeting with the family that very morning. It had gone better than expected. The Edwardian detached was set in an acre and a half of perfectly landscaped gardens and just walking up to the entrance made Suzie want to grab her Canon with the wide-angle lens. The girl was on the brink of tears at the start, but after two hours of discussing art deco backdrops, marquee hire and oversized champagne glasses, she was delighted. When they went on to describe Rachel's signature hors d'oeuvres that included smoked salmon on a lemon herb blini, and the photo booth, how Suzie would photograph the guests as if she was paparazzi, they were falling over themselves to give them the job. By the time Suzie was explaining repeat orders of photographs and featuring some of the pictures in *Cheshire Life* magazine, the father was almost writing a blank cheque. They could name their price.

They had less than a week to pull off a Gatsby style party for three hundred and when they got back to Rachel's and were sitting in her open plan kitchen with the morning winter sun streaming through, they were both giddy and slightly panicky. Then it happened.

Rachel had been talking about how it was going to be tight, not only because they had limited time to organise and plan the twenty-first Gatsby party, but because she was trying to arrange a holiday as well. She had it in her mind that her daughters should experience Father Christmas in a Nordic setting whilst they were still young enough to enjoy it. With Katie at fourteen and Jessica at sixteen, Suzie thought they were far too old already, but she knew better than to voice her opinion on matters like this with Rachel, so she kept quiet and went to fill the kettle instead.

'Phil thinks we shouldn't take them out of school,' Rachel was saying, 'but as I explained to him, I'm booked up all Christmas week. I've three big charity dinners to cater for in town as well as my consultation work with the council and I like to do a bit of volunteering around this time of year, if I can fit it in, so if we're going, it'll have to be at the beginning of December. It'll be the week after the Gatsby party so it'll be a squeeze, but Katie's fifteen next year. How much longer will she want to come on family holidays? And Jessica! Little Jessica is going to be an adult soon, she's leaving college next year so if we're doing it, it needs to be now and it's a price difference of thousands! Not just a few hundred, but thousands.'

Suzie had barely been listening. With no children of her own she couldn't really empathise with the whole 'school holiday' dilemma. She only understood that it was business; a higher demand for something meant a higher price. It went with the territory, if you were lucky enough to have children, then you had to endure certain things. Like paying more for a holiday, and besides, Rachel could afford it. Suzie only had to look at her big detached house, the car in her drive, the expensive coffee that was in her cupboard and the sound of her cleaner, Della, hoovering upstairs, to realise that for all Rachel's moaning about prices, she had the money in the bank.

She stared out at Rachel's large garden whilst the kettle boiled and thought instead about her honeymoon. In a matter of months she'd be Mrs Adam Staple. Lying on a sun bed, somewhere tropical, her new husband by her side and hopefully, if this party went to plan, a great new business on the go. In a few short years, if Suzie allowed herself to dream, she could be standing in a house like this, maybe not as big as Rachel's, but certainly similar, and perhaps, if she was really lucky, with a child of her own. She could be the one who was gleefully moaning about child-care and overpriced holidays. Suzie smiled, excitement fizzing inside her.

As Rachel went on to talk about how the experience of visiting Norway would be so much more educational than sitting in a classroom, Suzie got out the mugs and checked her phone. Adam hadn't yet called back. When she'd been paying for her coffee that morning, her bank card had been refused. Mandy was fine about it, said she trusted Suzie wouldn't leave the country, but it was embarrassing all the same. She needed to call the bank, but wanted to speak with Adam first. Her fiancé was the one who managed the accounts, sorted the cash, fiddled the books. He dealt with everything financial, so she wanted to check with him before she started up blue murder about a frozen card. Could be that he was holding something back for tax deduction or something similar, which she knew he sometimes did.

She idly tried to remember when he'd said their self-assessments were due, when she'd become a partner in his business, the dates of their fiscal year and what cash sales she'd had that month. Or if she should use the other bank card, the one he said to lay off for a couple of weeks, where she might have put it, when she realised that Rachel had suddenly gone quiet.

All the talk of thieving airlines and husky rides had stopped.

She turned around to see Rachel hunched over the laptop, her shoulders rigid.

'What's wrong?' Suzie asked, walking toward her, 'what's happened?'

Rachel didn't answer. She simply turned slightly so Suzie could see the screen. Twitter. Rachel was on Twitter and as Suzie made sense of the page, she could see that she was on the private messaging section of the site.

'I'm not sure what to think of this,' Rachel said and pointed to the top message. Suzie read it aloud.

'Meet me today at two, room booked at the hotel on Chester retail park. I'll bring champagne. Can't wait to see your hot body.'

She looked at Rachel who had gone pale, a confused look on her face. Leaning forward she looked at whose account Rachel was reading.

'Big Smiles 33,' she said. 'Is that you?'

Rachel shook her head tightly and navigated the screen back to the inbox. Suzie could see a whole array of messages; some pictures that she couldn't make out and all were addressed to someone named Shutterbug1718.

'I was on a travel agent's site,' Rachel said, staring at the screen. 'One that specialises in Santa trips. They're doing special offers via Twitter so I went to it. When I get to their page, I'm on Twitter and see I've got a notification. A direct message. Then I find this,' she waved at the screen. 'Then, I realise I'm not logged in on *my* Twitter account, I'm logged in on someone else's.' Rachel paused and looked up at Suzie. 'Automatically logged in.'

Suzie had taken a sharp intake of breath. 'So who else uses this laptop?'

Rachel had stayed silent.

'Jessica?' Suzie had asked. 'Is it Jessica's account? Is she meeting her boyfriend?'

'Jessica hasn't got a boyfriend!' Rachel spat out. 'She's too busy studying. She wants to be a vet, she wouldn't be meeting people in a hotel. And besides, she despises social media. She's on a digital detox, or something or other. The only phone she has is this huge old retro thing. She doesn't even text. This isn't Jessica.'

Suzie had paused for a moment.

'Katie then,' Suzie had suggested carefully. 'You think it might be...'

'Katie's fourteen!' Rachel said. 'I'd know if she had a Twitter account...'

'But...'

'We don't let her use any of these sites.'

Suzie went to argue, but Rachel put her hand up to stop her.

'We don't allow Katie on it and she understands. Cyber-bullying and all that. And the girls know they're not allowed on my laptop. This is a work laptop, the girls know not to touch it. The only people to use this are me,' she'd paused, swallowed, 'and Phil.'

Suzie had pulled out a chair at that. It was obvious. Phil had sent that message. He'd been on Twitter and forgotten to log out of his account. He was having an affair and arranging his rendezvous on his mobile, unaware that he was still logged in on the home laptop.

'Oh shit,' she'd said and then, 'I'm so sorry.'

Rachel stared at the screen in silence.

Suzie put her hand out. 'Oh Rachel,' she'd said after a moment. 'What a way to find out.'

Rachel had let out a confused little laugh, the air coming out of her mouth in little puffs.

'Don't be silly,' she'd said. 'Phil's in London. How could he be arranging to meet someone in Chester when he's in London?'

Suzie had raised her eyebrows.

'That's ridiculous!' Rachel had said. 'My Phil?' She'd looked at the screen, the message and shook her head. 'Impossible. No. Not Phil. He's in London. He caught the train there this morning.'

Suzie watched as Rachel took in a deep breath and logged out of the Twitter account.

'It's probably Della,' she said with two bright spots of colour on her cheeks. 'I'll have a word with her when you've gone. Speak to her about using my laptop, she knows she's not allowed on it. Silly girl.'

Suzie had been very still as she listened to Rachel talk about how it was most certainly Della, and how it was even possible that Twitter accounts could be hacked. She didn't say a word as Rachel came up with excuses as to what they'd both seen. They'd gone on to plan the Gatsby party then, but it had been under an atmosphere.

Rachel had taken out one of her personalised pens, a silver roller ball specially designed for the left handed, and laboriously written everything down as if she was afraid of opening up the laptop again.

Suzie had found it slightly infuriating as Rachel had filled the A4 pad, she'd wanted to grab the laptop and take it back to the Twitter account. She wanted to read each and every one of those messages, look at the images that had been sent and pull apart exactly what Phil had been up to.

She'd always thought Phil wasn't the type. He seemed so reliable, so *boring*. As long as she'd known Phil he'd never once done anything to surprise her. He was predictable, reliable; it was what she supposed Rachel found attractive about him. Whenever Suzie saw him, he was quiet, happy to go along with whatever Rachel was planning. Happy to be told what to do. But as Rachel talked about the party, Suzie re-evaluated her opinion of him.

She wanted to take the pen from her friend and ask about her marriage. She wanted to look at the messages and see if it was Phil, see if he wasn't predictable after all. But as Rachel talked about the arrangements to meet up the following day, she made it clear it wasn't up for discussion. So Suzie had left to go on her jog. Now, sitting opposite her broken friend, it looked as though Rachel had done exactly what Suzie had wanted to as soon as she'd left.

–

Suzie looked at Rachel, sitting in the wheelchair at the hospital with her head in her hands, and felt a great wave of sympathy. Rachel knew. Deep down, she knew that her husband was being unfaithful, even if she hadn't seen him at the hotel that afternoon. Rachel had doubted him enough to go there. She had her suspicions. She just couldn't admit it to herself, yet.

'It's okay,' she said and put her arm around Rachel's shoulders. 'I'm here now, I've got you. I'm not going anywhere.'

'Mrs Farrell?' a smiling nurse came toward them. 'They're ready for you now.' She went to push the wheelchair forward and Rachel looked to Suzie.

'I'm coming,' she said. 'I'm right here.'

The nurse nodded. 'You can wait for her outside the fracture ward then they'll be sending her home as soon as it's set. Shouldn't be too long.'

The nurse started to wheel Rachel away and Suzie walked alongside. They went out of the waiting room at a quick pace and just as they turned to go down the corridor, Suzie faltered in her step.

He was wearing a suit and tie. Carrying a briefcase with his overcoat slung over his arm, looking like the manager of some small car dealership. He came running over as soon as he saw them.

'Oh my darling.' He bent over and kissed Rachel full on the lips. 'When Della phoned I was distraught, thank God I was able to get home.'

'Phil,' Rachel said his name as if she couldn't quite believe it was him, 'why aren't you in London?'

'Got the train back as soon as I heard,' he'd said and Suzie watched as he looked at Rachel's ankle, shook his head in alarm and made sounds of sympathy.

'But I asked Della not to call you,' Rachel said. 'I told her not to.'

'Well she did,' Phil ran his thumb along Rachel's cheek, removing the dark stains of mascara. 'Thank God she did, because I'm here now. With you.'

He leaned forward and kissed Rachel's cheek and Suzie couldn't be certain, but she was sure Rachel flinched at his touch.

3

Rachel

They were in an unmarked car at the side of the road. As we came back from the hospital, the taxi pulled into our driveway and I'd seen them. A jolt of terror sweeping over me at the sight.

I watched as they got out of their car and braced themselves against the wind. There were two of them, an older one with greying, tight hair that looked like it was a perm, and a younger man about half his age with an overbite. They wore the kind of clothes that are sold in big supermarket chains and as they reached our house, they stared at us intently. They'd been waiting for our return, as I guessed they would be, and my heart thrummed against my ribs.

Phil didn't see them or, if he did, he stayed silent about it. Our taxi came to a halt in front of our house, where Della and the girls were standing. They'd seen our taxi pull in and had opened the door, the three of them staring out at us, a small group of anxiety. I'd opened the car door to get out, but Phil beat me to it. He pushed my crutches aside and lifted me out, leaving the driver and my belongings waiting. He ignored the two men walking towards us and carried me through the doorway as if we were newlyweds. Jessica and Katie started to fuss, asking me questions, asking Phil why he was home, whilst Della stood to the side, shaking her head and biting her lip.

'They wanted to come in,' she said to us, 'but I made them wait in their car. I made them sit out there until you came back from the hospital.'

'Mr Farrell?' one of the men asked. 'Detective Sergeant Bailey. I see we've come at a bad time, but if I could just have a few moments? Won't take long.'

His voice cut through the chatter and he smiled in the sudden silence. He had a way of standing that gave the impression he lifted weights, puffing out his chest and rocking on his heels. The younger one hung back, barely inside the house, obviously a little politer than his senior officer.

Phil placed me down on the chair by the coat rack, making sure I was seated before he spoke. 'Is this about my stolen car?' he asked them. 'Have you found it?'

Sergeant Bailey shook his head. ''fraid not.'

Without saying another word, Phil left to collect my crutches and pay for the taxi, leaving the two men waiting in the hallway watching us. I looked to my girls. Jessica put her hand to the back of her neck. She'd recently had her hair cut short and was still loving the novelty of the freshly exposed skin there. I gave her a weak smile and she smirked at me.

'Can't let you go out anywhere on your own, Mum,' she said as she came over to me. 'You okay?' I nodded and she looked at my cast, large and ugly. 'Can't wait to see how you accessorise that one,' she said and gave a small laugh.

I wanted to hug her, to wrap my arms around my eldest daughter for a moment and hide but Jessica wasn't like that, she needed personal space. She gave me a slight shrug, as if she could read my thoughts as Katie bounded to my side. She went to put her arms around my neck, then stopped abruptly.

'Ugh, what's that smell?'

I glanced at the police officers and felt myself flush. Katie was, as most fourteen-year-old girls tend to be, very dramatic. She held her nose as she looked at my stained shirt with disgust.

'Mum!' she said as she saw where I'd been sick earlier.

Jessica gave her a shove. 'Mum's been in an accident, stupid,' she told her. 'Back off.'

'You back off,' Katie immediately retorted and I closed my eyes.

'Katie, could you stop thinking about yourself for just one second?' Jessica asked and I looked at Della. It had been less than three minutes and they were off, arguing and bickering.

Della gave me a small smile. 'You okay?' she mouthed through the girls' chatter and I nodded back.

Phil's car had been stolen. He wasn't anywhere near the retail park when the hit and run had happened, he was on a train. He'd explained everything at the hospital, how his car had been taken, meaning that it wasn't him I saw that afternoon, it was *just his car*. Just his car. His stolen car. But even as he was telling me, I couldn't shift the image of what I'd seen from my mind. I'd been certain it was him I was following.

'We had to eat vegan curry,' Katie was telling me, 'because Jessica insisted she cook, when she shouldn't have because it was disgusting.'

'It was delicious,' Jessica said.

'I'm only ever eating what Della makes from now on,' Katie said and took my hand, 'aren't I, Mum? Because

Jessica shouldn't be allowed to cook. And being vegan is bad for you.'

'It is not!' Jessica said and started to list off all the reasons why a vegan diet was preferable. The police watched us, they made no effort to avert their gaze or pretend to be distracted. The younger one in particular seemed mesmerised by Jessica. With her newly short hair she had a look of a young Keira Knightley, lovely high cheekbones and dark eyes, completely unaware of how beautiful she was.

'Mum?'

I blinked rapidly. Katie had asked me a question and everyone was looking at me.

'Mum, are you okay?'

'Fine,' I told her. 'Completely fine.' My cast, which went up to my knee, lay heavily on the floor with my toes sticking out, the glossy nail varnish chipped. I smiled but it didn't feel how I wanted it to and when I swallowed I was surprised at how tight my throat was, how close I was to tears.

'Girls, could you...?' I looked to Della for help. 'Perhaps go into the den? Whilst I...?'

Della jumped into action. 'Cookies?' she offered. 'Or we've still got some popcorn, I could bring you that whilst you watch a movie?' She took a step toward the French doors that led into the kitchen. 'How about a hot chocolate?'

'I've got to get back to my studying,' Jessica said and went on ahead of them.

'I'll have a hot chocolate,' Katie said as they left and suddenly it was silent in the hallway. I looked to the open door. Phil was still out there, sorting out the taxi. I could hear him chatting, it felt like he was taking his time unnecessarily, delaying the moment when he had to come back inside.

'Kids,' Sergeant Bailey said after a moment. 'Got one that age myself, so I know what it's like,' he looked down at my leg. 'So what happened to you then? You are Mrs Farrell I take it?'

I told him, in few words, what I'd done. As I talked Phil came back in, quietly closing the door. He came to my side, putting his hand on my shoulder.

'The hotel on the retail park?' Sergeant Bailey asked when I'd finished, and shared a look with his partner, he shifted his weight and took out his notebook as my heartbeat quickened. I knew how it sounded, knew what they were thinking.

There was a long pause as he went through his notes, a bemused smile on his face. 'You're not going to believe this,' he said looking up. 'But there was a serious incident on that very same retail park this afternoon,' he turned to Phil. 'With your car.'

Phil stared back, his face blank. '*My car?* My stolen car?'

Sergeant Bailey gave a solemn nod. 'The driver left the scene,' he said, 'in your car.'

'So whoever stole my car,' Phil said, 'drove it to the retail park and it was involved in an accident and then they left? In my car?'

Sergeant Bailey paused, as if what Phil had asked was a difficult question. After a while he nodded. 'It was a hit and run.'

I heard a gasp and realised it was me. My hand was at my throat and I'd started to shake slightly.

'A hit and run?' Phil repeated. 'Bloody hell. Was anyone hurt?'

'Unfortunately, yes,' Sergeant Bailey said. 'They're stable at the moment, at hospital. In a coma. So you can appreciate why we needed to speak with you tonight.'

We were all silent for a moment. I could hear a small argument starting in the kitchen between the girls and I looked down, staring at my cast. At my toes with their slight greyish colour, the polished wood floor beneath, at the Persian rug I remembered buying in some expensive chain store. The drum of my heart was echoing around my body, I could feel it vibrating, feel myself shake with the force of it. I brought my hand down and clasped it in my other, my wedding ring glinting out at me.

'What time did you report your car stolen, Mr Farrell?'

Phil thought for a moment. 'It would've been when I got back to the train station,' he said. 'About, what? Four? Half past?'

Sergeant Bailey nodded thoughtfully and as he looked to me, my heart seemed to stop for a moment. As if it had jumped up in my throat and got stuck.

'And your collision, Mrs Farrell?' he asked gently. 'What time was that?'

I swallowed, my throat tight. 'I don't know,' I told them, 'I wasn't wearing my watch, didn't have my phone.'

He nodded, writing something down in his pad. 'Approximately,' he said, 'if you had to make a guess, what time would you say it was?'

I shook my head, swallowed, 'I would say… I mean… I was only there to see it as a venue, I was looking at the hotel as a venue. I run an events company and I was just checking it out, so I didn't really think about what time it was. I didn't look at the time.'

'But you were in the hotel?'

I nodded.

'And the staff were aware you had an accident?'

'They called the ambulance.'

'Of course they did,' he said and gave a smile. 'So that's easy to find out.'

I was getting short of breath, couldn't seem to take any air in.

'Just routine questions,' he reassured me. 'Nothing to worry about. And you,' he said looking to Phil, 'where were you this afternoon?' His pen hovered above his paper. 'Whilst your wife was having her accident and your car was being stolen?'

'Crewe train station,' Phil said quickly. 'I was on my way to London, for work. The train goes from Chester and changes at Crewe. I was ready to board the train to London when I got the call from Della,' he waved toward where Della was in the kitchen.

'And Della would be...?'

'She's our nanny, our housekeeper,' Phil said.

'And you're certain Della was here when she made the call?'

'Della was here,' I told him. 'I spoke to her, after my accident. I used a phone, called home and spoke to her.'

Sergeant Bailey made a note, then looked at Phil and gave him a nod to continue.

'So Della tells me about Rachel's accident and instead of getting on the train to London, I get a train straight back to Chester, to see my wife. And then...'

'And then you find your car gone.'

Phil nodded. I made an effort to breathe normally, to remain relaxed despite what my heart was doing. The repercussions of its beat were making my hands tremble, my chest shake. Fear was reverberating around my body.

I could see the hit and run in my mind, hear the crunch of bones, see Phil's face behind the wheel.

'Here,' Phil said and reached in his pocket. 'My train tickets if they're of any help. There's the one I used to get the train from Chester to Crewe, and these are for the second leg of my journey, the ones I didn't use going on to London. And here's the ticket I bought to come back to Chester, from Crewe train station. Proof I was there at that time.'

I stared at the tickets.

There was his train ticket. The ticket that Phil had bought that afternoon from Crewe train station at the time when I'd watched the hit and run happen. I had a strong urge to snatch the ticket, to examine it myself as it was passed to Sergeant Bailey. I held my breath as he studied it for a moment then tapped it against his pad. He rubbed his thumb along the top of one of the other tickets and then looked at it, as if to see if the ink was dry.

'Okay if I keep these?'

'Of course,' Phil said, and we watched as Sergeant Bailey handed them to his younger partner.

'And Mrs Farrell, your accident,' he looked at me. 'You ran into the back of someone outside the hotel on the retail park? Metres away from where the accident happened with your husband's car?' he had his eyebrows raised, as if he found it unbelievable. I nodded, not trusting myself to speak. 'I assume you've the information of the other driver? We'll need to check with them, with the hotel staff, the people involved. And I'll probably need to question you about it again,' he looked at Phil. 'Both of you, I'll need to take you to the station—'

'Hang on a minute,' Phil's voice interrupted. 'What happened with my stolen car has nothing to do with

Rachel. She's just out of hospital. She's broken her ankle in a minor collision that had numerous witnesses and you're talking of taking her to the station? Don't be ridiculous!'

I took in a shaky breath; Sergeant Bailey was watching me carefully and I could feel myself colour. I didn't know how to organise my features, was afraid I'd give something away.

'Now if you don't mind,' Phil went on. 'I'd like to take care of my wife. It's been a very long day. So please, come back when you've found the real criminal. The person who stole my car.'

They left at that point, but not before promising that we'd see them again. Soon.

I suppose I was expecting them to arrest someone. To say that they'd seen what I had, what the hotel staff had, but instead they'd confirmed that it was just Phil's car. I repeated it to myself as I let him carry me upstairs, whilst the girls bickered in the kitchen and whilst Della left for the evening, I repeatedly told myself that I was mistaken. It wasn't Phil that I'd been following, of course it wasn't Phil! I knew my husband and it wasn't him. I was being silly; it was the shock of the accident. It wasn't my husband. It was *just his car.*

I let him take me into our en-suite and help me undress and wash. I was a mess, crying and shaking and unable to form clear thoughts; no matter how many times I told myself it was my imagination, each time I looked at his face, I saw it again as I thought I had at the retail park, behind the darkened windscreen. I saw the body fly up in the air, the mess of it on the ground. I saw his face as he drove away. But then, I'd tell myself that it couldn't have been him. This was Phil, *my Phil*, the man I'd been married to for years. And I'd seen him talk to the police, hand over his train ticket as proof of where he'd been. I wasn't close when the hit and run happened. I was on the hotel car park, metres away.

I told myself I'd imagined it was Phil, so sure I was following him, I'd convinced myself that I'd seen his face, when I hadn't at all. When I'd been so far away it was probably impossible. And then the images would replay in my mind all over again and I felt like I was going mad.

Once I was in bed and settled, we realised we'd forgotten to get my medication from the hospital and he left to collect it. Being alone helped calm me down. I reminded myself of who my husband was. The man I loved. The man I'd been married to for fifteen years, the man who'd liked to read science fiction novels in the bath and had a weakness for chocolate buttons. The man who would choose a night in front of the television over a party, a pint of bitter instead of a glass of champagne. I knew him so well I could order for him at any restaurant, knew which shirt he'd pick out of a line at any department store, which tie. I booked our holidays, chose the decor for the house, organised our lives. He was the quiet one, the one who didn't do things on impulse or out of character. He wasn't capable of running someone over and leaving them for dead. That wasn't the man I'd married and by the time he came back, offering painkillers and a glass of wine, I felt marginally better about it all.

'Here,' he handed me the wine. 'You probably shouldn't, but after the day you've had…'

I didn't need any encouragement, I took a large gulp to swallow down the pills.

'Good girl,' he said and smiled. He looked tired, dishevelled. His suit was creased and his hair unkempt. I looked to his collar, open, his tie loose. I noticed the cuffs of his jacket were dirty; he'd folded them up, something I'd never seen him do before. I realised I knew nothing of his colleagues apart from the few that he chose to tell me about. I didn't know if he worked with a largely female team, if any of them were close, if any of them liaised between the Chester and London office as he did.

'Were you with anyone?' I asked him quietly, my heart beating, 'this afternoon? When you were at the train station, were you alone?'

He tilted his head at my question.

'Tell me the truth,' I pressed. 'Phil,' my voice was shaky, 'are you having an affair?'

He let out a bark of raucous laughter, shook his head and then picked up the bottle of pills. 'What's in these? What have you just taken?'

I swallowed. 'Please,' I said. 'Tell me who you were with and where you were today.'

He stroked my hair then went quiet, a puzzled smile on his lips. 'You know where I was.' He let his hand rest on my forehead as if checking my temperature. 'You feel okay?'

I didn't answer.

'I got the call from Della.'

'I never meant for Della to call you,' I interrupted. 'She's getting out of hand lately, not listening to me, the other day she went and…'

'I'm glad she called me,' Phil said. 'I would've been angry if she hadn't. I was at Crewe train station,' he went on. 'Alone. Not yet on the train to London so I didn't get on it. I caught a train back to Chester instead, back to you. Typical that the one day I really need to be home fast is the day my car gets nicked.' He took one of the smaller pillows and placed it under my cast, checking my face as he did so in case he hurt me. 'That's when I called the police, and now they're telling me it's been used in some horrendous accident. A hit and run. And at the same place you had your bump. Are you comfortable?'

'But your meeting,' I said. 'The big presentation. Weren't you meant to be in London for it? What about Felix? Didn't you say you couldn't let him down, that you were doing it together? I thought you were catching an earlier train for that?'

'Presentation got delayed,' Phil said. 'Clients cancelled so I caught up on some paperwork at the regional office instead. But what about you?' he looked at me. 'Weren't you going with Suzie for her big, exciting meeting? Why were you at the retail park running into people?'

'Checking out venues,' I lied quickly and then closed my eyes. Before today I'd never lied to Phil intentionally, but then, I'd never thought I'd be wondering if he was having an affair. Never thought I'd see what I did.

'Like what you saw?'

I blinked rapidly at him.

'The hotel,' he prompted and I shook my head, a tear falling as I did so.

'Was a bit cheap and nasty.'

We looked at each other a moment.

'Now,' Phil went to the door. 'I need to catch up on a bit of work. Felix has been calling, the presentation was cancelled today but it's been rescheduled and...' he held up his hands. 'Is there anything else I can get for you? I'll check on the girls, send Katie up to bed.'

I shook my head and tried a small smile, letting him go.

It made sense, what he was telling me, it made sense. I listened to the low murmur of his voice downstairs, the girls' chatter. I heard him laugh with them and I waited for the feeling of relief to wash over me. I reminded myself that it wasn't my husband I'd seen, it wasn't him I'd been following, he wasn't having an affair. What I'd seen on Twitter was a mistake, most likely Della. Most probably her arranging things she shouldn't be and I waited for a feeling of calm, for my heart to stop galloping and my head to stop swimming. I drank the wine until the concoction of alcohol and medication made me drowsy and repeatedly told myself that it wasn't Phil. *It wasn't Phil.*

Wednesday

Light showers with a chance of snow.

4

Rachel

'You awake?' He was dressed. Wearing a suit. He kissed me and I smelt his aftershave. 'How did you sleep? Was it terrible?'

I licked my lips. My mouth was dry, my tongue sticking. I tried to sit up and then winced at the unfamiliar weight of the cast holding me down.

'Let me help.' He lifted me up, putting pillows behind me and I looked at the alarm clock. It was ten past eight. Phil laughed at my expression.

'Thought you needed a lie in, we've all been creeping around trying not to wake you.' He passed me a cup of coffee and I took a sip, the warm liquid easing the discomfort in my mouth.

'You should've woken me,' I said. 'I can't believe I've slept so long.' I looked again at the bedside clock as if it were a lie. Usually I'm first up, downstairs putting on coffee and fixing my list for the day, long before anyone else in the house rises.

Phil smiled. 'Perhaps it was the wine. You shouldn't have drunk so much, I only meant for you to have a glass.'

I looked over at the near empty bottle by the bed, mildly confused. I was sure he'd only brought up a glass.

I must have had it, though, I could feel the repercussions of it behind my eyes, the steady, dull ache of a hangover.

'I've got to go,' he said and I looked at him, suddenly registering that he was showered, shaved, dressed. 'I'm on a conference call at ten and I'm needed in the regional office before that, and,' he raised his hands in defeat, 'I've to pick up the bloody courtesy car. Why they can't deliver it here before ten o'clock I've no idea.'

He went to his drawers, then the desk. He was collecting his belongings with strong sense of purpose and I shivered, there was a slight chill in the air.

'Is Della downstairs?'

'Not yet.' I watched as he put on his jacket and checked himself in the mirror, smoothing his collar. 'But we did keep her last night. She looked worn out when she left, so I told her not to rush in this morning.' He picked up his phone, studied it for a moment before putting it in his pocket. 'I've called a taxi and the girls are all ready to go. I'll drop them off on my way,' he smiled. 'Thought I'd do the school run for once.'

'A taxi?' I felt like I'd been underwater, like I'd been deep sea diving and was just breaking the surface. 'You're taking the girls? But Della should be doing that, can't you call her, get her to take them?'

He gave a laugh. 'No need, I'm here.'

I leaned over and took out my painkillers, swigging them back with the rest of my coffee, hoping they might clear my head.

'Phil, stop. Wait a minute. It doesn't matter if they're late this morning does it? What time did you tell Della to get here, let me give her a ring.' I looked about in vain for my phone then remembered it was in my handbag downstairs. Still on the kitchen table where I'd left it before rushing out to the retail park yesterday. It felt like it was from another life.

'Della will be here soon,' Phil said. 'Let her have a late start. She was brilliant yesterday.'

'She only stayed an hour over her normal time. Phil, just stop for a moment.' I tried to shift my position whilst Phil went about the bedroom collecting his things. I couldn't keep up with him, my head was foggy and I couldn't seem to wake up fully.

He paused and looked at me for a moment. He opened his mouth ready to speak but was stopped by Katie, she'd heard my voice and came charging into the room.

'Mum, finally!' she said coming in and kissing me on the cheek. 'You've been snoring your head off,' she laughed. Her black hair was piled up on top of her head and she was wearing more dark eyeliner than normal. She looked like a very young Amy Winehouse impersonator.

'You need to wash that off,' I began and she gave me an exaggerated eye roll. 'I mean it, Katie. School won't allow it and you look ridiculous.'

She looked at Phil and shook her head. 'Even with a broken leg she's still getting at me.'

'I've broken my ankle,' I corrected her. 'And I'm not getting at you, I'm telling you to take off that make-up.'

'I only came in to see if you were okay,' she said before flouncing out of the room.

'I'll tell her to wipe it off on the way,' Phil said as I went to protest. 'Or at school. Now, is there anything you need before we leave?'

'Morning, Mum. You okay?' Jessica asked before I could answer. She leaned on the doorframe, already in her coat, a big army thing that she'd got from the charity shop. It dwarfed her. She was clutching a pile of books to her chest. 'Dad's dropping me off at college on the way to his office,' she explained. 'He bribed me.'

'Bribed you?'

She nodded and took some lip gloss out of her pocket, expertly applying it whilst she spoke. 'Couldn't resist an offer of free pancakes.'

'Pancakes?' I felt disorientated. I was playing catch up and couldn't grasp what she was telling me.

'Phil,' I began, but he was already at the door, ushering Jessica down the stairs.

'Katie!' he shouted. 'You got your school bag?' he turned to me. 'Rachel, please, don't worry so much. You just relax.'

I went to say how I couldn't relax but he carried on talking.

'Your crutches are there but don't do anything until Della arrives, don't move until someone else is in the house, just in case...'

'Bye Mum,' Jessica called from behind him as she went downstairs. I wanted to shout at her to stay, not to leave me, but Phil was still talking, telling me how I should take it easy and rest up.

'Your medication is just there,' he was saying, 'and here's a glass of water if you get thirsty.' He grabbed the television remote and placed it beside me. 'Just have a rest until Della arrives.'

'I'm working at ten,' I went to tell him. 'You know this. I've got Suzie coming and...'

'Dad!' Katie shouted from downstairs. 'Taxi's here!'

'Phil!' I said. 'Phil, you can't go now.'

I needed to use the bathroom. The room looked suddenly overwhelming, like a giant obstacle course. I could hear Katie and Jessica getting ready to leave, doors

47

opening, and felt slivers of panic creep up my spine. I went to swing my legs off the edge of the bed, carrying the cast like a small toddler, but Phil ran over, dropping his overcoat on the unmade bed as he did so, his hands outstretched.

'Don't you dare!' he told me. 'Wait until Della is here.' He tucked in the covers tight around me. 'They say it might snow today so stay in bed. Wrap up warm.'

'Phil,' I said. 'I don't understand, why are you taking Jessica? Can't she stay until Della arrives? I need to get to the bathroom.'

I saw his face crinkle with concern and then:

'Dad!' Katie's shout again. 'If we don't go now we can't stop at Chilterns.'

I looked at Phil.

'*Chilterns?*' My voice was high. 'You're taking them to Chilterns this morning?'

Phil shrugged, a small flush working up through his neckline. 'Thought I'd treat the girls to early morning pancakes before school.'

So that's what Jessica was referring to.

'Phil? What the…?'

'Dad!'

He leaned over and gave me a quick kiss on the mouth, quietening my protests.

'I was thinking of the girls,' he said as he went to the door. 'It shook them up yesterday, you having your car accident and them seeing you like that. I thought they could do with a treat. Della will be here any minute and I'll be back in a couple of hours. Tops. Phone if you need me.'

'But Phil…'

'Why don't you try to get back to sleep? Take the day off?'

'You know I can't, Suzie is due—'

'Dad! Taxi!'

He looked at me with an expression of hopelessness and gave a slight shrug.

'I promised them,' he said, as if it quantified him running out on me. 'I'll be back before you know it.' He blew me a kiss from across the room and then charged down the stairs to the cheers of the girls.

And then, silence. My mouth left comically hanging open at his rushed exit.

After a moment, I reached for my crutches, my hands shaking. I couldn't wait for Della; I had things to do. I'd arranged that Suzie be here, I'd a party to plan, work commitments I couldn't cancel. And besides, even though Della helped with an enormous amount of our lives, nursing and helping me get dressed might be out of her remit.

I felt dizzy, nervous, as I gingerly heaved myself up. Nausea washed over me, either from the alcohol and medication or circumstance, I wasn't sure. I rested my weight on my good leg, and took a few deep breaths, cursing Phil. How could he be so attentive the previous night and then rush out and leave me this morning? There was no urgency, I could've phoned Katie's school, Jessica could've caught the bus into college, but then, perhaps he was right. Perhaps seeing me incapacitated was a shock to them; they weren't used to seeing me out of action. I wasn't used to *being* out of action.

I straightened myself, looked about the room and saw how I would do it. Once I had my balance, I hopped forward toward the dresser. I planned to use the furniture along with my crutch to make it to the bathroom, and then, my wardrobe. I'd have a dress or something I could put over my cast, I might not win any fashion awards but I'd be up. I'd be working. One thing I was sure of was that I couldn't stay in bed wallowing, my mind was too rattled, too restless. I needed work. I needed focus.

At the hospital the previous day, I'd arranged with Suzie that she'd pick me up at around ten. We'd talked briefly of how we'd work, how we could still go ahead with the Gatsby party despite my broken ankle and it was surprisingly easy to arrange. As most of the planning had been done, it was all down to delegating, phone calls and hiring temporary staff. I had a day of speaking with recruitment agencies in front of me and Suzie would be knocking on the door in less than two hours. I didn't have time to be panicky or anxious, or go over events in my mind. I had work to do.

I leaned against the wall, slotting myself between the dresser and the wardrobe to catch my breath. I was about to set off again, when I stopped. From the angle I was in, I had a clear view of the debris on top of Phil's drawers. Stuff that was normally hidden behind the lamp was on full view, loose change, crumpled bits of paper and receipts. He'd emptied his pockets there. I'd seen him do it last night. All the bits from his previous day, like breadcrumbs of where he'd been.

I was suddenly aware I was sweating, my heart thumping. I didn't need to look at any of that. I didn't need to investigate Phil's rubbish, but the events of yesterday started to crowd in on me. I closed my eyes, the rapid beat of my heart in my ears. I concentrated on the image of Phil handing over his train tickets to the police, of him explaining that it was his car but *it was not him. It wasn't Phil.* I didn't see Phil. Everything was normal.

I took in a deep breath, held it. My husband was not having an affair. He did not run someone over. I didn't see him commit a hit and run. Everything was *fine*.

I opened my eyes and saw his drawers again, the bits of paper on top. The bits of stuff from Phil's pockets. Evidence of where he'd been. I surveyed the room, working out how I could get there safely. Everything was fine, everything was normal, I just had to check, that was all. Just had to annihilate that prickling feeling in the base of my stomach, once I saw that his rubbish was just that, rubbish, I could get on with my day. If I went forward I could use the side of the bed and work myself along that, get to his bedside cabinet and then, it was only a step from his drawers and the rubbish on top.

The phone began to trill from the unit by the wall opposite and it threw me off. I went forward, but I was unsteady. My balance on the crutch not quite right and without the added support of the furniture I lurched, stumbling against the foot of the bed.

I fell against it clumsily, landing half sitting, half lying, on top of Phil's forgotten jacket and as I did, something fell on the floor. I heard it tap against the polished floorboards and looked down at it. It glinted in the weak sunlight. I stared at it for a moment, then when I'd regained my balance, picked it up.

It was a woman's earring, a silver hoop that had just fallen from Phil's jacket.

I turned it over in my hands as the blood began to roar in my ears. My nausea returned, my heart picked up its pace.

The earring was just like any other, pretty and delicate, except it wasn't mine. Couldn't possibly be. I knew with absolute certainty that it didn't belong in my house or in Phil's jacket, as no one in our family had pierced ears.

5

Suzie

'My bank card has been frozen,' Suzie said and folded her arms. 'It was declined yesterday morning at a coffee shop, which I thought was a one off, and today it's still not working. You've got too many security checks on it or something and it needs sorting.'

Sitting in a private room at the bank, she faced a young girl with dark bobbed hair and a set of thick painted-on eyebrows so symmetrical Suzie thought she must have used a stencil. They were just above the girl's natural brow line and Suzie couldn't stop looking at them; they were putting her off. Great big slugs, better suited to a mime artist than someone dealing with her finances.

'Won't be a moment,' she said and switched on the computer.

Suzie had had to argue for this appointment. She'd spent ten minutes on the city streets in the early morning praying the rain would hold off. Leaning on a bollard in front of the bank, ready to pounce as soon as they opened their doors, sipping coffee out of a disposable cup, watching the commuters get to work and the buskers get themselves set up. Eyebrow girl was the only person available, but still, she was better than nothing.

Either way, Suzie wasn't about to take any nonsense. She'd made a list of points to raise and mentally went through them as they waited for the bank's computer system to boot up. Even if Adam had done something, or if it was because she'd forgotten an instruction he'd given her about this particular account, she should've been informed before the bank stopped her card. The bank couldn't freeze her account without prior warning, it just wasn't right; they should be taking care of their customers, not humiliating them. They should've sent her a letter first, or at the very least a text. And more to the point, she needed some money. She'd looked at her cash situation last night and realised she'd very little, without going to Adam's safe or ransacking the till at the studio.

She checked her phone again. No missed calls from Adam, and no messages. She wondered where he might be. He was on a location shoot but she couldn't remember the venue. It was for the car thing he had a contract for, where he went out to one of their dealerships and took rows of boring shots of cars for the website and the newsletter; he could be gone for days when he did that. In fact, whenever Adam went off on a shoot, he could be gone for days. It was because, as he'd explained to her, he was an artist and the light was his paint box. As a photographer, he was at the mercy of the weather and it resulted in his work being erratic, spontaneous and unplanned. If Adam had good light and was near an interesting venue, he would go where it took him. He once came back from a portrait shoot three days late, as he'd been storm chasing. He was travelling back via a farm and had taken a detour that led him out in the country, but it had been worth it. The shots he got of the lightning and threatening clouds were tremendous. She had one of them in her flat, blown up in size and framed above the fireplace.

It was the reason why Rachel and Phil hadn't yet met him, and why her parents had only met him a handful of times. It was impossible to arrange anything as Adam didn't work to a schedule. He worked to the light. It was how he was, and if Suzie were being honest with herself, it was something else that she found attractive about him. She liked to boast that he was a jet setter, that he was spontaneous and his work was his passion. Adam was an artist and his work took priority over pedestrian things like dinner parties and drinks.

So it wasn't a worry that he'd been gone for longer than he'd said, but it was a little concerning that he hadn't answered her last message. She'd told him about the frozen card, explained that she couldn't find any other working cards and asked if she was alright to go to the safe for some cash. Normally he'd reply within a couple of hours. He must be somewhere out of signal.

She went to send him another message, then thought better of it. Her last relationship of twelve years had ended because apparently she was too 'demanding'. *'Too exhausting,'* Carl had said, which was utter bollocks because the only exhausting thing in that relationship had been Tina, his personal fitness trainer who had personal ideas about Carl that didn't include Suzie. But even so, she couldn't help but harbour a tiny bit of doubt as she put her phone away. She didn't want Adam back in range only to receive a series of hysterical texts from her. No, she'd be savvy about this frozen card, sort the bank out on her own, get some money without disrupting Adam's systems with the cash and then when he returned, he'd be pleased that she'd been as canny as he was about playing the banks at their own game.

'Is there any way you can speed this up?' Suzie asked and the eyebrows shot up in unison. 'It's just that I need to be somewhere.'

The room was small and airless. The only furniture was a shiny wooden desk with a computer and large telephone. Suzie could hear the low mumbles of people as they came into the bank, the odd laugh, the moan of a child. It was getting on for nine-fifteen and she needed to be at Rachel's for ten. They'd agreed yesterday at the hospital that they'd meet up and discuss things before making any decisions about the Gatsby party, but now it looked as if she was going to be late. And Rachel needed her, not just because of the job but because of Phil and whatever was going on with him, lying bastard. She'd half expected a phone call from her about it before now.

'Yes. Your account has been frozen,' the girl confirmed and looked at Suzie.

'I know that,' Suzie said. 'Hence the reason for my visit. If you could un-freeze it, I'll be on my way.'

There was a tight smile. 'We've tried to reach you and Mr Staple regarding the account as he's listed down as the main contact. The co-signatory? I understand he's your business partner?' The uniform the bank had issued her with included a red neckerchief that she pulled at as she talked. Suzie wanted to slap her hand and tell her to stop fidgeting.

'Well, yes,' Suzie said. 'I created this account. It's the New Business Starter. The one with the interest-free loan? But it's Adam, sorry, Mr Staple, my fiancé, that is usually your point of contact.' Suzie sighed. 'So if it's a security issue, or a late payment, it's Mr Staple that you need to speak to but he's on location. We're both photographers. He's away on a job photographing cars today. For a dealership. He should be back later this afternoon and he'll contact you but, in the meantime, you must please reinstate my card. I've a business to run and you can't just stop an account,' Suzie shifted in her seat. 'It's bad practice. I had no prior warning and it's been so frustrating.' She ran her hands through her hair, pulling the spikes upwards, and leaned back, ready for the girl to apologise.

'Yes, well, in his absence,' she looked at the screen and Suzie rolled her eyes impatiently. 'And as you are jointly responsible,' she smiled a little. 'We urgently need to discuss your overdraft.'

'Overdraft?' Suzie glanced at the square clock on the far wall, trying to calculate how long the journey to Rachel's would take in rush hour traffic. 'We've an agreement on that. It was the reason we opened this account in the first place, the interest-free loan and interest-free overdraft. Adam sorts that, the loan repayments and monthly deposits. He likes to do it in cash.'

The girl stared at her for a moment and then spoke carefully. 'But this account exceeds the agreement. You have gone over the limit and there have been no payments into the account in two months.'

Suzie shook her head. 'Well I suppose Adam could have fallen behind. He likes to come in and do it personally. I'm sure it's just a misunderstanding, if you take a closer look you'll see that it's really...' Suzie stopped talking as the girl was shaking her head. Her eyes had gone a little wider, her false eyelashes sticking out like spider's legs.

'If I could just...' she swivelled the screen around to Suzie and pointed to it. Suzie gave a heavy sigh. Without her glasses, she couldn't make it out.

'You created the business account with the Welcoming Business Loan just over four months ago. In that time, you've gone past the overdraft limit that we allowed you to extend for a short period of time, as per the new loan agreement. And now, it stands at thirty thousand. The agreement was repayments of eight hundred pounds at the start of each calendar month,' she pointed to another part of the screen, 'but there have been no repayments to the extended loan, and as you hadn't replied to any of our attempts to contact you, we've frozen the account.'

'What?' Suzie squinted at where she was pointing then went to her handbag for her glasses. 'You're telling me,' Suzie went on, 'you're saying we're, *how much overdrawn*?'

'Just over thirty thousand I'm afraid.' Her thick eyebrows furrowed together making her expression of concern somewhat pantomimed.

'I don't understand,' Suzie said, a cold, sick feeling swirling in her stomach. 'That's completely impossible. Thirty thousand in debt in four months? Adam pays into this account, he sorts out the repayments and we were certainly not told. This is the first I've heard of it! Thirty thousand? Impossible.' Suzie suddenly realised what the real problem was. 'I'd like to speak to your manager,' she said. 'I need someone who knows how these things work.'

The girl gave a nervous smile and pressed a button on the keyboard. A list came up on the screen, dates and notes.

'Miss McFadden, you *were* notified of this,' she said. 'The reapplication of your overdraft had to be sent to the area bank manager several times for approval and we have been sending you letters of notification. There are charges I'm afraid, bank charges because of the overdraft and we've been sending the letters to…' she paused as she read the address off the screen. 'Staple & McFadden Photography Services on Pilling Street? The last time we spoke to Mr Staple about the company's financial position, he assured us that he was just awaiting a payment,' she took a second, 'and I am the manager for this branch, Ms McFadden. I have been since you opened your account with us.'

Suzie stared at her. Adam was usually so on top of things like this, he made it his job to come into the bank and pay the cash in. He did it every week. Suzie had seen him do it, carefully counted wads of notes inside small brown envelopes, Adam checked them off ready to be taken to the bank in a little red notebook. She watched him, helped him pile the money into the counting machine sometimes and it was sexy, in a certain kind of way, seeing a man handle money like that. There was something old fashioned and raw about it, and although she was slightly ashamed to admit it, there was something about the piles of money that made her feel a little bit more alive.

'This can't be a surprise to you, Ms McFadden,' the girl said slowly. 'You co-signed the overdraft agreement. Look here,' she pointed back to the screen and Suzie put her glasses back on, 'that is your signature, isn't it?'

Suzie leaned in close. Sure enough, above her name was a scribble that looked very much like her signature.

'What's that for?' Suzie barked and the girl jumped a little.

'This is the final overdraft agreement,' she said, 'the extension. You agreed to the terms and conditions for repayment on the,' she peered closer at the screen, 'sixth of August.' She bit her lip. 'And this also means that the property on Charles Street is up as guarantee.'

'Charles Street?' Suzie felt a prickle of fear run up her spine. 'My flat?' She fell over her words. 'When I opened the business account you said that was just a formality. That you needed something against the loan, but the loan was only for five thousand.'

The girl gave a slow nod, 'and since opening the account and agreeing to those terms you've become over-drawn rather rapidly and not met your repayments on the initial loan.'

Suzie dipped her head against a wave of nausea.

When Adam suggested opening this account, he'd been very clear as to how they should work it. He did it all the time, he'd said, run the business almost at a loss for three years to pay minimal tax and no VAT.

'Just keep it ticking over,' was how he'd put it, 'make sure there's lots of expenses and not much profit and there won't be anything for the government to steal at the end of it.'

He had multiple accounts that he ran, and had been educating Suzie how you could manipulate the banks for the low interest rates and special offers. Switch money between them, get cash back on every bill you paid, take full advantage of their loss leaders like interest-free loans and credit cards. He had a few customers, like the car dealership, that paid directly into the accounts to give the appearance of a professional business, but for every other job he insisted on cash payments.

'Control the money,' he'd said. 'Use the banks instead of letting them use you.' But now, it seemed that Adam had forgotten about this account that he'd persuaded her to open up. It was thirty grand overdrawn and that wasn't right. Suzie hadn't seen one letter telling her as such; there was a serious mix up going on. Grabbing her bag, she got out her phone, desperate to see any communication from him, but there was nothing.

'Ms McFadden?'

Suzie looked up at her.

'If you're unaware of this, if you're telling me that Mr Staple…' she looked around the room as if there could be someone else to help. 'Are you saying, well, is there some element of fraud going on here?'

Suzie felt a jolt to her stomach, she laughed. 'Of course not!' she said and the girl blinked rapidly at her. 'Of course I know what's going on with my own bank account and fiancé. Print them out. Please,' Suzie said. 'The statements. The forms I signed. All of them.'

The young girl pressed a series of buttons and a printer began to whir into action. Adam would have an explanation. It would be the cash, Suzie realised with a modicum of relief. It would just be a matter of clearing the safe. Of course. That would be it. All that cash that Adam insisted on dealing with, no payments in cheques or transfers, only cash. The way he locked it all up and then drip-fed it out to the various bank accounts and businesses he had. He'd mismanaged the payments and somewhere along the way had forgotten to tell her about extending the overdraft.

'May I suggest,' the bank clerk said as she gathered up the papers, 'that you make an appointment to see one of our financial advisors? Your balance sheet is, well…' she swallowed as she looked at Suzie. 'I'm sorry, Ms McFadden and I'm not certain about your creditors but we do offer a very good service for those businesses that are in the process, or, look like they are in,' she paused, 'financial difficulties.'

'Financial difficulties?' Suzie repeated as the bank statements were passed to her. She looked at the figure on the bottom line. The word 'debit' in front of it.

'It's not something I normally recommend but, as you stand to lose your property, well, liquidation can be a solution. It's not the stigma it used to be.'

'Liquidation!' Suzie's voice was loud again. 'Don't be ridiculous. The business is not going into liquidation. I will not lose my flat. This is just a problem that needs to be fixed when I speak to Adam. It's something I can sort.'

There was a shocked pause and Suzie thought about apologising to her. After all, it wasn't her fault that Adam had forgotten to make the repayments on this account. This girl didn't know anything about Adam or how he liked to work his funds, so she wasn't to know that this was all just some silly mistake on his behalf.

'Listen,' Suzie leaned in, 'I'm sorry for, y'know,' she leaned her head to the side, 'getting a bit shouty, but I can easily sort this. I just need some more time. Just until I get hold of Adam so I can pay in the funds. We've got the money, I just need to transfer it.'

Up close, Suzie could see the fine lines around her mouth and realised she wasn't nearly as young as she'd first thought. Under all that make-up, she might even be the same age as Suzie.

'Any payment toward the debt would help ease the situation, and then we'd be in a position to come to an agreement on monthly repayments,' she said. 'But I'm afraid we can't give you very much time.'

'This afternoon,' interrupted Suzie. 'It's a misunderstanding. I just need to find Adam and get the details from him. Or, if I can't get hold of him, I'll get hold of the money. Make a deposit myself.'

After a moment, she nodded at Suzie and handed her a business card. 'My direct number,' she said. 'I'll handle this personally when you give me the details.'

Suzie got up. Her legs were shaky and not quite ready for her weight and she wobbled a bit.

'I'll need my bank card back working,' Suzie said. 'I've a business to run.'

The girl stared at her in silence with a look of pity and Suzie suddenly felt like strangling her again.

'I'm sorry…' she began but Suzie cut her off.

'You know what? It's fine,' she said, her voice abrupt. 'It's fine. Once I find Adam, we'll transfer the funds and then I'd like to close my account. The service I've had here is appalling, I'm going to move my business account to somewhere more professional.'

She slammed the door as she left, a line of waiting customers gawking at her. For a brief moment she wanted to shout at them all, to tell them to stop staring, and then she regained control. This was exactly the kind of thing Adam hated about banks, the way they made you feel so small. This was why they used them the way they did, this is why they took advantage and why she'd be closing her account here as soon as she could. She took a deep breath and checked her phone once more as she walked out to the high street. Where was he?

6

Rachel

It was about the size of a fifty pence piece.

I stared at the earring as if I had telepathic powers, as if concentration alone would tell me who it belonged to and what it was doing in the pocket of my husband's jacket, or between the sheets of our bed. I turned it over as my throat went dry, held it close and studied it, could it belong to a friend of Katie's? Was it a lost earring from a school friend of hers that she'd asked Phil to keep safe? Or Jessica, could it be from one of her friends? And if it was, why was it in Phil's jacket? It looked extravagant, not the type of thing the girls would want, too 'bling' for their friends. This was a woman's earring, a woman who had excessive tastes and it was in my husband's pocket.

I looked at Phil's coat, half hanging off the bed, and picked it up. It was his dark brown overcoat, the one he wore in the week over his suit. Part of his working uniform, it was the one he'd had slung over his arm when he came to the hospital.

It was probably the one I'd seen behind the wheel of the black BMW.

The hit and run suddenly played out in my mind, a body rising and falling, the screech of tyres. The woman's scream. I squeezed my eyes against it, feeling weak, as if

I could faint at any moment. My heart rattled and panic overtook me. Was it him? Did my husband do that? Was I just pretending to myself that I saw someone else?

I took a deep breath; it took a moment for the feeling of dizziness to pass. And then, once I'd managed to regain some level of control, I reminded myself of him handing over his train tickets to the police and his explanation of where he was. Did the person who stole his car have the same jacket that was in my hands? Could I have imagined seeing it? I was shaking as I looked at it. I dug my hand into a pocket and brought out an elastic band, a used tissue. I went to the next pocket. A wrapper from a mint and then, surprisingly, one of Katie's novelty keyrings, a small colourful parrot. That was it. Nothing else.

I swallowed, dropped his jacket back on the bed, wiped the sweat from my hairline then went again to the woman's earring. I looked at it from different angles, held it up to the light. Smelled it.

Phil had explained it all. I'd heard him tell the police where he was, made him repeat it several times to me; his train ticket said he was at the station, not at the retail park. My chest was tight and I remembered the message on Twitter: *Room booked. I'll bring champagne.*

I leaned forward, trying to get some air into my lungs, trying to calm down. I'd never experienced a full on panic attack, but I'd come very close over the years. Since the episode with Jessica's biological father, I'd had more than my share of white-hot terror onslaughts and knew the signs.

Once when she was a baby, before I'd met Phil, I started to hyperventilate in Tesco's. They took me to the customer service aisle and someone medically trained (or so I was led to believe) informed me I was suffering from asthma. I told them I didn't have asthma, my eyes wide, my breathing thin, it was then someone said the words 'panic attack'. I'd never heard the expression before. As I breathed into a paper bag that had been brought up from the bakery department, she asked me if there was anything stressful going on in my life. I looked at Jessica, a chubby one-year-old that the check-out ladies were keeping amused and then at my meagre shopping which was all I could afford and had started to laugh at the absurdity of the question. It was the laughing that stopped me from going to A&E.

I knew anxiety – I was a mother. I was on good terms with irrational worries, the waking in the night kind, concerned for what might go wrong. I knew what it was to care about the future and fear the worst, like many of us do, but this was different. This wasn't the usual panicky feeling, this was a deep dread, a heavy loaded rock in the base of my chest whilst my heart knocked as if it were about to stop altogether and my body shook. The room wouldn't steady itself, the dizzy feeling continued and the sensation was extreme. I closed my eyes and started to count, as slowly as I could, until it passed a little. I decided the trick wasn't to think about the whole thing, just a little bit of it. I opened my eyes and looked at the earring. Bite size pieces.

I gripped my crutch, my hand slick with sweat and for the first time was glad of the grey rubber around the handle. Once standing, the hoop held tight in my other fist, I looked over to Phil's drawers. The flotsam that lay there. The crumpled bits of paper from his previous day. Without a thought of my cast or the risk of falling again, I headed toward them. I used the edge of the bed as a makeshift low rail, with that and my crutch, I felt relatively steady.

Phil's drawers are tall and thin, bought from an antique seller in Liverpool and in perfect keeping with the decor of the room. They stand like a mini skyscraper, nestled in the corner. They're full of stuff he doesn't really need but can't dispose of, like skincare and aftershave. I ridicule him about periodically. He argues that it's similar to my vanity station, filled with stuff I don't use and his is a male version, but I still like to poke fun.

When he gets Christmas presents of toiletries, sent from his mother in France, I like to comment how it'll be going in his 'drawers'. He takes it in good humour and I never find out if he does put the shower gel and aftershave tonic in his drawers because apart from making fun about them, they don't interest me at all. I have nothing to do with them, which is why, as I made my way up to them, panting, sweating and wiping the hair out of my face, I realised I would never have paid attention to what he left on top of them behind the lamp. The few crumpled receipts I was about to investigate could have been there for days; they might not be useful at all.

I reached for the first bit of paper. It was illegible, I could only just make out a few numbers, a receipt for something. I threw it on the bed and reached my arm back up, it came across various coins, tissues and then, something hard. It was thick paper or card. I pulled it out, a small sightseeing map of Chester. I absently stared at the points of interest, the Cathedral, the Rows, the City Walls, the Amphitheatre, the blue wavy line that represented the River Dee, and it dawned on me that I'd seen this map before, recently.

I unfolded it and looked at it clearly, and it suddenly came back to me, I'd seen this map yesterday. I'd seen it at the hotel. When I'd been sitting with my ankle propped up waiting for the ambulance, the man in reception had been pointing out the location of the Roman Tours to a group of Spanish tourists. He'd been doing it on a map exactly like this one.

The young girl I'd crashed into used one of these maps to write down my insurance details when she'd been on the phone to Della, they'd had a stack of them piled on the reception desk. The other side of the card was split into four; it was a voucher scheme. In each quarter page, an advert for a hotel. It entitled the owner to a free lunch in the cafe at either the Chester Museum or Cathedral when presented with a booking receipt from one of the participating hotels.

I ran my finger along the names of the hotels that were taking part. They were all budget hotels, not somewhere that I could imagine Phil staying. But Phil had to have visited one to get this map and I couldn't think of a single reason why.

He did no corporate entertaining in Chester; he worked as a branding manager for a large pharmaceutical company. The main body of clients with whom Phil was dealing at the moment were all London based. That's why for the last eighteen months he'd been spending half of his working week in London. There were no clients in Chester, all of his time spent at the local office was management based. I studied the map that had come out of Phil's pockets, looking for notes, writing, anything that he'd used it for, but there was nothing. It made no sense. Phil knew Chester as well as I did, so what good was a map of it to him?

Room booked. I'll bring champagne. Can't wait to see your hot body.

I looked back at the drawers and stood up, leaving the map on the bed. My fingers felt the dusty surface and then another bit of paper. It was a receipt for coffee. One espresso, bought at Crewe train station the previous day, paid in cash. I let out a laugh at the sight of it. Felt a small cooling wave of relief wash over me. The weighty dread in my stomach shifted a little. Crewe train station. *Exactly* where Phil said he was and here was the proof. I breathed deep, revelling in the confirmation that my husband hadn't been at the retail park, he'd been at the station, *he'd been where he said he was.*

I swung my arm back to see if there was anything else. I felt a few more coins, a mint wrapper and then just as I was about to abandon my search, my fingers felt the edge of something. It was small, right at the back, a tight little ball of paper.

I brought it down and sat on the bed with it. It was stuck together, it was tacky and hard. It was printed on sticky paper, making it difficult to unwrap. I carefully picked away at a loose edge of the tight little ball, slowly starting to release a small corner. I tried to read the print, but it was hard, the ink wasn't clear and the way it had been screwed up made it almost impossible to read. I stared at what I'd managed to pull away and suddenly I recognised what it was. A parking ticket. The pay and display kind, the ones issued from a machine on sticky paper so as to enable the driver to stick it to their car window as proof that they're entitled to park.

I took a moment, then picked it back up, trying desperately to read more of it, to pull at more of it, but it was useless. All I could make out was the beginning of

69

yesterday's date and the word Crewe, the rest was unobtainable. I stared at it, trying to make sense of why a parking ticket from Crewe, which as far as I could make out was for yesterday, would be on top of Phil's drawers. I studied the print, making sure it was Crewe and not Chester, trying to read the date, to be certain it was for this year, this month. He'd told the police that his car had been stolen in Chester, I'd seen him hand over his train tickets to them as proof of where he was at the time of the hit and run, so why would he have a car parking ticket from Crewe? And if the car had been stolen, how did he have the parking ticket at all? Wouldn't it have still been in the car?

I looked at the earring in my hand, the map of Chester from the hotel and the illegible car parking ticket and began to howl.

7

Suzie

She left the bank and walked out into the high street. The familiar, overpowering scents of perfume and traffic fumes combined with food drifted towards her. It was cold, rain threatened and Suzie remembered the weather report mentioning snow, so she pulled her jacket tight. Ignoring the wind, she went over to the nearest bollard and leaned against it, the cold iron biting though the material of her pants while she thought hard.

Even though it was still relatively early, Christmas shoppers were swarming the streets. The buskers had set up in force, a man walking a tightrope dressed as Charlie Chaplin was playing a violin, a choir were gathering to start carol singing, and somewhere, further down East-gate Street, a man was shouting religious phrases, but Suzie was oblivious to it all. Shoppers bustled past her, buggies banged into her ankles, foreign tourists offered their apologies, but she was blind to it, lost in the paperwork before her.

Suzie had been working in an admin job when she met Adam, her days spent in stuffy council offices typing up reports and filing neverending paperwork. She'd been alone for almost a year by then and had found herself in the frustrating situation of being over thirty with no real friends and no way of making new ones. It had been a harsh realisation, when she split from Carl, that her social circle consisted entirely of Carl's friends and their partners. They dropped off, gradually losing contact one by one as Suzie moved out of Carl's life and Tina, his new girlfriend, moved in. She couldn't blame them. Who wanted to go out with the awkward ex-girlfriend? What did they have in common any longer now she was single and they were thinking about marriage and children? Suzie had lost not only her boyfriend and her hopes of starting a family, but vast parts of her social life and she found herself obsessing over it. Thinking unhealthily over Carl and what he was doing, and Tina, who, in another devastating blow, Suzie had recently found out was pregnant.

On more than one occasion she'd taken weekend walks revisiting her old turf, going deliberately past Carl's house in the hope of seeing Tina fat and bloated and Carl miserable, but she never did. What she did see, however, was her lonely reflection in the window of their sitting room and she didn't like the image, so after one particularly long weekend of gym workouts, visiting her parents and then a trip alone to a night club which sounded reckless but turned out to be mortifying, she decided enough was enough and went to get herself a hobby.

She checked through the night courses being held at the local high school and settled on 'Beginners Photography', because it sounded slightly glamorous and because it was held on a Friday night, the loneliest night of the week. She invested in the best camera she could afford and went with the hope of going forward with her life. The reality was a group of pensioners reminiscing about dark rooms and film and bemoaning the digital age, but it did have a good tutor who showed her the basics of composition and photo editing and within two weeks, she was hooked. She found she was quite skilled at being a photographer, directing groups of people, instructing them how to stand, how to look, how to feel. And the more photographs Suzie took, the more she fell in love with the freedom that the camera gave her. She no longer felt pitiful when she was out alone, with a camera hanging around her neck she felt empowered, and most of her free time was spent squinting through her lens and recording images.

Suzie had long since moved past 'Beginners Photography' when she met Adam. By then she'd taken hundreds of images of the city, from the Roman street performers re-enacting history to the architecture of the Cathedral and the landscapes of the city walls. She'd photographed shoppers in the cobbled streets, animals at the zoo and two colleagues from the council offices had asked her to do portraits of their children. She had looked at investing in a portable studio and when she spoke to old friends she rarely saw since splitting from Carl, she could avoid any awkwardness by talking about photography. It saved her.

'That's a nice bit of kit,' were the first words Adam said to her.

She was at the races, standing by the fence looking at the crowds hoping to get some images of drunken women. She had an idea she might sell them to the local paper as they always did a story on how debauched Ladies' Day turned out to be. She turned around at his comment, ready to tell whoever it was to do one, but when she saw him the words never came.

The majority of good looking men are usually described as handsome or clean cut, or athletic, or some other roundabout adjective that conjures the image of virile masculinity, rarely are they described as beautiful, but when Suzie looked at Adam, that's exactly what she thought. Adam was beautiful. He had thick brown hair falling in slight curls over his forehead, giving him a wild, untamed look. He had high cheekbones, dancing blue eyes, and when he smiled, his whole face lit up. He was tall, so much so that she had to crane her neck to look up at him. And he was older than her too, in his mid-forties she guessed, which seemed to provide him with a real sense of sophistication and maturity. She took in his broad chest, wide shoulders and all at once felt childlike and vulnerable in his presence.

'Are you a professional?' he'd asked and the awkward-ness vanished. Suzie had found herself answering. He was like that, Adam. He had a way about him. As well as his good looks, he had the ability to make you feel instantly at ease.

'Who d'you work for that lets you use the automatic setting?' he'd continued leaning down so he was close to her and as Suzie caught his scent and felt the electric-like current at his proximity, she'd told him she worked for herself and it went from there.

In less than four weeks they were a couple and two months later she quit her job at the council and started working for him, under his training. It was intoxicating, the time she spent with him. It was everything that she didn't have with Carl, an exciting, overwhelming, romantic love. It was all-consuming and although Suzie had always scoffed whenever anyone had previously mentioned the words 'soul mates', after meeting Adam, and the months that they'd spent together, Suzie knew she'd found hers.

It was Adam that suggested she start up on her own, create her own business with its own bank account. He operated several and explained how it was the clever thing to do if you wanted to take advantage of the interest-free loans and overdrafts the banks were offering.

'Practically giving money away to new customers,' he'd told her, and he was right, the offers to start-up businesses were unbelievable.

'We make minimal repayments back,' he'd explained after she'd opened the account, 'use the money they've given us to invest in some new equipment, and then in three years,' he'd clicked his fingers, 'close the account and the business. HMRC thinks you've made nothing because you've been running the business at a loss, so you don't pay any tax, when all you've done is kept your declared incomings low and closed one business to start up another. Basically, it's as easy as changing your business name. You just tell your customers you're expanding, and then, hey presto, you've got all the offers of a new business open up to you again. We could take out another interest-free loan then if we like. Get a house, go on holiday. The money's there for the taking. How about we put this one toward our wedding?'

It was a 'whirlwind romance' as her mother liked to call it. Seven months after meeting Adam they were engaged and they'd be married the following year. People found it shocking, she knew Rachel did, particularly as she'd never had the chance to meet Adam yet, but as Suzie said, 'Why wait?' She was in love; she knew he was the man she'd been waiting for and she wasn't getting any younger.

She made Adam co-signatory so he could handle her account along with his others. If Suzie was honest (although she would never admit it to Adam), she found it all confusing. As most of her customers were businesses, they rarely paid her in cash. Most of it was done via bank transfer, so she made the legitimate payments into the accounts and left it to Adam to fiddle his side, the cash payments.

If one account started looking too healthy, he gave her different details for clients to pay into, stressing how it was better in their pocket rather than the taxman's. She had cards on all his accounts, used the ones he told her to and, sometimes, he'd give her a wad of cash. It was easy for him as the majority of his clients were all members of the public. They paid in notes and coins. Adam explained that this was how he'd worked for years and from previous experience with her ex-boyfriend, cheating the taxman was something that Suzie understood.

There was a shout and then a cheer, the tightrope walker had finished his routine and Suzie looked up, watching, while in her mind she went back to the statements, to where Adam had forged her signature for the overdraft, to the potential loss of her flat in Charles Street. He'd said they'd sell that flat after they were married. Sell his flat as well and use the money to buy a semi somewhere out of the city, somewhere with a garden. A family home. They were going to start a family, once they were married; it was the next step. He'd promised.

The cold had made her stiff and she moved quickly to work her circulation. She made her way out of the centre and towards the Cathedral just as it began to rain. She dodged the groups of tourists and ducked instead to the side of the shops, under its covered walkway. Unlike the black and white half-timbered rows in the centre, the walkway by the Cathedral was made from imitation concrete columns and offered none of the cosy shelter, although she was out of the rain, the wind blew hard and almost took her breath away.

And then she was out, back in the open and facing the town hall where small wooden huts were being constructed. The Christmas markets were due to open in a few days and as Suzie walked past the imitation Alpine huts, the prickly feeling of fear she felt earlier returned. She made her way past the police and bus station and toward the multi-storey car park. She'd try Adam again when she got to the car. He'd have an explanation for it, he was probably in his flat now above the studio, emptying the safe and on his way to the bank, because, of course, his cards would also have been frozen. So wherever Adam was, whatever he was doing, he couldn't get any money out of the account either.

The thought of Adam cursing the cash machine gave her some reassurance; as he was out on a job he wouldn't have taken any cash as everything on location was to be put through as 'expenses' and needed to be traced. Silly sod. He'd be on his way back now, she was sure, he wouldn't be able to survive with a frozen card. By lunchtime it would all be sorted.

He owed her for this. She'd make him take her to the Grosvenor, a nice meal. Full works. She'd forgive him somewhere around dessert, she could hear how he'd apologise. Explaining how he'd got lazy with the repayments, how he'd decided to up the overdraft because of low interest rates or some such reason, how he'd decided not to bother her with the paperwork.

The car park was in desperate need of maintenance, the paint peeling away, the concrete slabs damp and she shivered as she got to her car. She'd insist he called her more regularly next time he was working away on location. No more of this laid back 'phone me when you can' nonsense. She was done pretending she was relaxed about this kind of thing. They were going to be married, she could be demanding if she wanted to be and right at that moment, she very much wanted to. There was nothing more she wanted than Adam.

The phone ringing in her pocket made her jump and she almost dropped it in her haste to answer.

'Miss McFadden?' Her stomach fell in disappointment. It was a man's voice she didn't recognise.

'Speaking,' Suzie said as she threw her handbag on the passenger seat.

'Miss McFadden, of Staple & McFadden Photography?'

'Yes, can I help? Although I am no longer taking wedding bookings, but I can recommend a very good—'

'Is Adam with you? Adam Staple?'

Suzie paused. She didn't like his tone.

'I'm afraid Adam isn't here at the moment, can I help or take a message?'

There was a long pause, she could hear him breathing. She switched on the engine, the car immediately fogging up with condensation and she gave an involuntary shudder.

'You know where he is? I need to speak to him. Urgently.'

'No,' Suzie said, turning up the heaters. 'Can I ask what this is concerning? If it's about a job, I can get him to call you as soon...'

'This isn't about a fucking job, love.'

Suzie startled at the use of a swear word so early in the conversation.

'This is about the money he owes.'

'The money he owes?' Suzie repeated.

'I didn't want to call the business number,' he said. 'But Adam's left me no choice. I was expecting him last night but he didn't show, so you tell him, when you see him, that if he doesn't see me today with what he owes, there'll be consequences.'

Her mind couldn't keep up with the conversation. She was about thirty seconds behind understanding what she was being told.

'I'm sorry, what? Adam owes you money?'

'Don't pretend you don't know. So either you get it to me, or he gets it to me, by the end of play today.'

She frowned at his words. The business line automatically transferred calls to her mobile if they weren't answered at the studio but she'd never taken a call from this man before, and knew nothing of what he was talking about. Adam never mentioned owing money to someone in person, never mentioned meeting up with anyone, and besides, how could he when he was away on a location shoot?

'I think there's been a misunderstanding,' Suzie began. 'There must be. Adam's away on a photo shoot, in Wales.'

'So you get it to me then,' he said. 'Four grand. Tonight.'

She let out a shocked laugh. Four grand! What he was suggesting was ludicrous. Nonsense. It was a prank, a joke.

'Listen,' she said. 'I don't know who you are, or what you think Adam owes you, but you're wrong.' She took a deep breath. 'Is this about the props? The Christmas and winter scene backdrops? Is that where you're calling from?' She didn't wait for an answer. 'Adam cancelled that order. They were cancelled and as we didn't receive them, we didn't pay the invoice, so if that's what this call is about…'

'I'll tell you what,' he interrupted her. 'I'll come to you. Pop over to the studio today, so we can have a little chat about what Adam agreed to. Then you can pay what he owes and we can go on from there.'

'I don't think…'

'He's not told you about this has he, love? No matter, I'll explain it all later when I see you.'

The line went dead and Suzie stared at her phone in disbelief. A car was slowly moving behind her, the man leaning out of the window, trying to get her attention. He was making exaggerated hand gestures, trying to determine if she was leaving and if he could have her parking space. She watched in her rear-view mirror and ignored him, trying to determine what had just happened. Four grand. Who could Adam possibly owe four grand to, and for what? All the props and photography expenses were paid by card, went through the business account so that they could be claimed back, could it be that he'd bought something for cash?

It suddenly occurred to her that Adam's safe was full of money and in his flat above the studio. That if it was a simple mistake of him being behind, of him forgetting to make deposits in the bank and repayments with things he'd ordered, then there was something she could do about that until he returned. She would take the money out of there. She would empty the safe, pay off the bank and get rid of the overdraft, but whoever had just called would have to wait.

Whatever Adam had bought, whatever he owed, wasn't a priority. She checked the time: it was near ten. She'd need to call Rachel, tell her she'd be late. Explain that she had to make a quick trip to Adam's and sort out his mess. She realised that an apology meal from him at the Grosvenor wasn't going to cut it anymore. Adam had made a royal mess of things, taking up her time like this. When he got back they'd need to have a serious chat about how their finances worked, she needed to know exactly what was going on.

She'd have him take her on a mini-break, she thought as she put the car in gear, by way of him making it up to her, somewhere in January perhaps. Somewhere luxurious and indulgent. She'd recently seen one of the celebrities in a glossy magazine in Seville. That would do. She'd find out the details and Adam could take her there and apologise for making her feel like this.

As she went to reverse she saw the bank statements sticking out of her bag and saliva filled her mouth as a wave of nausea washed over her.

'Adam,' she muttered as she drove out of the car park and into the busy traffic. 'What the bloody hell have you been playing at?'

8

Rachel

'Rachel?'

'Suzie? Is that you?'

There was a moment's silence and I used it to try and get back some control. The phone had started to ring again as I was trying, without success, to pull apart the parking ticket. I'd spent a good ten minutes crying at the sight of it, before picking it back up and starting to pick at it. I was trying to ascertain if it really was from Crewe and if it was dated yesterday when she'd called. I'd thought it was Phil and had quickly gone to answer it, hobbling over to the unit on the far wall. At that point, I wanted to ask him outright about it all. I was crying, verging on hysteria and if he'd been there to shout at I would've howled at him.

I wanted to scream, to ask him what was going on and get some answers. To show him the earring, the parking ticket, the map and have him explain all my worries away with some rational reasoning. I was desperate for it not to be true. I kept seeing the Twitter message, the hit and run play out in my mind, his car, then him telling the police he wasn't there, showing his train ticket as proof, and then there was this. A woman's earring in his pocket, a map of hotels and a parking ticket for a car that was meant to be in Chester.

'You okay?' she asked and I nodded, knowing that if I spoke, she'd be able to hear it in my voice.

Suzie was one of my oldest friends. In the last eighteen months since we'd gotten back in touch, we'd become close again. And now, as we'd started working with each other, she knew all parts of my life. She knew Phil. She knew the girls. She knew us. She knew me of old and there was nowhere to hide. If she heard my voice waver, if she heard the slightest falter, she'd know something was wrong and would be asking questions I couldn't answer.

'How is everything?' she asked quietly when I didn't speak. 'How's your ankle? Are you in pain?'

'I'm okay,' I told her wiping my eyes. 'The painkillers are working. My ankle is fine, just a little uncomfortable and the medication is making me a bit... woozy. A bit tired, but other than that, it's fine.'

She waited a moment.

'And everything else?' she asked, 'is that okay? I never got a chance to ask you at the hospital, and you didn't pick up your phone last night, but is it...? I mean, are you okay? Are you and Phil...?'

I heard the blatant sympathy in her voice and my cheeks went hot. I gritted my teeth at the way she made her words soft in tone. I could imagine her face filled with concern at the other end of the line, I knew what she was thinking.

'Did you ask him?' she pressed. 'About the messages on Twitter, was it him? Is he having an affair?'

When Suzie's last relationship had ended, when it became public knowledge that Carl, her then boyfriend, had left her for another woman, I'd been the one having this conversation with her. I'd rung her up and been sympathetic. I'd pitied her, asked her if she was okay, made my voice soft and gentle. I invited her to the house for coffee at the time; it was how we got back in touch, the rekindling of our friendship. I'd been the Good Samaritan, the one who helped her.

I was the one who was sure of my life; I was the one who could be gracious with my sympathy and kindness because my marriage was rock solid. And now I was ashamed. Ashamed and frightened of the position I was forced to be in, listening to the pity and concern in her voice now directed at me. I wasn't certain of anything anymore and it made me afraid.

'It's fine,' I said and my voice came out stronger than I expected. 'All fine,' I lied.

There was a beat.

'What did he say?' she asked. 'Did he deny it? Did you tell him about the messages? Because believe me, Rachel, speaking from experience, if he...'

'It wasn't Phil. I told you that.' I was being harsh but I couldn't stop myself, it was the way she was including me with her sorry experience with Carl. 'Phil would never cheat on me, it was a mix up. We can forget about those messages.'

There was a pause. 'Oh, well, okay then, good,' she said. 'I just thought, with you going there yesterday, after what we found...'

'It was a misunderstanding,' I heard myself telling her. 'The police came over last night and Phil gave them his train ticket. He was in Crewe yesterday afternoon. Phil wasn't in Chester.'

'The police?'

Blood rushed to my face again, I was sweating.

'Phil's car has been stolen,' I gave a false laugh. 'It was madness here yesterday, what with my broken ankle and Phil's stolen car!'

She didn't reply straight away. 'Oh,' she said and then, 'his car was stolen? In Chester?'

'What does it matter where it was stolen?' I snapped. 'It wasn't him. He was in Crewe yesterday afternoon. He didn't send the messages, it's all fine.'

'Right,' she said. 'Well, like you said, it was probably Della.'

'Must have been.' I picked up the hotel map and ran my finger along the crease where Phil had folded it. 'I'll have a word with her, tell her not to use my laptop again.'

We both took a moment. Suzie was driving I realised, talking to me on hands-free, I could hear the soft whoosh of the traffic around her.

'Listen,' Suzie said. 'I'm so sorry, I know this is shitty timing, but I'm going to be late. Adam's messed up the bank account and I need to sort a few things out, nip to the studio and then back to the bank. It's urgent or I wouldn't be going. I shouldn't be more than an hour at most, I know there's a ton of stuff to do, but do you think you might be able to make a start without me?'

My mind was so full of Phil that it took me a moment. 'The Gatsby party,' I said as I caught up. 'Of course, I can start the work from here.'

'That's what I thought,' Suzie said. 'If you could call round the temp agencies, hire the catering staff we need then I can do the rest when I've finished with the bank.'

'I'll call the marquee company, but,' I stopped as I realised, 'we need to measure up for that. I need to measure up in the back garden before anything else. Shit.'

'I'll only be an hour or so,' she said. 'Perhaps two at most. I could do it this afternoon? Get the measurements then and ring round?'

'That's tight,' I said shaking my head. 'Without the measurements we can't secure a marquee and as this is the busy season, we'll need to know if we can get one or if we have to look for something else. It's the first thing we need to do as it'll affect everything else we book.'

We were both silent, trying to think of a way around it. The house was too small for the number of guests that had been invited to the party. Securing the marquee was the first step in the planning; if we couldn't get one we'd need to think of another solution and we couldn't do any of that if we didn't have the measurements of the garden. That would impact on how many staff we needed to hire for the night, where we could prepare the food, where the band would be playing and where the DJ would set up. It was the first task to be done and it sounded like Suzie had things of her own to sort out. This job was too short notice, there was too much to be done in the time we had.

I looked down at my cast, my leg was throbbing and since my escapades around the bedroom searching the top of Phil's drawers, the pain had increased.

'If we cancel now,' I said, 'would that be better than making a mess of it? If we can't get a marquee...'

'We can't cancel!' Suzie's voice was shrill. 'Rachel, this is our big break, our first big job. I know you've broken your ankle, but I can do most of it. Please, we can do it. You said so at the hospital yesterday. It's just logistics. Just hiring people and delegating. I'll go there and measure up now. I'll call the bank and...'

'Della,' I said as the idea came to me. 'I'll ask Della.'

'Della?' Suzie asked and I nodded as the idea took hold.

It was perfect. If Della took me to the house then it meant we would be in the car together, alone. It would give me a chance to ask her about the laptop and Twitter messages without the threat of Phil finding out, because I realised as I'd talked to Suzie that I didn't want to speak to Phil about any of it at all. I didn't want to be there when he came home. If something was going on, if my husband was having an affair, if he was involved in the hit and run in some way, then I wanted to be certain about it before I asked him. I didn't want to see the pity in his face as he told me, I didn't want to hear my husband's voice go soft as he explained he was sleeping with another woman. I didn't want to be pacified, or given some rational explanation, I wanted to discover what was going on for myself and be ready if he admitted to it.

I picked up the earring, inspected it as I told Suzie involving Della was the perfect solution. Della could help with the party; I'd make her do what I couldn't. The cleaning and other household chores that she usually did could wait. I'd get Jennifer as well, my friend from the catering college, and hire her for the job. I ended the call with us arranging to meet later at the house, Suzie promising that this was a one off, that a quick trip to the studio and bank was all that she needed.

I understood, she was running a photography business just like I was running a catering business whilst we got this events company off the ground. It took a certain skill to be able to juggle things, to be able to run two or three businesses together as I did. It took me a while before I got organised with my work and besides, she was right, this party was too good an opportunity to pass up. Once we had the measurements it was simply a case of hiring staff, ordering props and food and delegating.

My ankle was throbbing, I collapsed on the bed and I hastily took some more painkillers to take the edge off. I hadn't yet eaten and the acid in my stomach churned, I was slightly dizzy. The earring was still in my hand, the phone in my other, and without thinking I dialled the number. I knew it verbatim and once connected, I asked to be put through to him. It took all of two minutes.

'Felix?'

'Rachel! What a pleasant surprise! How's that ankle of yours? Phil tells me you had a car accident?'

'Fine, fine, thank you.' My voice was trembling, I wasn't quite sure what I was doing, only that I was doing it.

I'd dialled the London office, knowing Phil wasn't there and was now speaking to Felix, his colleague, his partner in the big deal they were in the process of securing for the company.

'I just wanted to apologise,' I said, and surprised myself by how calm I sounded, how in control. 'For ruining the big presentation that you two had set up yesterday.'

'Apologise?'

'Well, I know it was postponed,' I went on, ignoring my racing heart and my throbbing leg, 'but it was my fault that Phil had to cancel. If I hadn't had my silly accident, then it could've gone ahead...' I let my voice trail off and waited for him to fill the silence.

It worked.

'The presentation wasn't postponed,' he said, 'so no need for apologies. You really don't need to ring me for that Rachel, although it is lovely to hear from you, how are the girls?'

'It wasn't postponed?' I asked, ignoring his question, 'so Phil didn't cancel it?'

'Oh yeah, Phil cancelled it,' Felix explained and I heard a phone ring somewhere behind him in the office, a rustle of papers, 'but he did that on Monday. He called the clients on Monday afternoon, said it was due to him not having the numbers together. He needed to get some more data so he wouldn't be able to get to the London office at the time he thought, he said...'

'So Phil never intended to come to London yesterday morning?' I pressed. 'He knew he was going to be late? You didn't call him?'

There was a pause.

'He went to the regional office,' I went on. 'Phil was at the Chester office yesterday morning?'

'He took the morning off,' Felix said slowly. 'Said he had to sort out some personal business, listen...' His tone changed. 'Rachel, I'm sorry if I've said something out of line here, if Phil's not told you that he booked time off...'

I could hear it in his voice, the uncertainty, the veiled concern. I realised how it must have sounded, how me calling him out of the blue and asking him where my husband was implied the very thing I wanted no one to know.

'I'm sorry, Felix,' I said quickly. 'Of course Phil wasn't there yesterday morning. Of course he took the morning off! I've got myself all muddled, got my days mixed up. It must be the medication, making me have a senior moment!' I gave out a laugh. 'I just wanted to apologise for him not being in at all, and to catch up, how are the boys? Tell me, is Alfie still mad about penguins?' I endured five minutes of painful small talk and ended the call as quickly as possible.

Sweat was soaking through my nightgown, my hands shaking. If what Felix had told me was correct, then Phil never intended to go to London when he left the house yesterday morning. He knew the meeting was cancelled because he had already cancelled it. Phil had taken the morning off and he'd lied about it.

When he kissed me goodbye, he told me he was heading for the London office. But he wasn't. He was going somewhere else entirely.

9

Suzie

Adam's photography studio was on the outskirts of the city centre and the flat he owned was above it. The property was just a ten-minute drive from the car park near the bank at most but the traffic slowed to a pitiful pace just outside the amphitheatre. She looked over at it, a semi-circular piece of ground surrounded by a busy road and overlooked by a hotel. A group of school children were at the far end, a multi-coloured flock of padded jackets in the rain and sleet. Three ladies pulling travel cases behind them stared down at the group in puzzlement. Everyone was wearing a pained expression; even those in the vehicles around her and it seemed to be a direct reflection of her mood. Only the children, out of school and on a field trip, seemed to have any energy as they scuttled about on the sandy ground.

Suzie had never been impressed by the amphitheatre; she supposed it must be something to be standing amongst the ruins of the largest example in Britain, but it never moved her. The painted far side wall where it was blocked off reminded her of a fairground ride, the 'added scenery', and there was also the fact that it was surrounded by industrialism. Unlike other parts of Chester where you could mount a flight of stairs and be above the city, or go through a hidden walkway and be sheltered by the city walls, hidden or taken away from the everyday, this relic was plonked in the middle of it all. The council and businesses had just built around it. Car engines and their horns, hotels and pubs all enclosed this great historic ruin and seemed to diminish its history.

Adam, however, was of a different opinion; he loved it. When they first got together he boasted that he lived, 'just past where the gladiators performed'. His studio and flat above were more than *just past*, but she could forgive him that. Adam was a storyteller, you only had to look at his photographs. She Googled it once, the amphitheatre, and read that it was also used as a medieval rubbish dump but she'd not tell Adam that. He would never say he lived, 'just past where they used to fly tip', so Suzie kept that one to herself.

The school children got in line and started to file toward the exit just as the traffic inched forward and Suzie gripped the steering wheel. She didn't realise it, but she was formulating a prayer of sorts. Please let Adam be in the studio. Please let him be home. Please let him have the answers.

The road followed the great sweeping direction of Grosvenor Park and took her around a long corner. She craned her neck, leaning forward, hopeful for a glimpse of the studio. She fully expected to see the shutters up. Following the one-way system, she banged on the wheel in frustration as the road took the row of shops out of her view. The traffic stopped and started at an agonising pace, her windscreen wipers creaking with every stroke. She gritted her teeth and when she finally arrived she was jittery and angry. She imagined hitting him hard on his chest whilst also clutching at him, her fingernails digging into his biceps. She wanted to feel his breath on her face, his arms around her, his body dwarfing hers, she wanted him to take care of this bank situation and the debt, and be on her way to meet Rachel.

She swung into the car park and stared up as a heavy slug of disappointment hit her stomach. The studio windows were dark, the back door locked, and in the designated car park, the space allotted to Adam's car was empty.

–

The first time Suzie cheated HMRC was for six skirting boards in a semi-detached on South Wirral. To be fair it had been Carl, her ex-boyfriend, who'd been the real criminal, but it was the first time Suzie had been actively involved. She'd been with Carl for eighteen months by then. He'd just set up on his own, branching out as a painter and decorator. He was working constantly in those early days, so that night, when the owner of the semi-detached arrived to pay for the skirting boards, Carl was out on another job.

'So sorry,' she'd said as she'd pushed the notes into Suzie's hand. 'Carl said to put a cheque in the post, but I know he needs the money for supplies so thought I'd drop it off on my way home. Tell him he's done a wonderful job, we're delighted with the way they reflect the light.'

She'd taken down the woman's name and address, the details of the job and thought herself very efficient, half imagining that she could be Carl's PA. When Carl arrived home, she presented it to him. After he'd counted out the crisp twenty-pound notes, he went to his invoice book and ripped out the corresponding page. He put it together with her handwritten receipt and tore them both into tiny shreds.

'Shouldn't you leave that in?' Suzie asked. 'For your records?'

'Why should I leave it in,' said Carl throwing the paper into the fire. 'When I never did that job in the first place?'

He chuckled at her expression and kissed her forehead as if she were a naive child. Then, over a cold beer, he explained (if a little patronisingly, Suzie later thought) how, if you were smart, you didn't have to bother with tax like normal people did. Like she did in her job, like the rest of the working population did.

'You only have to look at all the rich,' he'd told her. 'Those actors and people on the telly, aren't they always being done for tax evasion? They're all doing it.'

Opening his invoice book, he showed her how he fiddled it, every fifth cash job didn't happen. That cash was theirs. They paid no tax on it and they could spend it how they liked.

He told her it was something that everyone did, if they were clever enough, and Suzie, with wide eyes, completely understood. They bought a Chinese takeaway and a bottle of really expensive Sauvignon Blanc with the money that night and Suzie felt special and dangerous all at once. It felt like being a criminal without committing any real crime, certainly no crime in the sense of someone else getting hurt. A 'victimless crime', was how Suzie thought of it.

They were getting one up on the system, that was all. Taking it back from the taxman and it gave Suzie a sense of self-righteousness. It felt like a form of protest. And in the back of her mind, she knew that if it all went tits up it would be Carl, not her, that would be in trouble. After all, she paid her tax whether she wanted to or not, proof was the amount taken from her pay slip every agonising month.

Carl's business not only survived but thrived. They spent the cash on holidays, new clothes and meals out and they could afford to save. Within two years they'd enough to put down a deposit on a house. Two of Carl's friends had their own businesses, one as a landscape gardener and another as a car mechanic, and although none of them ever said as much, she was sure they did the same. She looked at the cash brought out on a Saturday night, saw their new cars and fancy clothes, and made the assumption that everyone who could do it, did.

And if it hadn't been for Carl and cheating HMRC, they wouldn't have got the joint mortgage. Suzie wouldn't have paid it off for five years and she wouldn't have got half from the sale of the house when they split up. She'd still be in her parents' house instead of being able to afford her flat in Chester. She'd be catching the bus instead of driving her car. Using some old phone instead of her new one and without any kind of gym or fitness club membership. Life would be very different. So it was, Suzie thought, perfectly reasonable that Adam did the same.

But now, sitting in the empty studio, bank statements in hand, she thought she might have left a little too much to Adam. As she checked the answer machine, the realisation that she should've been more involved shone in her mind like a neon light. This wasn't the odd cash job of a painter and decorator, this was thirty thousand pounds in debt. Adam was much more sophisticated than squirreling away payment for the odd job here and there. He had several businesses and bank accounts that he managed, hers included, and he fiddled them in a way she knew nothing about and now, she didn't know what to do for the best. And what was worse, she couldn't get hold of him to ask. She'd never thought she'd need to. He was her fiancé. The man she loved and the man with whom she would have children.

When his voicemail clicked in, this time, she left a message.

'Adam,' her voice had a tremble to it. 'I've just been to the bank. I've seen how overdrawn we are on my account and I've seen the loan agreement.' She took a long, deep breath. 'Why didn't you tell me? I'm not totally inept. I could've helped. I'm not angry,' Suzie went on, 'I just wish you'd told me.' Her voice was wobbly, she sounded pathetic and she straightened her back. 'And I wish you'd call me back. Not only to sort this out, but I've had a call from some bloke who thinks you owe him four grand. I don't know what you bought off him, but you've forgotten to pay and he's talking about visiting the studio today to see you. He was...' Suzie paused, it sounded feeble to say he was mean, but that's exactly how he sounded: mean and nasty. 'Aggressive,' Suzie finished. 'I should already be at Rachel's by now, so...' her voice became a little firmer. 'So I'm going into your flat. I can't see any alternative than to get some of the cash. I'm taking some of it to the bank so call me. Call me as soon as you hear this,' Suzie paused for a moment. 'I love you,' she said and ended the call.

Taking out the spare key from the cash register in the studio, Suzie went up the narrow staircase at the back of the shop that led to Adam's flat. She knew the combination to the safe, a mix between both their birthdays. All she needed to do was get out some of the cash, make some kind of deposit to keep the bank happy and then she could talk about it all with Adam later.

The flat was a mess. The door led straight into his kitchen and it wasn't how Suzie usually saw it. A plate filled with crumbs, a half-drunk coffee cup and a plastic wrapper of some kind littered the counter. She closed the door and then, as she took her first breath, put a hand over her mouth to stop herself from inhaling the smell. There was a strong stench of something rotting, something dying.

'Adam?'

The unexpected shock of the smell in his flat made her feel vulnerable and without thinking she'd called his name. She took a moment, in the silence, her hand over her mouth and nose and watched a bluebottle work its way along the kitchen worktop. She took a step forward and was about to call him again when she saw the overflowing bin to the side of her. Three empty tins of mackerel. The juice had dripped onto the floor tiles and left a sticky mess. She cursed under her breath and began taking out the full bin bag and cleaning up the floor. Trying not to retch, she replaced it and left it by the door, ready for her to take to the outside bins when she left. The smell hadn't entirely gone, but removing the rubbish had brought back some of the anger she'd felt at the bank and she cursed him for leaving everything in such a state.

She went into his lounge area and saw several magazines and newspapers on the coffee table. His three photography books (expensive, glossy things with full page graphics) had been pushed to the side and in their place were the local paper and a magazine. Suzie picked it up. She stared at the cover: bold headlines, bright colours, a young actress laughing with the words '*Super*

97

sexy, shiny hair can be yours!' written in pink, along with five smaller pictures of teenagers who must be famous in some capacity.

She looked at it a moment longer before flicking through the pages. It wasn't a magazine she'd ever read as it was clearly for young girls, the kind that was filled with bright images and sensational gossip. She dumped it back down on Adam's coffee table, bemused.

There was a can of something on the floor and her foot knocked against it, she dived down to rescue it before anything spilled and cursed Adam. Whenever she'd visited his flat it was always spotless. So in order in fact that she'd joked more than once about him having OCD concerning his uncluttered and very tidy space. He usually had a bottle of wine open in the kitchen, a candle giving out some luxurious aroma and would always clean up after himself. Rinsing the glasses before they left, running a cloth over the worktops and plumping up the cushions on his sofa. It was confusing and somewhat enlightening to see it like this, to see it actually *lived in*.

Some shoes lined the wall that led into his bedroom where his bed was unmade with a pair of jeans and socks on the floor. She smiled, he clearly didn't expect to be gone for long and better she knew before they started living together exactly how messy he really was. There'd always been a small part of her that had wondered at his neatness, she'd tease him about this when he got back. Tell him she was relieved to find out he had some faults after all.

She walked into the small room to the side of his bedroom, which Adam had as an office. Here things were still organised as usual; his laptop, notes and files were arranged on the desk. Several filing cabinets and shelves of paperwork were against the back wall and a small ivy plant was hanging from the ceiling. Here was where he counted the cash, made notes and dealt with everything concerning his businesses. Here was as she expected it to be.

She went to the side of the desk, to a cupboard door where he kept his safe. A small iron safe, grey with a dial type door, the kind you saw in old movies. How he got it upstairs she had no idea, but he had and it was where he kept his money. *Their money*, she corrected herself. Money they were saving for their wedding, and their future.

Suzie had got cash out of it before, had seen how much he kept in there and was confident it would be at least ten grand. She'd never actually counted it, but she was sure it was a reasonable amount. Enough to pay off some of the loan and keep the bank at bay.

A rush went up inside her chest as she opened the cupboard door. The safe door was slightly ajar. She heard herself moan as she pulled it back.

It was empty. Bare shelves.

There was no cash, only the money counter, empty plastic coin bags and some tape for wrapping up the notes.

She put a hand to her forehead that was now prickled with cold sweat.

No money.

She was thirty thousand in debt, about to lose her flat and Adam wasn't returning her calls.

'For fuck's sake!' she shouted, as she fell to her knees.

10

Rachel

I was only twenty when I met Phil. Jessica was just a year old and I was living with my mother having returned there, tail between my legs, when she was seven months. I'd tried to make a go of it with Jessica's father but two teenagers and a surprise pregnancy was hard going.

I see now that it was the worst decision I could've made. Not the separation from Jessica's father (who got another girl pregnant within the year), but going back to my mother. She was single at the time and going on blind dates with a frenzy.

My mother isn't the type of woman who does well on her own. She's only bearable when she's got male company, and it's only a new lover that she'll listen to. Her mind overthinks and if she doesn't have someone to tell her to 'cut that crap out' her neurosis goes on overdrive. So life at home was tense.

I'd been working at the chemist two months when I met Phil. Even now I can remember him: wearing a suit, dark brown with a pale blue tie. I was watching him before he even came into the pharmacy. I liked the way he moved; he was very self-assured. He swung his arm a little as he walked, in time with the swing of his hips.

'You're new,' he'd said, walking right up to me and I'd blushed. He'd laughed at my embarrassment and I'd joined in, amused by the reaction he'd caused in me.

'When did you start?' he asked and listened with real interest when I told him. He was a medical sales rep back then, often visiting the surgery and presenting to the staff but he'd always stop by to see me.

I was a single mother; no real money, no qualifications, a distrust of men and a bullying, controlling mother. Phil changed everything. He managed to charm not only me and my daughter, but also my mother. And when I moved out, ready to start my life with Phil, my mother said the only nice thing I can ever remember, 'Keep tight hold,' she'd said, 'you two have something good there.'

If I'd been told the future then, I'd have laughed. If I'd been shown images of myself with trembling hands as I got myself dressed that morning, the sweat on my forehead as I hobbled to the sink to wash, the anxiety over my husband's actions and fidelity clear on my face, I'd have laughed back then and said it was impossible. Unbelievable, unthinkable. Phil was my saviour, my knight, the happy ending to my fairy-tale.

But the knight in shining armour routine was done fourteen years ago. People change. Look at my mother. She remarried, moved to Devon and became a Buddhist. We've a strained relationship now. I tend to keep her at arm's length, avoiding her calls and emails, but when I do talk to her, she tells me about mindfulness and freedom from material possessions. She tells me I'm self-obsessed and greedy, and perhaps I am greedy, wanting a safe, predictable life for me and my family, but so what? Doesn't everyone?

We have a large kitchen diner, open plan, wooden floors and plenty of space. It's the room I love most in the house. We had kept to minimalist decor, white walls, the Scandinavian look. The simplicity of it was soothing as I made it to the kitchen table with the laptop lying there, and collapsed on the chair panting. I'd had to come downstairs on my bottom and my whole body ached with the effort. My cast was painful, a dull ache that the medication hadn't completely soothed.

Rain was hitting the window, it was coming down heavy and I shivered slightly; I was wearing a cotton wrap dress, more suited to August than November, but it was the best I could do and it provided no comfort from the chill in the air.

The phone rang just as I was pulling the laptop toward me and I froze. The nearest one was in the hall by the front door and I couldn't make it there in time. I waited, listening to see if they'd ring off or leave a message. I heard the answer machine kick in. My cheerful voice apologise to whoever was on the other end of the line and invite them to leave a message. There was a pause, an intake of breath, and then a familiar voice that made my heart gallop.

'Mr Farrell? It's Detective Sergeant Bailey here, just following up on last night's call.' He took a moment. 'I'd really like to speak to you, and Mrs Farrell, about the run of events that took place yesterday. If you could call the station, as soon as possible, the number is...' I couldn't listen to any more of the message, the pounding of the blood in my ears was roaring. The police had called again. Did they know something? Worked something out that I hadn't?

I pulled the laptop toward me and opened it up, Della hadn't yet arrived and for that I was grateful. I'd no idea what time Phil had told her to come and I had a vague notion that she was taking the piss, but I couldn't speculate on that now. I needed to see the Twitter messages. I needed to know if it was Phil who sent them.

The dial on the screen slowly turned as I waited for the Wi-Fi to connect, for the page to upload. And then, when it did, I let out a groan of frustration. Instead of taking me straight to an account, as it had before, a page uploaded asking me to log in. I thought how I got to the messages yesterday and went back to Google, typed in the Santa holidays I'd been looking at, desperately searching for the Twitter icon I'd clicked. I found it and again, was presented with the home page asking for log in details. I banged my fist on the table, desperately trying to remember the username from the messages I'd read.

BigSmilers I typed in, hoping that the username would be stored and recognised but nothing came up. *BigSmiles, BigSmiling, BigSmiler.*

I clicked on 'forgot password' and it prompted for an email or phone number. I froze, if I put Phil's mobile number in, the message would go directly to him. I was at a loss. I thought a moment and then went into the calendar function. It was something I used heavily to organise my work and it was also where I put in Phil's movements. I went back over the previous weeks, his trips to London. How long he'd been there, when he'd returned. Were they all lies? Was he seeing another woman in Chester on all these dates instead?

I looked over yesterday's entry, *Phil in London*, I'd typed for the Tuesday morning, but he wasn't in London. He'd taken the morning off. He'd lied.

'Where were you?' I hissed at the screen. 'Were you in Crewe or on that bloody retail park?'

I needed his phone, his diary. I needed to read his emails but I had no idea how. I leaned forward and put my head in my hands. Immediately the hit and run played out in my mind: Phil's BMW charging forward, the screech of tyres against the ground.

'Shit,' I said as saliva filled my mouth. 'Shit, shit, shit.'

I took a few deep breaths that had no impact on my thudding heart, and went back to Google.

Hit and Run. Chester.

It was the first result.

Officers appeal for information.

Police were called to Grosvenor Retail Park yesterday afternoon following reports that a pedestrian had been hit by a moving vehicle outside the Mexican fast food outlet. Officers were informed that a man had been involved in a serious collision with a black BMW, which failed to stop after the collision at around 2.30pm. The pedestrian, who suffered serious injuries and is believed to be in a coma, was taken to hospital where he is now receiving treatment. His condition is currently described as stable. Police are now appealing to the public. Anyone with information in relation to the incident should call…

A cold sweat had built on my shoulder blades, on my upper lip, between my breasts. None of it made sense. None of it.

It couldn't have been Phil, not *my Phil*. I could extend my imagination to him having an affair, I could stretch to that, but I would not accept that he had anything to do with the hit and run. He was a good man. He wouldn't drive off after doing something like that. I couldn't understand it, it just didn't make any sense. I'd seen that car, *his car*, travel at speed. As if they intended to hit whoever they were charging at. It wasn't an accident, not what I'd seen, so it made no sense that Phil, my Phil of all people, would do something like that.

The front door slammed and I jumped.

I grabbed the map and screwed-up parking ticket and thrust them in my pocket as footsteps made their way toward me. I had no idea what I'd say to him, how I'd ask him, tell him. I wasn't ready. I wasn't prepared. I snapped the laptop shut and went for the earring but it escaped my fingers, it slid out of my grasp, moving further down the table. I stretched as far as I could, but my cast pinned me to the chair.

'Hello?'

It was Della and I looked up in shock, relieved it was her but horrified to be caught out. I stretched as far as I could to the earring but to no avail.

'I'm so sorry I'm late. Did you get my message? I called your mobile a few times but you didn't pick up. Has everything been okay? Did the girls get to school? Phil said last night he'd take them, did he? How's your ankle?'

She appeared in the French doors, soaked from the rain, her hair hanging down in long tendrils making her look much younger than she was.

'I thought you'd be in bed!' she said when she saw me. 'Are you feeling alright? Is it okay if I put this in the dryer?' She held up her coat. 'I'm not sure it'll dry on the rack. It'll only need ten minutes or so. I'll do that and then get on with cleaning the kitchen, unless you need me for anything else? Do you want me to help you back upstairs? Back to bed?'

She came toward me, her face wet, and smiled. Then her expression froze when she saw my face.

'What's wrong?' she asked stopping at the side of me. 'What's happened?'

She looked down and saw the earring, the hoop that lay just out of my reach and picked it up. A small murmur escaped me, but it was too late. She was holding it in the light.

I went to say how it was mine, how it was Katie's or Jessica's. The story of some made-up tale on the edge of my lips, but then her face broke out into a large grin that stopped me from talking.

'My earring!' she said. 'You found it.'

I watched as she put it quickly into her earlobe with the practised moves of someone who does it daily. It was Della's earring.

'I lost this yesterday when I was cleaning your room,' she said. 'Looked all over but couldn't find it.'

I stared at her. It was Della's earring, fallen from her ear when she was cleaning my bedroom, as I paid her to. Not fallen from Phil's pocket but fallen from my bed. I slumped in my chair, exhausted.

'Your earring.' I nodded. 'Of course it's your earring,' I said and closed my eyes, suddenly drained of all energy.

I thought of Phil, the idea of him having an affair with the wearer of the earring that was now back in Della's ear. The logical explanation for how it had come to be in my bedroom.

'I think I'm going insane,' I told her and found myself starting to laugh.

11

Suzie

Suzie took a deep breath and opened her eyes. The safe was empty. Left open. No money.

'Okay.' She concentrated on filling her lungs and then letting the air slowly out. 'Okay.'

She tried to think of a logical explanation but all she could recall was the memory of Carl confessing his love for Tina. Carl speaking quickly over a cheap meal of tagliatelle carbonara, stressing that he hadn't done anything. He hadn't so much as kissed Tina, but he wanted to, he very much wanted to and that was enough.

It hadn't been a surprise. Suzie had known her relationship with Carl was in trouble because there'd been 'the signs'. Little clues that Carl was straying and, at the time, she'd ignored them all. They'd stopped having sex, that was the first sign. Not so much as a fumble in over three months and then Carl started going to the gym obsessively. He'd started talking about his new personal trainer called Tina non-stop, and was sprucing himself up to meet her. New sports gear, new haircut and stinking of aftershave. And the selfies! It was the reason she came off Facebook, so many self-congratulating photographs of Carl, taken by Carl. Carl tensing his biceps, Carl drinking a protein shake, Carl bare-chested in the garden, Carl with a drink in his hand and the words, 'Beer-o-clock!' written underneath. So many little clues that he was trying to impress someone that wasn't her. They became obvious as soon as he said it was over. She'd known then that Carl was cheating, so surely if Adam was having an affair she'd have spotted the signs?

She thought back over the past few days. They'd had sex. Just three days ago, half drunk in her flat and he'd been very passionate. Very loving. He'd insisted they took a bath together afterward, washing her hair, gently massaging her back with a sponge. And he'd been talking about the wedding, helping her plan. Only last week they'd chosen the track for their first dance. They'd settled on 'Better Together' by Jack Johnson; Adam had suggested it and Suzie had been delighted. It was perfect. He'd downloaded it there and then. Played it in her flat whilst she'd been preparing their evening meal, him pouring her a glass of wine and singing along. They'd even had a little dance in the kitchen whilst the chicken browned.

Her eyes snapped open.

'Impossible,' she said and took another deep breath. 'Impossible.'

There was absolutely no way Adam had left her, she was sure of it. He had *not* done a runner. They were in love, proper love. He wouldn't leave her like this, if he knew how much she wanted to speak with him he'd be home in a flash. Besides, wasn't that his laptop on the desk? Weren't his clothes still in his wardrobe? His shoes still littering the floor? No, Adam had not left her for another Tina.

She stood up and walked back out into the lounge and stood for a moment in the silence playing different scenarios out in her mind. Perhaps he'd been mugged. He was on his way to the bank, money in his pockets when he was attacked and beaten, the cash stolen. Perhaps he'd got caught up in his job, followed the light and got out of range on his phone unaware of how much he needed to be back. That was much more plausible. Or perhaps, Suzie thought with a lurch in her stomach, something had happened to him.

She marched back into the office and looked around for his diary for any clue as to where he was. Wales. She was sure he'd said he was going to Wales. She picked up the test sheets, the notepad, the bits of receipts ready for him to file, but there was nothing about his appointments. She thought about going to the diary in the studio but she knew he kept his location work on the calendar in his phone. He didn't make any hard copies of his appointments just in case he should be investigated.

'Bloody hell, Adam!' she hissed. This avoiding tax was all very well and good until something like this happened. When she needed to know where he was and where he'd put the cash.

Biting her thumbnail she went into his bedroom, hoping to find something there. Stepping over his clothes on the floor, she went over to his unmade bed and picked up his pillow. She held it close to her face and took a long breath in of his scent whilst looking over at his bedside table. There was nothing other than a half empty glass of water. She threw his pillow back on his bed, then after a moment, lay down. She couldn't think what to do and for a moment, she was lost.

Her phone bleeped in her bag and she scrambled up for it. She had a message. Going into the lounge, she grabbed it and felt the plunging drop of disappointment as she saw it wasn't from Adam, but Rachel. Della hadn't yet arrived, but as soon as she did, Rachel would ask her to take her to the Gatsby house and they'd meet Suzie there. She ended with, *Don't be too long!* and Suzie felt her stomach clench.

'Well, at least she's got Della,' she said as she put her phone away, but she wasn't entirely confident that it was for the best.

Suzie imagined Della trying to measure up in the garden accurately, help them pin up the fabric backdrops and move about props with her inane questions and inability to listen and shook her head. She'd be a liability. From what she'd seen of Della, Suzie was sure she'd break everything, not take instructions and generally get in the way. She was okay to mop a kitchen floor but not qualified to take exact measurements and arrange catering for three hundred, and there was something about her that Suzie didn't quite trust.

After speaking with Rachel she'd had the idea that they'd use someone from the catering college instead. Rachel often hired students for her own gigs from Jennifer, a teacher she knew who worked there, and they'd agreed on employing them with this one, so why not hire one of them full time for the week? But she needed to sort out the money situation with Adam and that conversation with Rachel hadn't happened and now Della was the hired help. She shook her head. So be it. She had to get this sorted out first.

She couldn't think. Couldn't concentrate on the party with Adam missing and the safe empty. She quickly typed back a response, telling Rachel that she'd got waylaid. That she might be late, but would get there when she could. She didn't want to alarm Rachel. Not yet. There was no point in telling her the full story. Besides, Suzie didn't know it. Once she had the logical explanation, she'd explain then. For now, she asked if Rachel would sort out the marquee, clarify the boundaries of the party area and she'd get on with organising the props.

'Adam!' she hissed, and checked her messages again. Just in case.

There was only one thing she could do, so after a quick search, she made a call to a hospital in Wales. This is what she'd seen them do on the television, in the dramas and films. When someone went missing you checked with the hospitals. Perhaps Adam was in there now, he'd had appendicitis or something on the job.

After a short while, she was put through to admissions and after giving his name and address was told quite clearly that no one with those details had been admitted.

'But he's missing,' Suzie had said, her voice shaking. 'I've not heard from him in over a day and this is an emergency. I'm sure he said he was going to Wales, can you check again? How many hospitals are there in Wales?'

There was a slight pause.

'If he's missing, love, and you're concerned, then you want the police. Not the hospitals. Try them.'

Suzie sat for a moment. Of course. The police.

They would know and should anything terrible have happened to him, so would she. They'd have been knocking at her door by now, all solemn faces and asking to come in. Feeling slightly relieved that he wasn't dead at least, she went to her phone but paused before making the call.

If Adam had just got delayed on his shoot he wouldn't thank her for getting the police involved. He'd be livid. The police would interfere, start sniffing around, she'd be bringing attention to his businesses, they would ask questions. Want to know where he was last. They'd probably want to have a look at the studio, maybe even his flat and then what? When they saw the open safe?

'*Too demanding. Too Exhausting.*' Carl's voice was in her head again, the reasons he'd gone after Tina. But if she didn't find Adam she could lose her flat, her business, everything.

She closed her eyes and took a deep breath. Facts, that's what she needed to look at. Adam had not contacted her in a day and a half. He'd been missing for less than twenty-four hours. But this was not unusual for Adam, he often spent more time than he intended when he went away on a job.

There was no money in the safe.

Again, not completely unusual. Adam rented a safety deposit box somewhere in Manchester. She knew he kept large sums of cash there, cash he'd not been able to declare, and she'd seen the safe empty before now.

Her bank account was overdrawn by thirty thousand; he'd forged her signature to put the loan against her flat.

She took in a sharp intake of breath. What was the logical reason for that?

This was harder to understand. Adam fiddled businesses, avoided tax, so it was possible he'd done something with her account in the interests of getting a better deal and the bigger loan against the flat was just a formality. Something he'd forgotten to tell her. It was plausible that he'd simply not told her when he did it because it was all under control and it hadn't occurred to him to tell her. She was not happy he'd forged her signature, but she could have that out with him once he finally called her back.

Feeling a little calmer, Suzie put her phone away. She'd not call the police just yet, if Adam wasn't back by the evening, then she'd ring. He wouldn't be able to argue with that, especially if he'd not replied to any of her messages by then. She took out her purse, forty pounds. Enough to last her a couple of days and the bank could wait a few more hours. They weren't taking back her flat today. There was no need to be hysterical. No need to panic. She could work, wait it out and if she hadn't heard from Adam by the evening, then she'd report him as a missing person.

A missing person. With missing money.

12

Rachel

I watched as Della bustled about the kitchen. Although no one had eaten in there that morning it was still a mess. Jessica had left her study notes on the table and Katie's plate and mug from the previous evening was out along with magazines, spilt coffee and other debris.

It was Della's earring. There was a perfectly rational explanation for it being in my bedroom. Did that mean there was a rational explanation for the map? The car parking ticket? His lies?

'Rachel?' Della was at my side and I jumped a little. I hadn't heard her come over. 'Shall I put the heating on?'

I nodded and watched as she went into the hallway, her slim figure cutting a trim silhouette against the morning light. She was wearing a close fitted jumper dress over thick tights that displayed her curvy figure to its best advantage. Had she always dressed like that? I seemed to remember her usual attire was jeans and a jumper.

'Shall I ask Phil if he wants coffee?' she asked, as she came back into the kitchen. 'Is he in the office?'

Adrenaline whooshed through my body.

'He's not here,' I said, and made an effort to sit up. 'He'll be home later.'

'Phil's out?' Della asked, and then: 'Of course. Is it his stolen car? Has he gone to sort out a new one? He said last night the police hadn't found it.'

She ran a hand through her long auburn hair. It was past her shoulders, slightly wavy, and I could never understand why she didn't tie it back. She was forever pulling and pushing it away from her face. I mentioned it to Phil once and he'd replied that he thought it was nice, in a hippyish kind of way. I put my hand up to my neat bob that finished around my chin.

'Della,' I asked. 'Can you stop a moment?'

She put down the cups that she'd been taking to the sink. 'What is it?' she asked, coming over to me. 'Do you need some help?'

I looked at her for the first time in a while. I really looked at her. Della had been with us for years. She'd come to us as a shy nineteen-year-old, in between studying for her child-care qualifications, and in desperate need of employment. Her gran had recently been diagnosed with dementia and it seemed she had no other family around her. With both her parents gone, Della needed money and needed it fast. Her gran was being taken into care and Della had found out whatever credit or savings they'd been living on had gone, forcing her to leave her studying and get a job.

As she was telling me her heart-wrenching story, Katie had wandered in. She'd been ten at the time and Della had immediately hit it off with her, both suddenly dropping into their own conversation about some boy band I'd never heard of, and I'd hired her on the spot. She was genuine, extremely naive and trusting. I liked her, the girls liked her and she took care of everything wonderfully. She ran our household, slotted into our family perfectly and did everything without me even having to ask.

But now, as I studied her, I saw the fresh-faced nineteen-year-old had morphed into a mature twenty-three-year-old without me even noticing. She was wearing make-up, expertly applied and some kind of musky scent. Her face had thinned out, showing off a set of distinct cheekbones and I realised she was no longer naive or unsophisticated.

'Did you see Phil yesterday?' I asked and she took a moment.

'Only when he brought you back from the hospital,' she said. 'He was in London wasn't he?'

'Yes,' I said and a vision of Phil and Della together suddenly popped into my mind. Them together in our bed, her earring falling out in the throes of passion. The thought gave me a jolt and I paused, straightened myself, smoothed down my dress. 'Phil said he was on his way to London,' I told her, 'but, I think he might have taken the morning off instead. You didn't…?'

She looked at me blankly.

'You didn't see him here did you?' I went on, watching her carefully. 'In the house?'

'No,' she looked off, toward the hallway. 'I did all the bedrooms yesterday, vacuumed, dusted, I had my earphones in, so unless he was…'

She trailed off.

'You didn't see him at all?' I pressed. 'Not until he brought me back from the hospital?'

She flushed, a crimson blush flooding up from her neck.

'I'm sorry about calling him,' she said. 'I know you said not to, but I panicked. I went to ring Suzie, like you said, but ended up calling Phil instead, I was so worried about you.'

I smiled, nodded.

'Honestly Rachel, you gave me such a scare yesterday,' she went on. 'When you called, you sounded so...' she paused. 'Unlike yourself.' She swallowed and I saw all the muscles in her throat work. 'I don't know what I'd do if anything happened to you.'

And to my surprise, her eyes flooded.

'Della!'

'You gave me such a fright,' she said quietly.

'Don't be silly.' I leaned forward as she wiped her eyes, put my hand out to her. 'I only had a small bump.'

She nodded. 'But you're family. And when I heard you on the phone, your voice all...' she shook her head, wiped her face roughly and then gave a forced, bright smile. 'Sorry, it's just... I tend to be a little over dramatic about these kinds of things, since...' she shook her head.

I had no idea how Della's parents had died. I had never thought it appropriate to ask, but suddenly I got a little understanding.

'Oh Della,' I said and opened my arms out to her.

She came forward and we hugged. I could smell her shampoo as I held her, the musky scent and I knew at that point any idea I had of Della and Phil together was ludicrous. She was still very much the shy girl I'd employed, still genuine and trusting.

'Listen,' I said as we pulled apart. 'I need a favour.' I glanced at the clock, it was getting on for ten thirty and Phil would be back at any moment. 'As I'm not able to do much,' I pointed to my cast, 'I was wondering if you wouldn't mind helping out with the party today?'

'The party?'

'It's not much,' I went on, 'just a bit of measuring up, but you'd be doing me a massive favour. If you could drive me there, help out a bit, we'll only be a couple of hours at most and then as soon as we're back you can leave. Get off early.'

She looked to the kitchen, the abandoned pots on the counter.

'Leave that,' I told her. 'Don't bother with any of that today. Just help me. Do what I can't.'

She nodded and helped me into my jacket. I was gaining confidence on my crutches and with Della's help I managed to make it to the front door fairly painlessly.

'Do you want me to see who that is?' she asked and I looked at her blankly. 'The answer machine,' she explained. 'It's flashing, you've got a message. Want to see who it is?' She went to press the button, leaning over, her finger ready.

'No!' my voice came out louder than I intended and she jumped back. I didn't want to hear Sergeant Bailey's voice again. The pausing between his words, the accusations lying heavy in the air. I didn't want to listen to it with Della, to have to answer her questions, see the look on her face as she worked out the run of events yesterday. Let Phil be the one to listen to it, let him deal with the police and what they wanted to know.

'Let's just go,' I told her. 'Let's go now.'

–

I was sweating, my head banging and my leg was painful but once inside Della's car, I felt a modicum of peace. I was out of the house, I hadn't had to see Phil. Hadn't had to talk to the police or discuss what the police wanted with Phil. I had the day to myself to think, to sort out my thoughts before having to face any of it.

Della drove us through the busy traffic and once we got to the A41 and out of the built-up areas with fields on either side, I steadied myself and broached the subject.

'I know I'm a little to blame in this,' I began. 'As I might have not made it quite clear, but please, *please*, do not use my laptop.'

I watched her face as she drove, looking for any signs of remorse. My stomach was churning, I desperately wanted her to flinch, to crumble and apologise, but instead, she kept her eyes on the road and frowned slightly.

'I understand that sometimes, you may have a few moments when everything is done,' I went on, 'and I'm not at all angry, but please, please, don't go on my laptop.'

'I didn't,' she said and I looked at her. 'No, Rachel. I didn't. I wouldn't.'

I took a deep breath.

'I found something on it yesterday,' I began, 'you hadn't logged out of your Twitter account and it caused all kinds of misunderstandings, so please...'

'Really,' Della said. 'I didn't! There's no way I would go on your laptop. I know it's got all your work stuff on there and you keep it on the high shelf so the girls can't get at it, and besides, I don't know your password.'

'Password?'

Della took a moment, the small hedgerows and empty fields whizzed past us as she drove. The sunlight was low in the sky, almost blinding.

'Phil set it up?' she said. 'After you found Jessica on it? You said she couldn't use it because of all your work stuff and that if she wanted a laptop, you'd get one of her own and then you had that massive argument about it because Jessica wanted an iMac. She said yours was too primitive, and she didn't want anything that wasn't top of the range. You called her ungrateful and it went on for weeks, remember? So you asked Phil to set this up so she couldn't go on yours at all.'

I looked out of the window in shock. Of course. How could I have forgotten? We'd offered to buy Jessica a laptop after finding her on mine but it resulted in her being demanding and completely unreasonable. We'd argued and were about to relent when she announced her 'digital detox' (along with her vegan diet) and that she'd only be using the computers at college from now on. It was still a bone of contention with Phil, him suggesting getting her a mid-range one instead of her using the ones at college and her refusing, opting to work in her lunch hour rather than bring work home. Even now when she found us staring at a screen, be it our phone or laptop, she'd quote statistics at us about how they rotted your brain and caused all kinds of scary symptoms.

'Of course,' I murmured. 'How could I have forgotten that it needs a password?'

We were quiet a moment, Della changed gears and glanced over at me.

'Perhaps it's a virus?' she suggested. 'Sometimes, when you download something, you download a virus along with it,' she went on. 'Happens all the time. You just need someone to take a look at it, or buy some antivirus software. It's easy to install.'

'But someone was on Twitter,' I said, still staring out of the window. 'I was in another person's account. On my laptop. I went into Twitter, and it logged me in to someone else's account.'

We were both silent.

'Perhaps it was Katie then,' she said and I looked at her. 'Your password, if it's easy to guess, then it's Katie. Whatever you've found on there, it's probably to do with her.'

'Impossible,' I said quickly. 'Katie's fourteen, she wouldn't know how and besides, she knows she's not allowed.'

Della said nothing.

'She wouldn't,' I insisted, 'Katie wouldn't do that. She's not like Jessica, once she knows something is out of bounds, she respects our decision.'

Della opened her mouth to argue but I carried on.

'Besides, the messages I saw weren't from a fourteen-year-old. They were…'

I stopped. I couldn't tell Della the nature of the messages. What they'd said. Katie was at school yesterday afternoon. She wouldn't be at a hotel drinking champagne any more than she would be at the zoo feeding monkeys. It was ridiculous. I stared out of the windscreen, watched the passing hedgerows.

A feeling of nausea washed over me and the sunlight was suddenly blinding, it was too hot and I needed to open the window. A blast of icy air shot through the car, cooling my face and neck. I closed my eyes as it washed over me. *Why was I pretending? The messages must have been from Phil. I'd seen him, I knew where he'd been.*

I opened my eyes and found Della staring at me.

'Are you sure you should be working?' she asked. 'Only you seem…'

'I'm fine,' I told her, 'absolutely fine. Take the next right,' I told her as I saw where we were. 'It's the second left after the roundabout.'

Della stared at me a moment and then nodded as she followed my directions in silence. We'd arrived. I had a party to organise. I took a deep breath and swallowed down my nausea. My heart beating, thudding against my ribs and the open window making me shiver. *It must have been Phil*, my mind repeated as I tried to behave normally, as I smiled at Della and told her where to park.

Phil's Twitter account. Phil having an affair. Phil driving at the retail park.

13

Suzie

She was putting away the rubbish when she saw him, stuffing the overfilled bin bag from Adam's flat into the outside skip when she saw a figure at the front of the shop. He was pacing up and down, staring up at the drawn shutters, a mobile phone in his hand and she guessed it was his Jaguar alongside hers in the tiny car park.

Suzie put her head down, she had no time to talk to customers now, and she went toward her car as quickly as she could without being seen. When her phone started to ring, she looked up and their eyes met momentarily.

She fumbled in her bag, eventually fishing out her phone. 'Hello? Adam?'

There was silence on the other end.

'Adam,' she pressed. 'Is that you? Can you hear me?'

'It's me, love.' He was walking toward her, switching off his phone and ending the call. 'I'm the one ringing. And you, I take it, are the lovely Suzie.'

Suzie looked at her phone; the call had ended. It hadn't been Adam, it was this man in front of her, smiling and putting his phone back in his pocket and stretching out his open hand to her for her to shake. He was mid-fifties, possibly early sixties, and the way he was dressed didn't match the luxury of the Jaguar she was stood beside. He had on a heavy black jacket, clearly worn and his jeans were scuffed. He was also wearing black slip-on shoes, old fashioned things that were an odd combination to put with his jeans and it reminded Suzie of when she was small and would meet her parents' friends at functions. How men would put jeans together with a pair of formal shoes and think it represented 'smart casual'. She tentatively shook his hand. It was warm, clammy and he smelt of cigarettes.

'Nice to meet you, love,' he said and his voice sounded familiar, the way he called her 'love' and suddenly she made the connection. She raised her chin, put back her shoulders and resisted the urge to wipe her hand on her jacket.

'I told you before,' she said going to her car. 'Adam is away on location, he won't be back until later.'

'And I told you,' he said, taking a step toward her, 'that I'd come here and explain what Adam's been up to, why he owes me four grand.'

Suzie glanced at her parked car. Rachel was waiting for her and, at that very moment, Della was most likely making a mess of measuring up the garden. She needed to be in her car and on the way to Tattenhall ten minutes ago. She needed to be calling the Manchester safety deposit boxes, asking them if Adam had an account with them and finding where he'd put all the money. She needed to be so many other places than talking to this man about what he thought Adam owed him.

'Listen,' she said trying to walk past him. 'I've not got time for this. I'm sorry, but I have to go. Adam will be back later, you can talk to him about it then.'

'Oh, you've got time,' he said and put his hand on her car door, moving his body so he was in front of her car, blocking her escape. 'You're his fiancée, right? He told me about you.'

Suzie flinched, with moving in front of her, he was too close. She had specific personal boundaries and he was breaching them, purposely making full use of the fact that he was a good couple of feet taller. He was trying, and succeeding, in intimidating her. She took a step back.

'Who are you?' she asked.

'Mark,' he said and smiled. 'Shall we go inside?' he nodded to the studio. 'Out of the cold?'

'The studio's closed,' Suzie said. 'And I really need to go.'

'Of course you do,' Mark said, but he didn't move.

His jacket was leather. It went down to his knees with huge pockets on either side. He crossed his arms and it moaned with the effort.

'I don't know anything about this,' she went on. 'It's got nothing to do with me.'

He smiled slightly and stayed still.

'Whatever Adam bought from you, props, cameras, I don't know, lighting was it? Whatever it was, you'll have to take it up with him. I know nothing about it.'

There was a moment's silence before he gave a laugh.

'Adam's not bought anything off me,' he said after a while. 'No love, you've got that wrong.'

He stepped forward and Suzie automatically stepped back. She mentally cursed herself for responding to his tactics.

'You're getting married next year, aren't you?'

Suzie checked the busy street. A few pedestrians walked by, completely unaware of Suzie and this man at the side of the shop. The car park was in plain view and hidden at the same time. The studio was on a busy road, the small lane leading to the car park at the back of it almost hidden. Traffic zoomed past, no one noticing the hidden area where she stood. If she were to scream or shout for help would anyone hear her? No one knew she was there. Did she tell Rachel she was going to the studio? Did Rachel even know where the studio was?

'Next June if I'm not mistaken,' he was saying. 'Adam's told me about it, says you want a lavish wedding, that it's what you deserve. Big dress, big party,' he splayed his fingers out to emphasise his words. 'Well, all that costs money, love,' he said and Suzie stared at him. 'Money that your fiancé borrowed off me.'

'Borrowed?' Suzie's heart quickened. 'You're saying that Adam borrowed money from you?'

Mark nodded. 'He was in a tight spot, needed the deposit for something. The venue perhaps? Hotel?'

Suzie thought for a moment, Adam hadn't mentioned booking anywhere; he'd left it all to Suzie. She was the one who'd made the bookings, provisionally paying a small deposit on a quirky boutique hotel in the city centre. She'd booked the entire first floor and the balance was due early in the new year.

'Honeymoon then,' Mark said, 'perhaps it's a surprise romantic break for the two of you?'

They'd not discussed the honeymoon. Adam had talked of Thailand. He'd been several times and said that he wanted to take Suzie to Phuket, show her the three-wheeled Tuk Tuks, the orange-robed monks and glorious beaches with white sands and crystal blue sea. He'd talked of a resort he knew that was five stars, only the best in food and entertainment and he'd also said that they should fly business class as it was the only way to travel. Had Adam borrowed money and booked the honeymoon as a wedding present to her? It sounded like something he'd do, and perhaps he'd taken money from this man standing before her so it was kept a secret. So she wouldn't find out. But now, like the bank, he'd forgotten to make the repayment.

'Romantic bugger, isn't he?' Mark asked, giving a laugh. 'He said the money was for something special, I helped him out. Let him have it when he was in a tight spot, but the thing is, he was meant to meet me last night and make a repayment, only he didn't show.'

'He's got caught up,' Suzie said. 'He's on location and got waylaid. He's due back imminently. I'll let him know you've been here.'

Mark waited a moment. 'He owes me four grand,' he said in a low voice and Suzie nodded.

'And I need a payment of five hundred. Today.'

Suzie let out a laugh.

'It's no joke, love,' Mark said and his expression was serious. 'I lend with strict instructions, strict rules. You borrow off me and you make repayments when I say or there's consequences.'

Suzie didn't like the way he said the word consequences. He stared at her a moment and then held up his hands.

'My apologies,' he said. 'I can see that this has all come as a surprise to you, I'll leave it for today.'

He took a step back and Suzie let go of a breath she didn't realise she'd been holding.

'You tell Adam to get in touch when he's back.'

Suzie nodded as she watched him go to his Jaguar.

'Oh, and you tell him it's four and a half grand now.'

'What?' Suzie asked.

'You heard me, love,' he said. 'Interest. My hands are tied, I can't go making special rules for one and not the other.' He gave her a smile. 'Don't worry about it. Just tell Adam and if he doesn't come back, I'll pop round and see you again. I need five hundred in the next few days, and if Adam can't get it to me, then I'll be coming back to see you.'

'But…?' Suzie started and he came over to her again. She walked back, until she was backed up against her car.

'My number,' he said handing her a card. 'In case Adam shouldn't return and the debt passes over to you.'

'Passes over to me?' her voice was high, shrill.

'You're on Charles Street, aren't you? One of the little flats over there?'

'What?' she said. 'How do you know…?'

'I make it my business to know, love,' he said and smiled. 'See you in a few days, Suzie.'

She watched as he got in his car and slowly manoeuvred it out of the car park. As he was passing, he waved at her; a friendly gesture, as if they were old acquaintances and he'd not just made some kind of veiled threat.

Once in her own car she looked at the card he'd just give her. There was no company name, no address, just his name and a number.

A slow realisation brought with it a panic like cold chill. Her breath was a mist in front of her and her mouth went dry. That man knew who she was. He knew where she lived. That was no representative from a lending company or bank. There was nothing professional about the way he'd just spoken to her.

'Fucking hell, Adam,' she whispered. 'A loan shark?'

14

Rachel

The house was magnificent, better than I remembered and I could see from Della's face that she was impressed. It was a grade II listed building with exposed timber frames against the brilliant white, and had creeping vines around the doorway. It was something the owners had talked about at length yesterday; what we could and couldn't do to the interiors and what type of insurance we'd need. As nearly every building was a listed something or other in Chester, I'd heard it all before, but I was surprised to see it was news to Suzie. She'd made copious notes on paintwork and features. It was something I'd need to discuss with her. I'd got leaflets and websites I should tell her about, but not today.

We set up a makeshift office in the large orangery at the back of the property. The clients, Mrs Laydon and her daughter, had been pacified with an explanation of Della being a new member of staff and, after reassurance on how my broken ankle wouldn't affect the party they'd left us to it. They'd gone out to get their nails done, leaving us in the house alone.

The gardens surrounded us and it was easy to instruct Della where to measure for the marquee as I could easily see what she was doing. I was on the phone to the company, discussing the layout and what flooring they had available, immersing myself in the distraction of concentrating on the logistics when Suzie finally arrived. I'd sent her several texts asking where she was and when I heard the tap of her heels against the tiled floor, my heart quickened at the thought of what I had to ask her. I had no idea how I was going to raise the subject without dissolving into a mess, but I needed to know. I had to know exactly what the Twitter message said.

Because as I sat there, discussing coloured swags for chairs and Georgian style windows, I'd started to convince myself that I'd got the details of it wrong. I told myself that, okay, perhaps Phil was having an affair. He'd lied to me about going to London that morning, so perhaps he was going to meet his mistress. Perhaps he was sending messages on Twitter to meet up with his lover – I could just about deal with that. But what I couldn't deal with, what I couldn't accept, was him being involved with what I saw at the retail park. *Phil just wouldn't do that.* I was struggling to associate Phil with driving at someone and leaving them on the ground. I needed Suzie to tell me that I'd got that part wrong. The time, the day, wasn't what I thought. And his train ticket kept on coming back to me, I held onto that like a life raft. I needed Suzie to tell me the dates were mixed up. Phil could be having an affair, but he didn't try to kill someone. I went to ask her why she was so late, but was taken aback by her expression. Her face was set, her mouth a tight line, her eyes anxious.

'Adam's not got back to me,' she said by way of explanation. 'He's got caught up on some bloody job.'

She sat on the flowered sofa opposite me, her arms and legs crossed, her oversize handbag on her knee.

'I'll strangle him when he gets home.' She looked up then as if she'd caught herself out. 'Sorry, sorry.' She shook her head. 'How are you? I got your texts so I knew you weren't in dire straits otherwise I'd have been straight over. Is it okay?' She looked to my cast. 'Has it been alright this morning? I know you said that you're fine, but are you? Really?'

I nodded. 'Just booked the marquee,' I told her. 'They've thrown in the heaters for free and I'm just about to sort out the seating, lighting and decor. I've called Jennifer, the lady from the catering college and she's available.'

Suzie held up her hands. 'Oh, Rachel, you're amazing! I half expected you to be in bed, not here, doing this. I'm so, so sorry that you've had to come here alone, well, without me. And look,' she sighed. 'You're so on top of it all. I have one call from the bank and it creates all sorts of problems, yet you've got a broken ankle and you don't even break a sweat! I'm so sorry.' She took a moment and saw Della outside, going over her measurements. 'However, I have rung the prop place and they're expecting me this afternoon. I've sorted out the van hire so I can do that.'

I went to say something about taking Della but she stopped me.

'I'll be fine going alone, really. I've been before when dressing studio shoots and besides, I need to make it up for being so late. If I do that this afternoon, and,' she nodded to Della who was counting out her strides on the far side of the garden, 'if I'm right in guessing that plod-along there is measuring up for the marquee, then we'll be fine.' She smiled tightly, 'it's just, I went to the bank

132

this morning and the stupid woman there wouldn't… and then this man appears at the studio, and he tells me, well…'

She didn't finish her sentence meaning it wasn't as simple as she'd thought yesterday. Her bank card had been declined and then an urgent meeting at the bank; it didn't look good but I wasn't going to ask.

'And I can't get hold of Adam to tell him, so that set me back,' she gave a long sigh and watched Della. 'He usually replies straight away. Must be out of signal and not even realised, silly sod!'

I'd heard enough from Suzie about how brilliant and good-looking Adam was, but aside from speaking to him on the phone, I'd never met him. It was ludicrous really, he was her fiancé, swept her off her feet, she had told me. She was engaged to him within six months of meeting him. She used words like 'soul mate' and 'the one' when talking about him, yet he never seemed to be around.

He always seemed to be working 'on location', a vague term that Suzie batted about whenever she spoke of him. I'd planned to invite them over for a dinner party, or at the very least a few drinks, but with work being so busy, and Phil spending so much time in London, it never seemed the right time. And besides, Adam's work often took him away from her. His photography business required him to travel all over. She said it like it was glamorous but to me, it sounded like hard work. I didn't enjoy Phil being away. I hated the weighty responsibility of the house and children on top of running my business. I didn't like to be on my own, rattling around in the evenings, scared of every sound and creak of the house. But Suzie, she seemed to relish Adam being away, as if it gave an air of freedom to their relationship. A breezy flexibility.

I didn't see her so much when she was with Carl, her ex-boyfriend, so I didn't know the ins and outs of their relationship, but I knew they'd been together a long time before he ended it. As I watched her talking about Adam's absence and lack of communication so airily, I wondered if her attitude was to blame for that. Everyone likes to be needed after all.

'It's because this job is so last minute,' Suzie was saying as she picked at a loose bit of thread on her pants. 'I was meant to be doing admin today so I got caught up in that, and then there were some phone calls I had to make about my other shoots and of course, with Adam being delayed I had to sort out his commitments. But hopefully, that should all be sorted out by this evening and the rest of the week will be clear.' She looked up at me and smiled brightly. 'I'll be all yours. Totally. Complete focus tomorrow, promise.'

'So everything is...?'

'All sorted,' she said. 'I won't be this late again. Full day tomorrow.'

I smiled back, and then, checked on Della. She was writing down her measurements in a small pad I'd given her. The sky had a dark, threatening look to it and although it wasn't raining yet, it looked like it might at any moment. She'd be back with us soon; there was limited time for me to ask Suzie my questions without Della hearing.

Suzie followed my gaze. 'So it was her on Twitter I take it?' she asked. 'She's the one who's been on your laptop sending messages?'

I felt my stomach tighten. I took a moment, choosing my words carefully.

'Those messages,' I said. 'Can you remember what they said?'

'They were arranging a meet up for sex, weren't they?' Suzie answered. 'I'm surprised she was on Twitter and not Tinder or Snapchat, isn't that what the kids all use now?' She folded her arms and watched Della with narrowed eyes. 'And she should've been working for you then. Yesterday afternoon. You might have been paying her for meeting God knows who for champagne and sex.'

I had to look away; the impact of her words had struck me like a slap. *Champagne and sex*.

The map of Chester from Phil's drawers was in my pocket, as was the screwed-up parking ticket. I could take them out and show them to Suzie, tell her what I thought I saw at the retail park, tell her about him lying to me, ask her what she would make of it.

'But what exactly did they say?' I pressed, still not meeting her stare. 'Can you remember? Were they definitely for a time yesterday, or did we get the date wrong? The place wrong? Was it definitely at that hotel? On the retail park?'

Suzie was silent. There was a gust of wind from outside and I looked up to see Della struggling with the tape measure. It floated about her like a gymnast's ribbon. I'd told her not to release the end from the spike in the ground until she'd retracted it, and yet here she was, fighting against the length of it as it whipped about her.

'It was for yesterday,' Suzie said slowly. 'It was for a meeting at 2pm. At the hotel on the retail park.'

I nodded.

'But you know that,' she went on, 'we saw that message together.'

She paused for a moment and we both watched Della struggle with the winding handle on the open frame tape measure. Another gust of wind took the dangling tape up and Della gave a little shriek in shock. She looked up then, caught us watching and laughed. I smiled back.

'It wasn't her,' Suzie said. 'Can't be, otherwise you'd be telling me how you gave her a warning. Giving me a heads-up if she was going to be sulking. You wouldn't both be laughing because she can't use a tape measure.'

I stayed looking outside and heard Suzie shift in her seat.

'Rachel?' she asked quietly. 'Was it Phil? You know you can tell me. You can tell me anything.'

Every muscle in my body contracted.

'Rachel?'

A few drops of rain fell and Della looked up to the open sky.

'I'm here, is all I'm saying,' she went on. 'Yesterday, at the hospital, before Phil came, you were trying to tell me something. Did you see him at the hotel? If you want to talk, Rach, you can. When I found out about Carl it cut me up, so I know what you're going through. You can tell me who he was with, what you saw...'

Phil's black BMW.

'I could come over,' Suzie went on. 'After I've got the props. Take you out, share a bottle of wine. We don't have to talk about Phil if you don't want to. If you just want to get away for a bit.'

A man being knocked over and left for dead. The screech of tyres. My husband's face behind the wheel.

But he said it was stolen, I mentally screamed to myself, *his car was stolen! He was in Crewe at the time. The police have his train ticket, if they thought it was Phil, they would have arrested him last night.*

'Is there any other way?' I asked and she jumped up, came over and sat in the chair next to me. My voice was strange, alarming. 'I mean, could I have got into someone else's Twitter account? Hacked in through the website I was on?'

She was silent. I knew she was staring at me but I couldn't look at her.

'No,' she said finally. 'Impossible.'

The rain had started to fall. Della had given up on winding the tape in by the handle and was gathering it up as best she could. She was making her way back toward the orangery.

'It was him, wasn't it?' Suzie asked. 'You did see him yesterday and that's why you went into the back of that car and broke your ankle. You saw Phil.'

My heart picked up a gear. I felt the panic lap around me.

'It's okay,' she was saying. 'When Carl did it to me…'

'Phil's not like Carl,' I said, looking at her directly.

She stared at me for a moment in silence before her face fell into an expression of pity, and for the first time in my life I wanted to hurt someone. I wanted to scrape my nails through her sympathetic face and feel her skin slide beneath my fingers. I couldn't stand to see the pity on her face, couldn't stand to be made to feel so helpless.

'Rachel,' she said gently and I felt tears prick at my eyes. 'You're not *afraid* of Phil are you?'

I blinked and the tears dropped onto my cheeks.

'Oh Rachel,' Suzie's arms were suddenly around me. 'You don't need to be scared of him. Scared of this! I'm here. I'll take the bastard on, you tell me now, tell me what happened, who you saw him with and we can work it out. You can stay with me for a bit. I'll sleep on the sofa. Come with me, to my flat. When Adam gets back, I'll tell him, tell him what's happened and he'll take us both out. He'll spoil us both, we'll go for a nice meal somewhere.'

I looked at Suzie. She was making a genuine offer. She wanted me to leave my house, my girls, *my life* and go to her small flat in the city. Stay in her bed whilst she slept on the sofa. Go out for a meal with her and her fiancé, whom I'd never met, as if that would make everything better. Tell the girls, the parents from their school, the people I worked with, our friends from the golf club that I was now in a small flat in the city, that I'd left Phil to go there? I started to laugh, a pathetic convulsion at the thought of exchanging my life for the one Suzie was describing and her face hardened.

'No,' I said as I saw I'd offended her. 'Suzie, it's not that. It's a lovely offer and thank you, really thank you, but it's not that simple.'

'Not that simple? You see your husband cheating and you'd rather stay with the lying bastard than come stay with me?'

I shook my head, wiped my face.

'I've got the girls to think about,' I said. 'I can't just walk away.'

'If he's done it once, he'll do it again,' Suzie said and I looked up at her sharply. 'It won't be the first time,' she said, 'never is. It's just the first time you've caught him.'

I went to argue but the door opened and Della walked in with a gust of icy air, her cheeks were red, her eyes bright. 'I think I got it all, oh,' she looked up, 'hi Suzie,' and then, when she sensed the atmosphere, 'is everything okay?'

'Everything is fine,' I said quickly.

'Is it?' Suzie asked and I stared at her.

'Fine,' I repeated and Suzie nodded, gave a small shrug.

'Okay,' she said and stood up. 'I need to get the van, it's a forty-minute drive to the prop warehouse so I'd better get going.'

I nodded as she went to leave. 'But Rachel,' she said as she was at the door, 'my offer is there, whatever you say you *didn't* see Phil doing yesterday, if you want to talk about it, ring me.'

I watched her go, heard the sound of the engine starting up and was about to instruct Della on re-measuring, when I sensed she'd gone very still at the side of me. I turned to her, she'd gone pale, all the colour from being outside seemed to have drained from her face, she was staring at her mobile.

'Della?' I asked. 'Is everything alright?'

She looked up, glanced at me and then went back to her mobile, to staring at the screen.

'It's the police,' she said. 'They left a voicemail, a Detective Sergeant Bailey. He wants me to call him, wants to talk to me about the events of yesterday.'

My heart began to gallop, my stomach was tightening at her face, the way she was looking at me, her eyes wide. 'Rachel, is everything alright?'

15

Suzie

Suzie adored visiting the prop warehouse, it was one of her favourite things to do. She would wander through the aisles picking up novelties, gazing at the curiosities and imagining how they would look in a photograph. She'd read the tags attached to the items detailing the history and period, and immediately think about how she could style it, how it would reflect the light, but unfortunately, it was something that she rarely got to do. Her current gigs required little props from outside. She sometimes forced her styling on the B&B's and hotels she photographed, introduced a Victorian breakfast tray here, a vintage writing set there, but usually, it went against the client's idea of how the photograph should look and ultimately, her styled shots never made it off her laptop.

Suzie walked into the warehouse and breathed in the scent of musty air and thought how she'd soon be a regular. Instead of stolen visits, these would become a necessity. It was as cold inside as outside and she zipped up her jacket as she walked in.

'Farrell McFadden Events,' she announced. 'Rachel Farrell has an account with you here? I need enough nineteen-twenties props to fill three rooms and a marquee.'

For the rest of the afternoon, Suzie was lost in the enjoyable task of choosing oversized champagne glasses, large feather fans and cardboard cutouts of people dancing the Charleston. By the time the hire van was filled, it was dark and she was hungry. She'd hardly eaten anything all day, hadn't had time to do anything other than pick out props and, worryingly, there was still nothing from Adam.

Not one voice message, not one missed call. She'd checked his Facebook, Instagram and Twitter account and there'd been no activity on those either. Her stomach churned, an acidic bite that accompanied her as she left the prop warehouse and saw four missed calls from the bank and two texts from Rachel telling her that the marquee had been hired. Della had proved to be useful, and they would meet tomorrow at the house again to finalise the catering staff.

Poor Rachel. It was clear that Phil was having an affair and, what was worse, was Rachel had seen him and was now in denial. She'd seen something on Tuesday, Suzie wasn't buying that she'd simply been 'messing with her radio' and gone into the back of another car. No, it was obvious in Suzie's mind. Rachel had seen Phil with his mistress. They'd probably come out of the hotel whilst Rachel was on the car park, and unaware his wife was watching, he'd most likely kissed his lover right in front of her and gone off, completely oblivious that he'd shattered his whole life into tiny pieces.

Once the shock of it had eased, Rachel would realise what a bastard Phil was and Suzie would be right there for her when she did. It would be hard, so hard. When it happened to her it had been relatively easy. There were no children involved and as it was Carl who ended the relationship, he'd practically given everything to Suzie without argument out of a sense of guilt. Rachel needed to make sure she got the same. In fact, Suzie thought as she drove back to Chester, Rachel should get more than half as well as the family home as she was the main care giver. She resolved to speak with her again tomorrow, see if she could find out exactly what happened. They may not be as close as they had once been, but Rachel was her oldest friend, she'd be there for her in any way she could.

It was late when Suzie arrived back in Chester, she wanted nothing more than a hot bath and a glass of white wine but that was impossible. Throughout most of the journey, she'd been in a battle with herself. She didn't know what to do. She could hear Adam's voice in her head, chastising her for calling the police. For bringing unwanted attention to his business, inviting the law to snoop around and what of the loan shark? Mark? That was illegal wasn't it? What if the police found out Adam had been lending money illegally, would they prosecute him for that? And what was he doing with all this money? A honeymoon sounded lovely but Adam had cash for that. None of it made any sense to her.

Sitting at the crossroads, waiting for the lights to change Suzie made a decision.

'Fuck it,' she said and put on her indicator to change lanes.

She was going back to Adam's flat. Back to the studio. There must be something she'd missed earlier, something in there. An old book of contacts, the name of the car dealership he was working at, something. She needed to call all of the people he knew, everyone he might be working for and see if they knew of his whereabouts. That was the first step. She didn't need to be so dramatic as to call the police just yet. Adam loved her, he was her fiancé;

he wasn't like Phil, or Carl, he was the real deal. He was out there somewhere, probably panicking at not being able to get in contact with her and explain his actions. And it was only two days, it felt like a lifetime but it was only two days that she'd been trying to get hold of him. It wasn't weeks or months; it was hours that he'd been out of touch. Most likely his phone was dead, he'd lost track of time and didn't realise what was going on in his absence. If there hadn't been all this trouble with the money and her bank card not working, she most probably wouldn't have been worrying about him not being in contact at all.

The flat was in complete darkness, the car park deserted. It took Suzie a moment to build up enough courage to get out of the van. She had to wait a while, it was ridiculous to think that Mark, the loan shark, would be making a return visit after this morning, but she waited all the same. The last thing she wanted was a repeat performance in pitch black, it had been bad enough in the light of day.

When she felt calm enough, she went into Adam's flat and switched on every light. She went back into the office, saw the empty safe and a moan escaped her lips. And then, she saw his laptop.

'Bingo,' she said, opening it up and then, 'shit' as she realised it was out of charge with no charger in sight.

His bedroom drawers revealed nothing of interest, and it was the same with the bathroom cabinets, the kitchen drawers and the hall units. She only found the items of everyday life, underwear, toiletries, utensils. A search on her phone gave her numerous car dealerships in Wales, the first page listing over twenty-one. It was too late to call any of them, so instead she went on a thorough search of his flat in the hope of finding an address book, or contact list, something or someone she could call.

It was only when she was ploughing through the DVD rack in the lounge that she came across a notepad. It was sandwiched between *Aliens* and a *Game of Thrones* box set. It was a thin cheap thing with gold writing on the front, '*Be young, be happy,*' was written in swirly writing and it was so unlike Adam that she almost immediately discounted it, but opening it up, she saw it was full of his writing. Small words in blue ballpoint. A shopping list. What looked like the lyrics to some old pop song and the rest filled with what appeared to be directions.

'Turn right at the roundabout,' she read aloud, 'fourth left after the traffic lights. Bungalow. Twenty-six.' She turned the page. 'Junction thirty-four,' she murmured reading his scribbled writing. 'Straight on until Dog and Anchor pub, second right. Asda car park. Yellow jacket, average build.'

She frowned as she went through the pages, all hastily written, all in Adam's writing and all leading to places that were unidentified with brief descriptions of what appeared to be people, but only as in so much of what they were wearing.

'Blue jumper, holding black umbrella, with small whippet,' she huffed as she read through them. 'Shopping centre, Argos, brown duffle jacket.' Adam never wrote anything, it was so unlike him.

'What the…?'

She put the notebook down. Why would Adam be using this instead of his SatNav or Google Maps? And why no names or numbers, only descriptions of people? Not in all the time she knew him had she seen him use this notebook, or any notebook for that matter. He liked his gadgets, always did everything via his phone so to see his written directions like this was confusing. She picked it back up and flicked through the notebook again, looking to see if she recognised anything. It looked old, out of date. Perhaps it was from the nineties, a time before she knew him when he didn't rely on his phone so much, and then she saw it. A small number on a ripped page at the back, just about legible.

Without thinking, she grabbed her phone and dialled.

An automated voice told her that the number did not exist. She tried again, exchanging the eight for a three, but nothing happened. Suzie looked to her phone, checked the signal and then dialled again. This time, it started to ring and her pulse quickened.

'Hello?' the voice sounded asthmatic, wheezing and breathy. It was male, no one she recognised. 'Anyone there?'

'My name is Suzie,' she began.

'Who?' they interrupted. 'I don't know any Suzie.'

The voice had a slight accent she couldn't place, each word ending as if it was clipped short.

'Suzie,' she repeated and ran a hand through her hair. Her face had got hot, she didn't know what to say, she wasn't prepared. 'I think you might know my fiancé, Adam Staple?'

There was a sucking in sound at the other end of the line, as if they were dragging on a cigarette or drawing something through a straw.

'Don't know him,' came the reply and the line went dead.

Suzie froze for a moment, then pulled the phone away from her ear and looked at it in disbelief. She looked at the number again, wiped her sweating hands along her thighs and dialled. This time she didn't wait for a response.

'We just spoke, and I'm trying to get hold of my fiancé, Adam Staple. This number is written in a notepad of his and I was just wondering if he was there? Or perhaps you might know where he is?' she let out a chuckle. 'He has his phone with him, you see, and it has all his contacts on it. I don't know the numbers of any of his friends, so I thought, if you were his friend, you could perhaps…?' she let the question hang in the silence.

'I'm not a friend,' the reply came back slowly. 'We've done a bit of work together in the past, but we're not friends so I can't help you.'

'Wait,' Suzie said quickly as she was sure the call was about to end, 'please. It's quite urgent I find him and I've got no one else to call, I don't know any of his friends…'

'You involved?'

Suzie took a moment. 'Involved in what?'

He didn't answer and Suzie felt the phone was about to be put down on her again.

'How long?' she asked quickly, 'how long have you been doing business with Adam? Was it recently?'

'Since we came out,' he said, 'seven years ago.'

'Came out of where?' Suzie asked. 'Was that when Adam was working abroad? Where you on the overseas jobs with him?'

There was a bark like laugh. 'Is that what he's calling it these days? Overseas jobs?' he gave a cough. 'I've heard worse.'

'So you weren't abroad with Adam?'

'I was inside. With Adam. We met inside, only, he got out early, on parole. In Liverpool for years, couldn't get anything out of him then.'

'I'm sorry,' Suzie began. 'You're telling me that you were inside, as in *jail* with Adam? Adam Staple? I don't think…'

'Listen,' the voice interrupted her. 'You tell Addy when you see him that I'm not on this number anymore, but tell him I'll be in contact when I've got a new line. And a word of advice,' he paused, 'don't go ringing any more numbers saying that Adam's gone missing. He's most probably got caught up in his work again, like we used to. Jobs that we take on can sometimes, well,' he laughed, 'they sometimes don't quite go to plan.'

'What jobs?' Suzie asked. 'Adam's a photographer, his jobs always…'

'Other jobs,' the voice was harsh. 'You've no idea what's going on, best to keep it that way and stop inter-fering. Tell Adam you've called me, tell him we've had this chat and see what he does. If you're planning on marrying him it should be him that tells you, not me.'

'Tells me what?' Suzie pressed. 'And who are you? Who shall I tell him I called?' but she was talking to herself. He'd already put the phone down.

She stared at the number, dialled it again quickly but there was nothing. Silence and then, number not recog-nised. Suzie slumped back on her heels, stared at the DVD cases around her, the small book filled with his writing. Adam had been in jail. If what this man had told her was correct, then her fiancé, the man she was about to spend the rest of her life with, had a criminal record that she knew nothing about.

She thought back to the empty safe, the way he fiddled the HMRC, the way he always dealt in cash, the loan shark and covered her face with her hands as the tears started to fall.

16

Rachel

I did the catering once for a mindfulness course being held at a holistic therapy centre over near Chester Zoo. There's a lot of land over that way, big wide spaces and just off one of the roads, down an uneven dirt track, was a farmhouse that had been converted into a therapy centre. They did the usual stuff: aromatherapy, reflexology, massage and had started an intensive one-day course in mindfulness.

I was asked to provide a light lunch for twenty, as well as snacks for comfort breaks that were planned throughout the day. I did an assortment of vegetarian sandwiches, two pots of vegetable soup, bowls of fresh salad and had planned a cream tea for the afternoon break. They loved everything apart from the cream tea. When I asked why, they talked of 'sugar crashes'. The peaks and drops in blood sugar levels that lead to mood swings, anxiousness and irritability. Not appropriate for a mindfulness course that included meditation.

Noting my interest, they invited me to join them to experience some of the teachings planned for the day. It was Easter at the time and I had another meeting already booked, but I managed to stay for an hour after I'd delivered and arranged the food. In that time, I learned about the breath, how to focus my attention on it and keep it there to tame a wandering mind.

It wasn't much, but it was enough, and as I lay in bed, my mind scattering and jumping about, I tried to concentrate on inhaling and exhaling. On listening to the sound of my breath entering and leaving my body. I wanted to stop thinking. I wanted a break. I wanted my volleying mind to stop showing me Della's face as she said the police wanted to quiz her. I wanted to stop hearing Sergeant Bailey's voice on the answer machine. I wanted to stop the whooshing rush of adrenaline that coursed through my chest every time I thought about the hit and run.

Della had called Sergeant Bailey whilst I was with her. I told her to, I tried to keep it light, made my voice sound as easy as I could.

'It's probably just a routine thing,' I told her. 'Why not ring him back now, see what he wants?'

Turns out he wanted to quiz her about exactly what she was doing on Tuesday afternoon. He needed to know exactly what time I called her and exactly what time she called Phil. I heard her tell him how long she'd been working for us for, what her relationship with us was like. I could her hear stammer her answers out, heard her agree and say 'anytime'. And when the call had ended she said that they might need to question her again, they might need her at the station as their investigation continued. I think I nodded as if it was all very normal, as if I knew what police protocol was in these situations and then I gave her a task so she wouldn't talk about it anymore.

How long would it be before the police came here again? When I came home the answer machine message from Sergeant Bailey had been deleted, Phil made no

149

mention of the call and neither did I, but how long before they knocked on the door again?

Phil had lied to me about where he was going that morning. I'd seen a message on Twitter that only he could've sent. I see his car and I think, I'd seen him plough someone over. *I think I saw my husband kill someone.* And the thought terrified me. Paralysed me. I wanted to talk to him about it but I didn't know where to start, wasn't sure I wanted to hear the answers and I was so tired. Exhausted.

I lay in bed and thought how the police would slowly be piecing it all together. They would have interviewed the staff at the hotel by now, seen the time of when my ambulance was called for and realised that I was there at the exact same time as the hit and run. They'd probably, right at that very minute, be discussing what an improbable coincidence it was.

I could see Sergeant Bailey's face in my mind, the way he shook his head at the probability of it all. The way he'd told us that he would need to question us again, soon. His voice on the answer machine, asking us to return his call. Sergeant Bailey would be checking CCTV, looking for Phil's movements, calling up the regional office. Perhaps even speaking to Felix and realising Phil's lie as I had done.

I Googled it again. As soon as I got home and Della had left, I brought up the news report about the accident on my laptop, the police file asking for witnesses and I read it again. It only mentioned a 'pedestrian', it didn't even say the gender and it said the time as an approximation. Who was that person lying on the ground? The body that I'd seen fly up in the air? Why were they run over like that, the car aiming for them, targeting them?

Breathing in, I counted to ten, my heart pounding, and held my breath.

Blood thumped about my body and I listened, strained to hear movement. Phil was downstairs, the girls in bed. Katie had spent the evening practising songs for her Christmas show at school and I'd listened to her. All evening. Before and after the takeaway pizza, whilst writing Christmas cards, whilst Phil watched television in the front lounge, Katie and I stayed in the kitchen and she sang.

Phil handed me my medication and that was the only contact I'd had with him. I felt drowsy, emotional. I was a wreck. Jessica joined us for a while, she brought down some henna, a black ink that she began to paint on her forearm and for once I didn't ask her what she was doing, or why she was making a mess, or why she felt the need to decorate her lovely smooth skin. I watched her. Watched both of my lovely girls for about twenty minutes, whilst Katie tried to learn the lyrics to her songs and Jessica made fun, with the smell of henna filling the kitchen, everything felt normal. I didn't want it to end. I revelled in it, soaked up every second. Jessica looked at me and burst out laughing at the tears on my cheeks.

'You've reduced Mum to tears!' she told Katie, who looked at me in shock as I shook my head.

'Your singing is beautiful,' I'd told her and they'd both stared at me. 'You're both beautiful,' I said and I didn't care how weepy I was, or how Katie was matching my level of affection with disgust at my sentimentality, I loved them both and needed them to know.

And then, Katie said something cruel about Jessica's henna design and the moment was lost. They bickered and Katie flew up to her bedroom accusing me of favouritism and I could do nothing to calm either of them. My cast was heavy on the chair opposite, my face wet and my head pounding and the fear and panic of what I was trying to ignore was threatening to take over.

At eight I went to bed. I was so tired. I didn't want to be alone with Phil and now, nearly five hours later, he was still downstairs.

I exhaled, my air coming out in a rush.

My cast was on the pillow again; his walking sock covering my toes. I'd planned to do it myself, but as he heard me trying to get upstairs he came out of the lounge and laughed at my attempts to climb the stairs. He'd carried me up like the previous evening but when we got the bedroom, I'd shouted for Jessica. I told her we needed her help but that wasn't true; I wanted Jessica in the room as a chaperone. A witness, like the female nurse who stands by the door in the doctor's surgery when you're under-going a personal examination. The safeguard that stops anything untoward taking place. Anything improper. I instructed Jessica to plump up cushions and gave her menial jobs whilst Phil was there so I could protect myself from myself, because I didn't know what I was going to do. I just didn't know what to do. I was scared. Terrified.

It was painful, my ankle and my knee, where the cast was rubbing. I'd done too much, already put too much weight on it and as well as the pain there was the building itch. They'd warned me of this at the hospital, said not to put a knitting needle down my cast but to try blowing the hair dryer down there instead. Phil massaged moisturiser into my knee where it was starting to go red and he'd asked if I wanted a cool towel or a pack of ice to get some relief but I'd shook my head. I couldn't even talk to him.

Jessica offered the hair dryer but the lead wasn't long enough and I took hold of her hand as she came to kiss me good night, I gripped it, unable to let her leave. Phil had kissed me then, told me he loved me. He'd stroked my hair as I'd cried and Jessica had shaken her head at my obvious show of emotion, and as they left. I heard her ask him something about an early menopause and heard them both laugh.

It was only after he'd switched off the lights and closed the bedroom door that I realised he'd taken my crutches and mobile phone with him. If I wanted to go to the bathroom in the night, I'd have to get there on my hands and knees.

I breathed in again and held it.

My body was charged. There was a terrifying buzz in my chest as panic swept through like an electric current. I struggled to breathe and had to concentrate on each inhale.

There was a bang of a door and I jumped. I knew from the sound that it was the back door, the one leading from the kitchen into the back garden. It's oak, a great dark wooden thing that you have to pull hard, as the wood has swollen around the doorframe. I've listened to Katie slam it enough times to recognise the sound.

I held my breath and listened. Very faintly, I heard it. The squeak of the back gate opening and closing and then footsteps on the gravel drive. He was going somewhere. I sat up, trying to move my cast to get out of bed but the room was dark and I was pinned down. Even if I crawled it would have taken me an age to get to the window. Instead I listened in the dark. Taking shallow breaths, sitting bolt upright, staring into the blackness. The footsteps got fainter as the terrain underfoot changed from gravel to pavement. I listened and waited and after a while, I lay back down pulling the duvet up to my chin.

He'd left. Gone. To where or what or who, I didn't know.

I listened in the dark and waited for sounds of him returning but there was nothing, nothing apart from the rapid beat of my own heart.

Thursday

A harsh northerly wind brings a drop in temperature, showers expected.

17

Rachel

A forty-degree washing cycle takes around an hour in our machine and that includes a fast spin. It's called a 'daily wash' and it's our go-to setting. I know we should be doing it all at thirty degrees and using an eco-friendly detergent. I know that, it's on my list. The list that I somehow only manage to remember in the early hours, but it's something that as yet I've not managed to implement. The things we wash on a hot cycle are towels and bedding. They go on at sixty, usually on Fridays. The difference between a forty and sixty-degree wash on our particular brand of washing machine is the light. A forty-degree wash has a little blue light that flashes; anything hotter becomes a red light.

It was six thirty in the morning and the red light was flashing. The red light under 'daily wash' was glowing on and off in the utility room, an alarming notification that a hot wash was now complete, which meant it would have been put on when Phil came back from wherever he'd been. I stared at it blinking on and off and thought I might be sick.

It was the shower that woke me, the sound as it was turned on, the low hum as the motor booted into action. I sat up, surprised to have been asleep. I looked about the room as if I were abroad, unsure of the position of the furniture and it took me a moment to remember. It was five in the morning and I patted his side of the bed, it was intact. Even in the dim light I could see that there were no sheets thrown back and the decorative pillows were still in place. I stared at the strip of light coming from under the en-suite door, watched the shadow of his movement and listened to the familiar faint splash and hum of the power shower and then I slowly lay back down.

I stayed very still as he carefully clicked off the light and tiptoed across the room. As I felt the weight of his body climbing into bed, I pretended to be asleep. There was a smell to him, a faint trace of something. Acrid and harsh. I couldn't place it. I barely breathed. I stayed there for an hour and a half, and then, when his breathing got deeper and I was sure he was asleep, I got up.

I opened the washing machine and pulled out what was inside, a jumper. A pair of jeans. Socks and underpants, a woollen bob hat. In short, a full outfit of Phil's. I held them, dripping and wet. A hot wash done in the middle of the night for a few clothes. What had he been doing that warranted a sixty-degree wash?

'I thought I could hear you.'

I dropped the clothes. It was Phil, shuffling into the kitchen whilst tying up his robe. His hair was ruffled, stuck up from where he had slept on it whilst damp. He flicked on the light and we both squinted. When our vision had stabilised, he looked at me, leaning against the washing machine. His wet clothes in a heap on the floor, and I shook my head slightly, suddenly tearful. My ankle was throbbing; I'd had to crawl to get downstairs to my crutches that he'd left in the hallway. The pain combined with my panic, made me want to cry in despair.

'What's going on, Phil?' I whispered, blinking rapidly.

He came closer, saw what I was holding and gave an attempt at a laugh. 'Went out for an early morning jog and fell over. I was running by the river, it's a mudslide over there. Torrential. Wouldn't be surprised if there's some flooding with all this rain.'

He yawned, a large over animated version of a yawn and went toward the kettle. 'Want a coffee?'

I took my crutches and followed him into the main kitchen, I watched as he got out the jar of instant, went to the fridge for the milk, busied himself with menial tasks, he turned and smiled.

'There was no running gear in the washing machine,' I said, 'just jeans and a pullover. You don't run, Phil. You never go out for a run.'

'Didn't want to wake you getting a change of clothes,' he picked up the sugar bowl and held it aloft. 'I'll make yours sweet.' He put two generous spoonfuls of sugar in a mug. 'I think you need it.'

'Phil—'

'And how you managed to get down those stairs,' he shook his head. 'You should've woken me. It's not good to be moving about so much on it.'

'Phil, I—'

'It'll come loose you know? Those casts are on for a reason. They say to rest for a reason. You can't just pretend—'

'Phil!'

He stopped and turned to me. I took a deep breath, my hands were tight on my crutches and even though I wasn't wearing my robe, I was sweating.

'I know you lied,' my words came out in a rush, 'on Tuesday, when I had the accident. When your car was stolen. You never planned to go to London, you took the day off. I called Felix.'

His eyes flickered.

'He told me that you were the one who cancelled the presentation, you booked the morning off,' my voice caught and I had to rally myself before carrying on, 'so you lied to me. And I saw where you were. I saw you.'

He stared at me. 'You called Felix?'

'I saw you in your car,' I went on, 'I was following you. I was at the hotel and I saw your car, by the fast food restaurant. *I saw what you did, Phil.* But then, you said your car was stolen. It wasn't you. You said you were at Crewe train station, showed the police your train ticket, and I thought I must have imagined it. I tried to kid myself that it was someone else, that I'd seen someone who just looked like you. But it wasn't anyone else, was it? It was you.' I waved at the washing machine. 'And now you're sneaking off in the middle of the night and coming back and washing your clothes. I can't take it,' I let out a sob, 'I can't tell myself I might've got it wrong anymore.'

'Rachel,' Phil said coming toward me, 'what is all this?'

I stared at him, silent. My jaw was clenched and there was an ache in my throat from the tightness.

'I know what you did,' I whispered and he gently put his hands on my shoulders.

'You're shaking,' I let him guide me toward the kitchen table. 'You must be freezing, here,' he took off his robe so he was stood in his boxers and T-shirt and wrapped it around me. 'Sit down.'

I stayed quiet whilst he brought over the coffee and a box of tissues, I hadn't realised I'd been crying and was surprised when I wiped my face and the tissue came back wet. We stared at each other as the rain hit the windows outside, as the boiler ignited and the pipes rattled with the central heating.

'Now,' he said. 'Tell me from the beginning. Tell me what you think is going on.'

'I was watching you,' I said closing my eyes. 'On Tuesday. I saw what you did. But when you said your car had been stolen, I thought maybe...' I shook my head. 'Why didn't you stop, Phil? Was it because you panicked?' I opened my eyes and this time, I could feel the tears fall. 'Who was it? Was it someone you were seeing, having an affair with?'

'What?'

My face crumpled. 'I didn't believe it, couldn't believe it. But then, the messages. There was no explanation for the message I found on Twitter and I found the map, on top of your drawers where you empty your pockets and a screwed-up parking ticket from somewhere in Crewe. I didn't know what to think, and then, Felix tells me you booked the morning off, so you lied to me. You lied to me.'

As I was speaking my heart picked up its pace, I could feel the panic build as I talked. Feel it lick at me and it was suddenly hard to take in a full breath.

'Your accident,' he said quietly. 'You're talking about Tuesday? When you had your accident and my car was stolen. You said you were trying to tune the radio, hadn't noticed that the car in front of you had stopped and that's why you went into the back of it.'

'You drove away,' I whispered. 'How could you? Cheating on me, on our family and then to leave that person,' my hand went to my mouth. 'What did they do

160

to you? Was it a woman? Someone you were involved with? And the police, they called here…'

'Rachel, you need to stop now…'

'You almost killed someone,' I choked and hiccupped around the words, I felt like Katie when she was very young. When she wouldn't be able to get past the emotion of a thing to form the sentence. 'You left them. You've been having an affair, haven't you? Arranged to meet someone and then, something happened and you ran her over. Is that it? Was it panic? Was it all just panic?'

I swallowed hard, trying to gain control, and as the realisation of what I was accusing him of took hold, his face closed down.

'Affair?' his voice was high. 'What the fuck, Rachel?'

I wiped at my nose. 'Just tell me why you did it, explain it to me. The affair is one thing, but nearly killing her and then leaving her for dead…' I shook my head. 'Who is she? Tell me what's going on so I understand, did she threaten you with something?' I blinked as more tears fell. 'I need to understand, Phil. I need to know why.'

'I can't believe you called Felix over this…' he was saying but I couldn't let him speak, my words were coming out in a tumble.

'I thought I was going mad. I thought I was crazy, but it was you wasn't it?'

He stood up and went to the sink, pouring away his coffee.

'You were driving weren't you, your car wasn't stolen was it?'

I stopped, my breathing shallow, my face swollen and eyes puffy from crying.

'I just need to know why,' I said. 'Why, Phil? Why?'

After a moment he turned around, leaning against the sink, folding his arms.

'So let me get this straight,' he began. 'You find some map of Chester and an old parking ticket. You call Felix, who doesn't even know what day of the week it is himself half the time, and he tells you I booked the morning off and so you think I'm having an affair? And what's worse, is that you think I ran over this person I'm having an affair with and left them for dead?'

I held my breath. He laughed, a hollow bark of disbelief.

'I am not having an affair,' he said. 'Rachel, look at me,' he lifted my chin so he was staring at me directly. 'How you think I would even have time to conduct an affair when you know how hard I'm working is beyond me. Just how am I supposed to be doing it, hey Rach? Tell me that. Meeting up at train station platforms? Romantic liaisons in the buffet cart?' He shook his head. 'And as for the hit and run. My car was *stolen* on Tuesday. You saw the police, you heard me tell them, I gave them my train ticket. That's the reason the police are calling, because the *person who stole my car* ran someone over. I was at Crewe train station when it happened.'

I stared up at him.

'And Felix. Did he tell you that he booked Tuesday off?'

I blinked rapidly.

'This presentation is a shambles, Felix is a shambles,' he sighed. 'He's got a gambling addiction, did he tell you that? He's booked more time off for counselling and therapy in this last month than I have all year.' He shook his head. 'He's over a hundred grand in debt, did he mention that?'

'Felix?' my voice was shaking. 'But his boys, he never said…'

'Well he wouldn't, would he? So when he tells you that I booked a morning off, how would he know? He's cancelled three times this week due to stress so, please, don't take into account anything Felix tells you.'

I wiped my face, trying to get my head around Felix and the news that he has a gambling addiction. Trying to remember exactly what he'd said when I called him, did he mention that he wasn't in the office on Tuesday either?

'I grant you it's an odd coincidence,' Phil was saying. 'You being at the same place as my stolen car was used for a hit and run, but now you're telling me you saw this accident happen? And you think I was *involved*? You told me, you told *the police* that you didn't see anything. You lied to the police.'

'MUM!' Katie bounded into the kitchen. I took a sharp intake of breath, shocked at her entrance. I hadn't even heard her coming downstairs. She was wearing her pyjamas, shorts and T-shirt decorated with small cartoon characters in garish colours. Her long hair fell about her shoulders, her face still puffy with sleep making her look so young.

'Can we go to Chilterns again? It was so good yesterday, and I'd like to try that crepe, the Nutella and banana one. Will you take us? Will you?'

We didn't move, Phil still had his eyes on mine and I ran my hand through my hair, over my face, turned away, trying to hide it from Katie.

'You can have cereal,' he said slowly not moving and Katie went to demand something else but he stopped her. 'Go and get dressed for school.'

She didn't move.

'Now.'

She started to protest but Phil looked at her, stopping any argument. She stared at him for a moment then slipped back off upstairs.

'Jessica will be down in a second,' he said. 'Stop crying and stop all this. The girls don't need to hear it.'

There was a thump from the floor above us and we heard Katie shout. She shouted something at Jessica, and Jessica shouted in return. The bathroom door slammed making me jump and I winced as the movement reached my ankle.

'But I thought I saw you,' I whispered and his eyes locked on mine, 'I thought I saw your face, and there was this message. I found this message on Twitter...'

There was a great bang from upstairs and we both looked up to the ceiling. Katie started to howl.

Phil squeezed his eyes shut. 'Stop this, Rachel.'

Katie was screaming now, crying. She was clearly hurt and Jessica was ignoring her, I could hear her heavy feet moving about inside the bathroom.

'I saw the message on Twitter,' I told him. 'On my laptop. That's why I went and I keep telling myself that it can't be you, that it's just not possible, but things keep telling me otherwise.'

He was staring at the floor, a small muscle twitching at the side of his jaw.

'MUM!' Jessica shouted from upstairs. 'I think Katie's hurt herself. MUM!'

'Give me a good reason why it can't have been you,' I asked him. 'That this is all my imagination. Why it wasn't you sending the message on Twitter? Why you couldn't possibly be having an affair? Give me a reason why you have nothing to do with any of this. Tell me what that map was, what the parking ticket was? Tell me, Phil, please.'

Jessica's footsteps thundered downstairs.

'Mum!' Jessica said as she charged into the kitchen. 'She's gone too far this time, she's ruined my lip gloss and lost my hair straighteners. She thinks she can just take anything of mine, you've got to do something!'

I turned away, hiding my face.

'Is everything okay?' she asked after a moment.

'Go get yourself ready,' Phil said. 'Get yourself and your sister dressed and ready. I don't want any arguments.'

I heard her make a huffing sound, and then, 'Mum?'

'I'm fine, Jessica,' I said with great effort to keep my voice steady and without turning around. 'Go get ready for college.'

I heard her wait a moment where she decided whether to ask further questions and then her footsteps going back upstairs. Phil took in a deep breath then exhaled loudly from his nose. I watched as he looked up to the ceiling, running his hand down his unshaven neck. I waited, holding myself until he spoke.

'The girls need to go,' he said slowly. 'I'll take them in, like yesterday.' He looked at me. 'You need to cancel work. Phone Suzie and tell her that you won't be in. It's ridiculous you're still going ahead with that job. It's clearly too much. You need rest.'

'Phil—'

'Rachel, I've heard enough,' he held up his hand, his palm facing me as if stopping traffic. 'You've got to stop with this hysterical…' He looked about the kitchen and then waved. 'All this. I don't know where you get your ideas from and to be honest, you're starting to scare me,' his shoulders sagged. 'C'mon, I'll help you upstairs, get you back into bed. You need sleep.'

'Where were you last night?' I asked. 'You went out after midnight. That wasn't for a run.'

He came over and picked up one of my crutches, holding it out for me to take.

'I went to stop Lucy's cat from going through the rubbish,' he said. 'I heard it in the recycling. The lid is loose on the box, last time it got in, it cut its mouth on the tins remember? Lucy asked us to weigh it down. I went outside to do that then fell asleep on the sofa. I woke up groggy and against my better judgement, went out for a run, fell over, came home and washed my clothes. Satisfied?'

I took his hand, let him help me up. They were solid and reassuring under my arms, my head and cast seemed to be throbbing in unison.

'But Felix said—'

'Rachel,' Phil said, his face was close to mine. 'Felix is a member of gamblers anonymous. He's struggling with massive debt and having to explain it all to his family as well as everyone at work. He's under a huge amount of stress, not helped by you ringing him and quizzing him over my movements. He probably said whatever he could to get you off the phone.'

I swallowed. My head was pounding.

'Enough, okay?' he said gently. 'No more. I wasn't there. It wasn't me. I was in Crewe. You were watching the person who stole my car.' He kissed my forehead. 'I'm not having an affair, I love you and I'm not running people over.' He stared at me, his face inches from mine. 'Alright? Forget about all this now, I don't want to hear it again.'

I took my crutches, shook off his hands. I needed to collect my thoughts. My face felt puffy, my body ached. I felt as if I was at sea, the ground beneath me shifting, and I couldn't get a clear path through my addled mind. Phil's words were in my head, his rational voice against my own that repeatedly went around the same circuit. I knew it was all too much to be a coincidence, had to be, but then, what if I did just see someone who looked like Phil? If Phil was in Crewe, if he wasn't in Chester that day, then perhaps it wasn't him on Twitter and it wasn't him on the retail park… But then, if it wasn't him arranging meetings, who was it?

I was at the foot of the stairs when the phone rang, the noise making me jump and then cry out in pain as the sharp movement went down my leg. I heard Katie's voice answer and then a pause. I made my way downstairs to the hall table and the phone. If it was Suzie I would tell her to go on without me, I needed time. I needed to think, to get everything straight and then I'd ask him again. Ask Phil to talk it out with me when I had it clear in my mind. Give me the explanations for exactly where he was that day, why he had the map of Chester in his room, what that parking ticket was and where it was from. Katie's voice shouted from upstairs, high and loud.

'Dad!' she called, and I turned back to the kitchen, he was in the utility room, holding his washing. He looked at me and we locked eyes.

'It's the police,' Katie shouted. 'They want to talk to you.'

18

Suzie

The gearbox in the van was horrendous, it had a habit of getting stuck in first gear and twice Suzie had bunny-hopped her way along Chester's busy main roads to the sounds of blaring horns from fellow drivers. She'd given the finger to four people already and was cursing loudly as she pulled up to the roundabout leading out of the town centre after crossing the River Dee. As she waited for the traffic lights to change, a couple of pedestrians crossed lazily in front of her pulling along suitcases behind them and chatting animatedly. One of the women's boots slipped off just in front of her and they both shrieked and laughed at the hilarity of it and Suzie gripped the steering wheel. It didn't seem right that people were laughing and enjoying themselves when she'd spent most of the night in a state of acute anxiety trying to find out if Adam had actually been in jail. There had been a hollow feeling in her stomach all night, a great chasm, and with it a deep sense of embarrassment. No matter how much she reminded herself that Adam wasn't Carl, with each hour that passed with no word from Adam, the feeling intensified.

After several failed internet searches, Suzie learned that you had to apply for the kind of information that would tell you if people had a criminal record. You could only find out if you were an employer and if the person in question was applying for a certain role. It was maddening. She hadn't slept. She'd spent hours Googling crazy terms then ringing Adam's phone and leaving tense messages. She'd taken his laptop and notepad back to her flat and as she didn't have a charger that would fit, she spent the evening reading through the bizarre directions he'd written down in the small notebook. Trying to work out where they were. Looking for something, anything that might tell her what was going on.

Despite the cold weather her hands were sweating because, she'd come to realise, whichever way you looked at it none of it was good. Adam was missing, her money was missing and she might lose her flat. A loan shark was involved and she'd just learned that Adam was possibly in jail. *Possibly*, she reminded herself as she drove through the streets, because the man didn't actually confirm that when she asked him. He'd only said that they'd been *inside* together. Inside where, exactly?

It was no good; she would have to take the day off. Della would have to unpack the van full of props and Rachel would have to style the house as well as organising the catering. What else could she do? Already she'd ignored a call from the bank that morning, as well as one from Mark, the loan shark, and it felt like a small knife were constantly stabbing at the centre of her rib cage. It made it difficult for her to fully concentrate on anything.

It was nine thirty in the morning, rush hour and miserable. For days now it had been trying to snow. Great sleety blobs that reminded Suzie of some kind of mucus, like a child's snotty nose or a trodden-on slug, hit the windscreen. Her eyes were hot and stinging and she'd had to wear her glasses as her vision was getting soft from tiredness.

The car behind sounded its horn and Suzie fought with the clutch. The van jerked forward just as the two pedestrians made it to the other side of the road and they both stopped to stare at her, their mouths hanging open at her bad driving.

'Oh get lost!' Suzie shouted through the closed window and then, afraid they hadn't heard her, made a face at their gawping expressions. She'd do what she had to and be back on this road within the hour.

The traffic started to thin out as Suzie drove away from the city centre and followed the busy dual carriageway out toward Tattenhall. She went through the part of Chester that wasn't so pretty. High-rise buildings, bleak and isolated, done in a kind of nineteen-sixties brutal architecture that were a strong contrast to the pretty black and white constructions found in the centre. It seemed grey, this part of the city. Grey with concrete and industrialism. Road signs signalling slip ways for the motorway and instructions for which lane she should be in bombarded her and then, she was out, continuing along the dual carriageway and in seconds found herself immersed in the country.

Flat, expansive fields lay on both sides with twiggy trees and shrubs dotted along the roadside. She took a deep breath and put her foot down, it was a straight road to the house where the Gatsby party was to be held and Suzie let her mind wander as she drove.

She was thinking of what identification was needed to get into a safety deposit box and if it was opened by a key, as she imagined, or something else. She was trying to place the insurance documentation that she'd taken out with Adam. It would probably be needed to prove she was his business partner, when turning into the driveway she found it almost full. As well as the hire car of Rachel's and the two Land Rovers of the people who owned the house, there was a small catering truck. Suzie pulled up beside it, white with stainless steel panelling and a latch on the side so it could be lifted. It was the type you see outside nightclubs selling burgers and chips, but without any bright logo or pictures of greasy food.

'That's Jennifer,' Rachel announced as Suzie walked into the conservatory. She was pointing to the far end of the room to indicate a woman with short brown hair and a deep tan who smiled and held up her hand in greeting, which Suzie did in return.

'She's the one I was telling you about. She teaches at the catering college and has agreed to help,' Rachel grinned and shifted on her crutches, 'so I'm going back with her today to discuss the menu and plan the logistics. She's talking me through the catering van to transport the food and what staff we'll need on the night. I think she's rolled in a few of her students and I want to talk to them about what's expected.'

She gave Suzie a big smile but her eyes, which were puffy and red, didn't join in with the expression of delight.

'I'd be useless here,' she went on, 'I can't help pin fabric backdrops or empty the van of the brilliant props that you collected yesterday and besides,' she flashed the false smile again, 'that's your domain. I thought it'd be better if I left you and Della to it. Get out of your way. Della can bubble-wrap any valuables whilst you decide on the arrangement of the rooms and I thought my time was better managed with Jennifer, ensuring that the catering is organised properly.'

Suzie stared at her. 'Actually,' she began carefully. 'I need to get away early myself today.'

Rachel, who had been getting balanced on her crutches, stopped and looked at her, as did Jennifer and Della who were fussing around with tape measures and bits of paper. Jennifer let out a nervous giggle.

'Adam,' Suzie said lifting her chin. 'My fiancé, well, he's… the thing is, he's…' the image of the empty safe loomed in her mind, and she couldn't bring herself to tell Rachel. To admit that she had no idea where he was, that he'd taken the money, that she was ignoring calls as they might be from a loan shark and that he might have a criminal record that she knew nothing about. A flush of heat worked up from her neck, 'been delayed,' she finished and Rachel nodded.

'He's still working away?' she asked and hobbled over to Della. 'If you could do as Suzie asks,' she said to Della. 'Whatever that may be and then, you don't need to come back to our house, you can go home from here.' She turned to Suzie. 'The two of you should be fine. More than fine.'

'Well you see…' Suzie began, taking off her glasses, but Rachel was turning to Jennifer, saying something about the menu.

'I'll just take Jennifer through to the kitchen,' Rachel said before Suzie could speak. 'Show her what we've got to work with and then we'll be out of your hair.'

Jennifer, who was wearing black and white chequered pants with a white overall, the uniform of the chef, giggled again at Suzie and lifted her shoulders in an excited way as Rachel started to leave the room.

'This house!' She put her hands together in a little clapping movement, as if to applaud it. 'When Rachel called yesterday she'd said it was just the usual, but this morning, when she gave me the address and said she needed me a bit more, well,' she grinned and Suzie noticed she had her nose pierced, a small diamond stud glinting in the winter light. 'I couldn't have been more pleased! We'll do you proud, don't worry, the food and staff will be brilliant. I'll get them all dressed up in black tie and we've got those silver platters. Very nineteen-twenties!' She joined Rachel, who was hobbling into the kitchen and started to talk animatedly to her. Suzie overheard the words, 'rolling in it' and 'alright for some'.

'Suzie?' Della, who had been fiddling with a roll of bubble-wrap took a few steps toward her. 'Where do you want me to start? Rachel said something about wrapping up all the valuables...?'

Suzie looked at Della and felt the stabbing of the small knife in her chest gain momentum. Della opened her mouth to ask yet more questions in that irritating way she had and Suzie almost ran out of the conservatory, following Rachel in two quick steps.

'Rachel,' she called out, her voice panicky. 'Rachel, can I have a word?'

Rachel and Jennifer were in the kitchen. Jennifer had a notepad out on the marble worktop and had scrawled something in big, loopy writing.

'Of course,' Rachel said and limped out from behind the breakfast bar. 'What is it? We're just about done here.'

'Alone,' Suzie said looking at Jennifer. 'If you don't mind.' Jennifer glanced at Rachel and let out another small laugh, before slowly moving.

'I'll just be outside then,' she said picking up her notepad. 'Nice to meet you, Suzie. Rachel, I'll wait for you in the truck.'

They watched her leave, Suzie noting how she gawped at the chandelier fitting in the dining room and ran her hand along the oak wooden door.

'Is everything alright?' Rachel asked once she'd gone and Suzie shook her head, rubbing her eye before putting her glasses back on.

'I really need to leave early today,' she swallowed, trying to get some control back into her voice. 'Adam's still not back and well, I need to sort some stuff out. And I need to borrow your laptop charger if I can,' she shook her head. 'I haven't got the type for Adam's laptop and I know you've got the same kind, once I can get into his laptop and see the accounts…'

Rachel was nodding, searching in her bag and bringing out the charger. She handed it over to Suzie and it was then that Suzie saw that she'd only put on the briefest of make-up, and that her hair, usually so groomed, was messy and in need of a wash. It made her look younger somehow, more vulnerable.

'And anyway, as I have to search through Adam's laptop, I was hoping to leave the props with you so I could get away.'

'But yesterday,' Rachel said. 'You told me that you'd be focused. The props and styling are your side of our business, Suzie,' she looked down to her cast, 'and I'm struggling here. That's why I contacted Jennifer…'

'About that,' Suzie interrupted. 'How much is she charging? Have you compared her rates? I know her type, she'll say one thing then charge another. Have you got a price because I don't think I can take the cut—'

'It'll come out of my share,' Rachel said quickly, stopping her from continuing. 'Don't worry. You'll still get your full amount.'

There was a moment where they looked at each other and Suzie felt her face colour.

'Sorry,' she said. 'I didn't mean that how it sounded. I'm sure she's lovely, really, it's just, well, I've budgeted for a certain amount from this job.'

'The cost of the wedding mounting up?' Rachel smiled. 'It's fine. I understand. I'll take the hit, don't worry, after all, it's me that went and broke my ankle.'

She looked down at her cast, the tip of it just peeking out from under her wide black trousers, and Suzie felt a sudden pang of guilt.

'How is your ankle?' she asked. 'I'm so sorry about all this, Rachel, I'm usually much more professional, it's just with Adam, it's thrown me. I can't seem to get a handle on anything.'

Rachel shook her head. 'Don't worry. You're here now.' She went to move, and then stopped. 'Suzie, is everything okay?'

'What?'

'This business with Adam,' Rachel said, shifting her weight. 'With him not coming back from his job yet, is everything okay?'

Suzie took a moment then nodded. She didn't trust herself to speak.

'Good,' said Rachel and Suzie saw relief on her face.

For a second she'd longed to confide in her, to tell her everything, how Adam worked the cash, how it'd all gone missing. The telephone conversation about jail, the loan shark, but looking at her friend, at her exhausted expression, she was glad she'd said nothing. Rachel had enough on her plate.

'Don't worry about me,' she said. 'You just get yourself better. How is everything with you? At home? You all… okay?'

Suzie dipped her head as she asked, trying to convey what she was really asking Rachel without saying Phil's name. Rachel nodded and for a long moment they looked at each other. If it had been a different day it would've been a different conversation, but there was no time. There was Adam to find, her money to find. She desperately needed the details to the safety deposit box, to search his laptop now that she could charge it, but first she had to dress this bloody house.

'When this calms down,' Rachel said. 'We'll have that drink you were talking about. Next week maybe?'

'That would be good,' Suzie smiled, and felt tears prick her eyes.

'And Adam as well,' Rachel went on. 'I'm going to start calling him Lord Lucan if he ducks out again; I've started to think he doesn't really exist. That you've made him up.'

Suzie let out a laugh, it was shrill and high.

'Well,' Rachel turned to go. 'Don't keep Della until silly hours, will you? She's not really employed for this kind of stuff.'

'I can't be that long myself,' Suzie found herself saying and she hated the way her voice sounded. 'I really need to get back.'

'Suzie,' Rachel said and suddenly the lightness to their conversation was gone. 'If we're doing this party then you need to pull your weight. I can't do it alone, that's why I've got Jennifer in. I don't know about styling and photography, and you've got Della. She might not be experienced but she's another pair of hands.'

'I know,' Suzie shifted her glasses back up her nose, they were slipping with the sweat, 'any other time and it would be fine, no problem. It's just with Adam not yet back, and the bank calling, I need to sort a few things out.'

'Can't they wait until next week?' Rachel paused, studied Suzie's face. 'Shall we call it off,' she said in a low voice. 'Is that what you're suggesting? Have we taken on too much, too soon? We could, I suppose, call Tailor Made Events, explain that…'

'No!' Suzie was surprised at how loud she said the word. 'We need this job. *I* need this job.'

'Then do it!' Rachel said and they stared at each other. 'The party is on Saturday. Wherever Adam is, whatever the bank wants, surely they can wait for a few days?'

Suzie found herself nodding. This job couldn't be cancelled, it was a large amount of money for relatively little work, and Suzie needed to be paid. That money had to go into her bank account if nothing else.

'Isn't Adam always working away?' Rachel sighed heavily. 'I don't see why it's suddenly a problem him not being around now. You can't expect to get paid without working, Suzie.'

Suzie watched her go, the anxious stabbing in her chest picking up speed. She needed money. She needed the pay from this job. She needed to find if Adam had hidden any cash and where it might be. She needed to be in so many places other than where she was.

From the conservatory, she heard her phone ring out. She ran forward, grabbing it and saw it was a local number. Not listed as a contact. Someone who hadn't called before.

'Hello?'

'Is Mr Staple there please?'

The sinking feeling of depression that hit her stomach was intense. 'No,' she felt herself deflate a little. 'If you're calling about a job, I'm afraid he's…'

'I'm calling from Chester council,' the woman said. 'Do you know where we can reach him? It's concerning his car, a VW?'

'What about his car?' Suzie asked quickly. 'I'm his fiancée.'

'It's been reported as abandoned,' she answered. 'And we need him to move it as it's on private land and there will be costs if we remove…'

'Sorry,' Suzie interrupted. 'You've found Adam's car?' A bubble of hope rose in her chest. 'Where is he? Tell me where he is.'

'His car,' the woman corrected her, 'has been reported abandoned on…' There was a pause and Suzie held her breath, 'the Grosvenor retail car park in Chester,' she finished and Suzie blinked rapidly. 'Just outside the fast food restaurant.'

19

Rachel

I read about a couple in a magazine who had a country wedding. After the ceremony, they took the wedding party outside where they had a tug of war of sorts with a thick rope. The groom's family on one side, the bride's on the other, and between them, a huge knot. As each side pulled, the knot was tightened. A poignant act involving all they loved to mark what they were doing. They had it above their bed, hanging there. In the picture, they were both sat smugly under this bit of old rope.

There was nothing above our bed, not even a picture. Just bare wall. Not one wedding photograph on show in the house. Not one picture of our extended family, of the ones we loved celebrating our union. If we'd had a proper ceremony, if we'd had the big group of friends and relatives around us, I wonder if things would've gone differently. If I'd insisted on the lavish party, entwining family and friends into our lives instead of a quick ceremony at the town hall followed by a pub lunch, would it have made any difference to the road our marriage had taken?

When Phil proposed I just wanted to be his wife as quickly as possible. My mother was in agreement, she thought that if someone like Phil was willing to take me and Jessica on, then best get him tied down as quickly as possible. Phil's family weren't of the same opinion, particularly Barbara, his mother. She wanted to take time and plan a big wedding, to hold some kind of ceremony suited to her taste and religion, and that would mean having a long engagement. Long enough for him to change his mind, I expect she was thinking and I can't blame her. Who wants their son to bring up another man's child? But Phil did, he had, and Barbara did warm to Jessica a little. She was never any doting grandparent, that's for sure; neither of them were.

I'm sure Phil's parents never really liked me, they retired to France shortly after we were married and within a few months, became almost strangers to me. I never called them, and they would call Phil, occasionally, and he would tell me of their news but I never pretended to be interested. Why should I? They'd moved away, made it clear they weren't going to be involved in our lives and I didn't see any advantage in putting up a pretence. I was too busy. I was re-inventing myself as a caterer at the time, studying so I could launch a business. And then, when Katie came along, their true biological granddaughter, they didn't behave any differently, so the alienation couldn't be all my fault.

When the kids were really little, it used to amuse me the way Barbara was when she did see them. They would make this big drama out of visiting us at Christmas and birthdays and she'd speak in a loud voice, miming out her words. Katie and Jessica both assumed she was hard of hearing until they were older. Now when they visit all conversation is stunted. Short sentences, quick questions. The girls hate it, although of late I have heard Jessica boasting of her 'grand-maman' to her friends and expect she's about to switch in her attitude towards them now she can see a free holiday in France on the cards. I've yet to tell her that they don't work like that. Phil's parents don't do invitations, family holidays or anything of the sort. They do wine tasting, small dinner parties and lots of cruises. It makes me wonder how they were as parents to Phil, what values they imparted on him.

All day, whilst Jennifer talked and finalised menus and ordered the food, I'd gone through my married life. I'd been wrestling with what he'd said to me that morning. He'd gone for a run, he'd been at Crewe, he didn't take the morning off, there was no affair. I analysed everything he'd told me. Suddenly, after years of being so certain, I found I didn't know my own marriage.

I turned my back to the bare wall, took my painkillers and with some effort, got myself comfortable on the bed. I pulled the laptop onto my knee and opened it up. The girls were downstairs; against my better judgement I'd asked Jessica to watch Katie. Offered to pay her even just to give me some time, a few minutes to work things out. After taking them to school, Phil had left to go to the police station.

'Found my car,' he'd said breezily when he came off the phone to them. 'It's a write-off, as expected. They're close to catching who stole it but need me to pop in, something to do with paperwork. I'll see you this evening.'

He'd smiled at me, kissed me on the forehead and before I could ask anything, he'd told me once again to stop with my wild imagination. He told me to quit work, tell Suzie I wasn't coming in and to get some sleep. Take the day off, watch a film, get some rest, and numerous other patronising things that were meant to pacify me.

I brought up the internet and, after a moment, did a quick search on how to hack a Twitter account. A short burst of laughter escaped me as I saw the results. There were pages and pages of them. Sites that offered software to do it, instructional videos, things to download, applications to go through.

A small part of me toyed again with the idea that perhaps I had, by going through another website, accidentally stumbled into someone else's account. It didn't answer the question of whose account I'd hacked into, of who was arranging to meet up in Chester, but there was a tiny possibility that it could've happened. It couldn't be ruled out and that was a small sliver of hope.

I closed the window and opened up another browser, pausing again, taking time to get myself ready as if I were on a diving board, ready to jump, and then I brought up the police report on the hit and run.

I held my breath as I read the account, then started to take shallow gasps as I realised it was the same story as before, the same wording. But at the end, was a small alteration. The word 'updated'. My heart seemed to pop in my chest at that word, juddering and beating erratically.

A burnt-out vehicle had been found. A black BMW believed to be the car used in the hit and run had been set on fire near Crewe cemetery. The fire brigade had been called out in the early hours of Thursday morning. There were no witnesses. No one was harmed.

The early hours of Thursday morning.

Last night.

They were asking for witnesses. The same number to call should anyone have information in connection with the burnt-out vehicle. I closed my eyes. Remembered the smell of Phil as he'd crawled into bed. The acrid smell I couldn't place at the time. I tried to concentrate on regulating my breathing. Phil's clothes in a hot wash in the early hours, him leaving the house at midnight. The crumpled-up parking ticket from Crewe. My heart was still making itself known, refusing to behave and I'd started to sweat, I could feel the chill of it on my upper lip.

The front door closed and I heard Jessica tell Phil I was upstairs, my eyes sprang open and all thoughts of slow breathing were lost.

'Rach? You up there? What did I say about going upstairs on your cast?'

I listened to his feet on the stairs, his banal chatter about Chester football club and how there was a fixture at the weekend that he might go to. I blinked, stared at the telephone number on the laptop screen in front of me as he came into the bedroom, the half conversation about football still on his lips.

'Your car was burnt out,' I interrupted. 'Last night. It was burnt out last night. In Crewe.'

He didn't move, half in the room, he stared at me from the doorway.

'You didn't go out for a run in the night,' I said. 'You went to Crewe cemetery. You went to burn out your car.'

He turned and closed the bedroom door quietly. I went to move, almost forgetting that my leg was in plaster and cursed it for making me immobile. Phil looked at me, and we stared at each other for a moment.

'You're doing this again?' he asked. 'You're still at it? Telling me where I've been and what I've been doing?'

I turned the laptop around so he could see it. I went to point to the updated part, the part about the burnt-out vehicle, when he came across the room and snapped it shut. The force of it made me jump. He took it from me and put it on the high shelf by the en-suite. Out of reach, balanced ridiculously beside my bottles of body lotion and perfume.

'Enough Rachel, enough,' he tuned to me. 'We've been over this. We said it all this morning. We've gone through it, now, *enough*.'

I watched him put his hand through his hair, go over to his drawers and empty out his pockets. I saw the debris of change and receipts that he put on top before taking out his phone and checking it.

'Where was the map from, Phil?' my voice didn't betray me. It sounded calm, soft almost.

He closed his eyes.

'The map of Chester, the one I found on top of your drawers,' I reached for my handbag beside me on the bed and rummaged inside, ready to find it and show him.

'Rachel,' his voice was a warning but I couldn't stop. There was too much unanswered. I'd been over it, my mind replaying things, a re-run again and again, the map, the messages, the parking ticket. His face behind the wheel of his car. It was all too much. It was sending me insane.

He came over and gripped my hands, stopped me from searching. He took my handbag and threw it off the bed. It landed on the floor with a soft thump.

'Just tell me,' I said. 'Tell me what the map was doing, where you got it from. Tell me why I found a screwed-up parking ticket from Crewe, tell me where you were last night, why you were washing your clothes.'

He stared at me intently, silent.

'Shall I call the police?' I asked. 'They'll tell me what they know about your car. About where it was found, and at what time. Shall I tell them you were out for a run? Came home and washed your clothes? Shall I show them the parking ticket, see if they can work out where it was from?'

'Rachel,' his voice was steady, threatening. 'You need to stop talking now.'

'I'll get Jessica,' I said. 'It is possible to hack into a Twitter account, I've found out that much, but those messages were still from someone in Chester. So if it wasn't you on my laptop, then maybe it was Jessica after all.'

'Rachel,' he said my name again, low and elongating the vowels but I didn't stop. Lack of sleep was making me reckless.

'Jessica!' I shouted. 'Come up here please.'

He moved then, quickly going to the door and his action made me jump. It hurt my cast and I winced.

'It's alright,' he said. 'Stay there, you don't need to come up.'

I opened my mouth to protest. I doubted she had even heard us, when he shut the door with a slam.

'Why don't you want Jessica to know?' I asked. 'She can easily tell me if it's been her on Twitter, on my laptop. I'll know if she's lying. Let me ask so I can rule her out, because if it wasn't her, then perhaps it was you?'

He didn't turn. He stayed facing the door, his back tense, his shoulders raised.

'You won't give me a good reason for the map, or tell me where the parking ticket is from, or why you were washing your clothes in the middle of the night,' I said to his back. 'So let me ask Jessica. Let me at least put the Twitter messages to bed. If you've done nothing wrong then—'

He turned and I stopped. The expression on his face silenced me. His eyes had gone dark, his face was tense, his jaw tight. It was so unlike Phil, I'd never seen him look like that before.

'You just won't stop will you?' he hissed out the question, his voice low and the quietness to it chilled me. He came toward me, walking slowly, 'You won't leave it alone, I tell you to, but you won't.'

I looked up at him, scared. I suddenly felt like I didn't know him at all, this man I'd been so certain of, he was like a stranger. He seemed alien, his face dark, I felt like I had no idea who he was.

'You really want to know, Rachel?' He ran a hand over his face and I saw it was shaking. 'Well, okay then. You're making me do this, remember that Rachel, it's you who's making me do it.'

He raised his hand and reached above me. Pulling something out from the overbed unit. Something from under the spare towels and sheets that were inside the storage cupboard. He pulled out an envelope, brown, A4 in size, with the words 'Please do not bend' written in red along the side.

'The police asked me to go into the station. They interviewed me, asked me where I was last night,' he said slowly. 'Where I was after midnight, if I left the house at all,' he looked at me steadily. 'I said I was here, with you. All night.'

My breathing became fractured. I shook my head.

'And if they ask you, you need to say the same,' he thrust the envelope at me. 'Open it,' he said. 'You want answers, Rachel? Well, here they are.'

I stared at the envelope.

'Phil,' my voice was trembling. If I could have moved away from him, if I could've gone to the other side of the room, then I would. 'Phil,' I looked up at him. 'You're scaring me.'

He dropped the envelope on my lap and moved away to the end of the bed. I swallowed, my throat tight.

'Phil?'

He didn't answer, didn't move and I looked down at where the envelope had landed. The name on the front of it, written in small bold letters made me pick it up. I looked back at Phil, who gave a small nod, his face set. I opened it up, took out what it contained.

It was a series of large photographs. Printed on glossy paper. I looked at the first one and couldn't focus on what I was seeing. It couldn't be, but it was.

She was sat on a high stool, her skinny legs crossed and dressed in sheer stockings. The lace tops squeezing around her thighs. Her feet encased in ridiculously high heels. Sparkly, red things with blocks under them. The kind you see in strip clubs, the kind of shoe that is associated with late nights, alcohol, smoky dark atmospheres and sex.

Her chest was bare. One of her arms was across her stomach, as if she wanted to raise it, to hide the swell of her breasts behind it, but hadn't. Her clavicle stood out, as did her ribs. I heard myself gasp. But, although she was half naked, it was her face that shocked me the most. Her heavily made-up face and backcombed hair, her eyes looking straight at the camera. *Her eyes*. And fear. There was fear in that face I knew so well. A frightened little girl playing dress-up. Lips red. Eyes dark. A streak of pink blush across each cheekbone. A small cry escaped me and I dropped it all, the envelope and the photographs.

Phil took in a deep breath. He sank his head down, leaned forward over the edge of the bed as if he were being pressed on by a great weight; his hair fell forward, obscuring his face.

'It can't be,' I breathed as my brain struggled to comprehend the images of my daughter. 'This is her?' I looked at him, '*This is our daughter?*'

'It's her,' Phil confirmed and my skin prickled with horror. 'It's Katie.'

20

Suzie

Suzie looked over at the vending machine. She was hungry. She hadn't eaten much of anything all day but she didn't like the look of the fatty chocolate bars or crisps inside the machine with their luminous packaging. They were bound to be chock full of chemicals and although hungry, the thought of eating them made her feel nauseous. She was feverish and jittery. The feeling had started when she took the call from the council about Adam's car and it hadn't left her since.

Adam was in Chester, had left his car at the retail park of all places and Suzie had ended the call with the council and immediately called the police. She'd answered numerous questions and waited whilst the information had been put into the police computer. Then, after a long wait, when she was told that Adam Staple had been admitted to hospital following an accident, and she'd gone into a kind of shock. That was the only explanation for it.

The police had told her to stay on the line, that someone needed to talk with her, but Suzie had dropped her phone on the hard tiles of the conservatory floor shattering the screen at the news. Adam was in hospital. He'd been at the drive-through, probably getting some food before coming home to her and had been in an accident.

He was at hospital. He wasn't missing, he hadn't left her. He was in hospital!

She was suddenly ashamed of all the doubts she'd had about him, how she'd questioned him. Suzie had turned to Della, told her to dress the house however she liked. Told her to do what she could and Suzie had left, got in the empty van and driven away from an open-mouthed Della straight to the hospital, and to Adam. She longed to speak to him, to hold his hand, to cry tears of relief and have him explain everything to her.

'Ms McFadden?' It was the nurse who had shown her into the family suite at the hospital, 'I'm sorry but no one is available to talk to you about Mr Staple's condition at the moment.' She came toward Suzie and perched beside her on the padded chair, whilst handing her a plastic cup filled with dark brown tea. 'There will be someone in tomorrow morning, or perhaps later, but I couldn't give you a time I'm afraid. There may be someone around in about an hour or two,' she smiled apologetically.

'I'd like to see him,' Suzie said. 'I am his fiancée. They said close family at the desk, well, we're due to get married next June.' Suzie got up and flexed her legs. She wasn't sure why she'd been brought into this room and told to wait. She just needed to see Adam. 'He must have been asking for me,' she said and the nurse frowned. 'It's possible he's forgotten my mobile number. He's useless with remembering things like that and if he's lost his, or it's out of charge, he wouldn't know my number off the top of his head. The police said he was admitted earlier in the week?'

Suzie waited expectantly. No one had actually told her what had happened to Adam or why he was in hospital. Dropping her phone had meant that the call to the police had been cut short, she wasn't even sure if the damaged phone was working, but by then she knew where Adam was. He'd been alone all this time, wondering why she hadn't visited him earlier. She'd got there as soon as she could and now she wanted to see him, to hold his hand, stroke his head, be with him. All this nonsense about having to wait, about speaking with a consultant or whatever before she saw him was absurd.

The nurse went over to Suzie and took her hand. She guided her back to the padded chairs and, in a gentle voice she delicately began to explain what the Critical Care Unit was for. She told Suzie about the high dependency beds and intensive care, the ongoing rehabilitation and as she spoke, a slow sense of horror rose up in Suzie. In her mind, Adam's accident had been serious, but not life threatening. A broken leg, a trapped nerve, possible appendicitis, something severe enough to prevent him from making contact, but not critical.

She looked at the nurse, felt her stomach contract and shook her head, she was unable to connect this description of Adam's accident with her own imagined version.

'Bleeding?' Suzie asked. 'Bleeding on the brain?'

The nurse nodded, both of her hands now across Suzie's.

'But he's doing really well,' the nurse said. 'We do expect him to gain consciousness soon. I'm so sorry to have to tell you like this, if we'd known Mr Staple was engaged, we'd have got you here this morning. To see the neurologist with the rest of his family.'

'The rest of his family?' Suzie blinked rapidly, she was repeating the nurse's last words as a question but she couldn't stop. It was ridiculous. It didn't make sense. 'Adam doesn't have any family.'

'The young lady?' the nurse prompted. 'I'm sorry, I'm not sure of the relation now, but there was a young lady here this morning. The neurologist spoke with her. I presumed that she'd been in touch, when you came to the desk and asked for Mr Staple, and explained that you were family, well, I assumed that you knew about his condition. That it was her who'd told you of Mr Staple's prognosis. I didn't realise that you weren't aware. You mentioned the police…?'

'I phoned about a missing person,' Suzie said and the nurse, registering how Suzie had come to be sitting in the family suite and hearing for the first time about her fiancé's state, closed her eyes in compassion.

'The council phoned me, his car was reported abandoned,' Suzie went on. 'And then I knew something had happened, so I phoned to make a missing person's report. I assumed he'd…'

She stopped. The nurse still had her eyes closed and was squeezing her hand a little too tightly. Suzie looked at her and thought about going to the door to call someone else, someone in a white coat and not a blue shirt. The nurse opened her eyes and they were wet, Suzie pulled back her hands. She didn't like the look of pity. She didn't like the way this nurse was tilting her head and giving her a small smile of sympathy.

'I'd really like to see Adam now,' Suzie said, standing up and giving her thighs a quick rub. 'I'd really like to talk with him about this.'

The nurse took a deep breath and slowly brought Suzie back to the chair. She explained it all again.

Critical Care Unit. High dependency. Rehabilitation. Unconscious. Coma. Bleeding on the brain.

The words were highlighted and underlined. Suzie found she was repeating them to herself silently. She tried to tell the nurse that it was impossible, that Adam couldn't have bleeding on the brain as they were getting married in a few months and they had a business to run.

The nurse nodded and carried on describing Adam's state, and every time Suzie objected, the nurse calmly explained it again. Somewhere along the way, tissues were brought out. The nurse went through it all, several times until she was sure that Suzie understood the severity of Adam's condition.

'So he won't be talking?' Suzie asked, 'or moving?'

The nurse shook her head. 'He's in a coma, which means he's unresponsive. He's also highly medicated as we're taking care of him. So there'll be a lot of equipment in that room whilst we monitor him.'

Suzie had stared at her tea, now cold, and repeated the nurse's answers to herself in her head. Adam wasn't responsive. The nurse went on to break down how Adam looked, what Suzie should expect to see in his room and, after a while, when the nurse thought she was ready, she took her along the ward to his bed at the end.

It was a shock. Even after all she'd been told, there was still a small part of her that thought he'd be propped up, reading his boxing magazine or one of those thick paperbacks he liked with the threatening images on the front. She wasn't prepared for the machines around him, for the tubes, for his swollen bruised face that made him look like someone else completely.

For a brief moment, she was certain it wasn't him. That there'd been a misunderstanding and this wasn't her Adam at all, but then she saw his hand with its square fingers and chipped nails. The hand that she'd kissed, that she'd held, and she took in a shocked gasp of air.

Once she'd recognised his hand, other bits of him fell into place. The traces of his curls peeking out from under the dressing, the mole at his collarbone like a lazy triangle and all of a sudden it was her Adam lying in this bed before her. Bruised and battered and barely alive.

She put her hands to her mouth as the nurse held her in a comforting way with one arm around her shoulders and the other at her elbow. Tissues were given and soothing noises made.

Someone came to the door and the nurse said in a soft voice. 'Not yet. I'll be there in a minute, I can't leave just now,' and Suzie found she was clinging to the nurse slightly and wasn't sure if the nurse meant she couldn't leave Adam just now, or her. Or both of them.

She was led over to the chair at his bedside and she had to concentrate to uncurl her fingers away from the nurse's hand. The nurse patted her and told her she could stay as long as she needed to. She read off Adam's charts in an optimistic way and repeatedly said the same clichés about 'doing well' and 'lucky escape' but Suzie barely heard any of it. The nurse left her sat by his bed, clutching his hand whilst she tried to locate the specialist again, or anyone who could shed some light on how her fiancé had come to be in such a state.

She looked at the version of Adam that was in front of her as the truth of the situation started to penetrate. It was getting late, her head hurt, but Suzie didn't take her eyes off him. She sat and soaked it in as she held onto his hand. The rhythm of the hospital ward encompassed her, as did the otherworldliness of her situation.

The ward seemed to have a motion about it that was close to soothing. The whisper of the machines, the constant whir and flash of them. The movement of staff, of other visitors, all calm, all softly spoken and all with heads lowered and bodies sagging with the weight of their circumstances.

Here was a place at the brink of death, God's waiting room. People who had barely escaped were clinging onto life whilst the living watched and as Suzie sat waiting for information, she sensed their hopelessness and started to fully grasp her own.

'I'm so sorry,' the nurse said as she came back into the room. 'But there's been an emergency and it's taken most of the staff I'm afraid.'

Suzie saw she held another plastic cup of the dark brown tea and she took it and sat back down in her chair at Adam's bedside.

'There will be someone,' the nurse said, checking over Adam and the things attached to him, 'but it might not be until the early hours. You're welcome to wait, or you could come back tomorrow?'

'He's a photographer,' Suzie said and the nurse stopped to listen. 'He can take anything, anything at all and make it beautiful. That's how we met. He caught me taking photographs and showed me how to do it properly. And under all that bandaging, he's got really thick lovely hair and his nose is usually straight and his eyes, they're bright blue.'

Suzie felt the nurse put her hand on her shoulder, a comforting squeeze.

'We're going to Thailand for our honeymoon, it's a surprise. He took out a loan for it,' Suzie said stroking

Adam's hand. 'He went and took out a stupid loan to surprise me with a wonderful honeymoon.'

The nurse made a noise, muttered something about putting plans on hold, and Suzie turned sharply.

'You don't understand,' she said. 'He is my life. *My life.* And it's not changing, any of it. So yes, I'll be waiting. I'm going to wait right by his bedside until you bring me a consultant or a specialist or someone who can come along and fix him because he is not staying like this? Do you hear me? He's not staying like this.'

'I understand,' the nurse said and Suzie swallowed. 'But I must ask you to keep your voice down and to stay calm. I realise it's a terrible shock but we do have other patients.'

Her nose had started to run and she nodded. 'It's just so unfair,' she said. 'We have so much to do. We've only been together a short while and we're meant to be going to the comedy club on Friday night.' She took his hand again. 'The one with all the fairy lights on the top floor so they look like stars. He was booking tickets. And he was taking me for cocktails at that secret bar. The one by the church on Watergate Street, where you have to go up the stairs and knock on the door to be let in? Adam told me it was quirky, that they'd put rose petals in my wine. I'd even decided what to wear.'

The nurse got the box of tissues from the side and handed one to Suzie. She waited as Suzie wiped her eyes and nose and then took it from her like a child and threw it in the waste basket.

'As soon as anyone is available I'll bring them straight to you.'

'It's just so cruel,' Suzie said, 'and I won't have it. This isn't how our story goes. Y'know? This isn't what me and

Adam are doing, we're getting married and buying a house and starting a family.'

The nurse took a moment. She looked at Suzie and then at Adam. Suzie sensed she was going to hug her or say something about his condition but instead she asked, 'Shall I get you another cup of tea?' and Suzie nodded.

Staring at his battered face, she could feel the life they had together being pulled away from her. It was being snatched. Stolen. She wanted to scream at how wrong that was. All their wedding plans, the expansion of the business and the new home that Adam had talked of buying, the home with an extra bedroom, the promise that they might start a family, it was being robbed from her. She could feel it dissolving as she sat in his hospital room and it was something she couldn't let happen.

'Don't worry,' Suzie said, stroking her thumb along Adam's hand. 'I'll sort this. Leave it to me. I'll make it alright darling. I will fix you; fix it all. I'll find the cash, make it right. I'll do whatever it takes.' She rubbed at her face and gripped his hand, 'I love you so much. Nothing is going to change. *Nothing.*'

21

Rachel

'I don't understand.' I looked at the photograph as if it had bitten me. 'What is this? This isn't her. It's not Katie, it's *not*!'

But it was.

Her face stared back from where the photograph had fallen, caked in make-up, her expression false. Pouting red lips, backcombed hair, exposed chest. It was my daughter posing like a bad page-three girl from the eighties. Her hip bones visible beneath the taut black lace, jutting forward; her small waist only just beginning to curve. The awkward shape of her juvenile legs as they hung from the stool, large knees, white flesh. God, she looked young, like a fawn, all bony limbs and the way she was dressed, the way she was posing, the thought of what she was suggesting... It winded me; I couldn't get a full breath.

Katie was not this girl in the photograph. She locked the bathroom door for fear one of us would walk in on her naked body. She screamed if I went into her room unannounced. Only last year I'd asked if she wanted to go shopping for a bra and she'd blushed. Told me that she'd already done that, a group of them had gone together. Got themselves measured at Marks and Spencer and she'd bought herself a couple of non-padded things with her monthly allowance. Jessica wasn't even allowed into her room uninvited.

And yet, here was her childish body trussed in black lace and red nylon. Her adolescent nakedness that she kept hidden from even me, *her mother*, claiming embarrassment and an awkwardness I could identify with from my own experience at that age. I looked to Phil, his face full of an indescribable expression as he watched me, softened with sympathy along with a fearfulness and I pushed the photograph away, batted and slapped at it, my hand working hard to get it off my lap and out of my sight.

'Where did you get it?'

Phil picked it up and put it back in the envelope.

'Where did you get that?' I repeated. 'Phil, you tell me *now* where you got that picture of Katie dressed like that.'

'I had nothing to do with them,' he hissed. 'For fuck's sake, Rachel,' he looked down at the envelope. 'I found them.'

'Who took this?' My voice was brittle. 'Was it was Olivia, or Tara, or one of the other girls she knows? A friend we haven't met? Did Jessica have something to do with them? Was it one of her friends from college?' I knew the answer. Katie had been in front of a white backdrop, a studio light to the side of her. They were professional photographs.

He went over to the bedroom door, opened it slightly and listened. After a moment, he closed it and came back toward me.

I held out my hand for the envelope.

He shook his head. 'You need to calm down.'

'Give it to me,' I demanded. 'I want to see them all.'

He paused, debating whether to show me. I leaned forward and snatched it from him, pulling out the photographs. There were three of them. My hands shook as I studied each one. Katie on a white fur rug, lying on her tummy, one leg bent at the knee, lacy knickers covering her bottom. Katie stood with her legs wide apart, wearing a mini dress. A mini dress that she'd bought for a school disco earlier in the year. I gasped as I saw her wearing it. I thought I'd sent it back to the catalogue. We'd argued over the length, she'd sulked in her room for a week over that. My stomach rolled, I was going to throw up.

'Is this it?' I asked and Phil turned away. 'Is this everything?' I demanded. 'Phil?'

He took a moment.

'She doesn't know,' he said. 'Katie. We can't let her know that we've got these pictures.' He started to put them away, sliding each one back into the brown envelope. 'This is important, Rachel.' He was staring at me. 'Do you understand? It's too late to ask Katie about it. Too late to confront her. After what I did,' he took a breath in. 'After what I did, it's too late. We can't tell her or Jessica, we can't involve the girls in this.'

I was under a waterfall, my head being pounded by the force. I was close to drowning.

'*After what you did?*' I whispered and he stared at me, then after a moment, nodded.

It came tumbling back.

The gruesome display of images that I'd been battling with for the past two days. I heard the crack of bone, the violent screech of the car. The body as it landed on the tarmac.

'You?' My voice was barely audible.

'Me,' Phil said. 'I did it.'

I could see the red caps and aprons of the staff as they came running out of the restaurant to the body on the ground. I could hear the woman's scream.

'But you were at Crewe train station, you said your car was stolen, you gave the police your train ticket…' I stared at him. 'It was you in the car that day,' I said. 'You did the hit and run.' My cheeks were wobbly, my tongue too large for my mouth. I'd been right all along. 'Why?' I asked, my throat tightening. 'Why would you do that?'

Phil slowly lifted the envelope and placed it back on my lap. It took me a moment.

'Katie?' I asked. 'You did it because of these pictures?'

'Last week,' Phil said. 'I came home early, do you remember? You were meeting Suzie at some coffee house in town,' he prompted. 'I'd travelled back early to surprise you, thinking you'd be at home.'

I recalled the time I'd met Suzie and had the missed call from Phil. I'd rushed home after listening to his voicemail, cutting the meeting with Suzie short. I'd been elated that he was back midweek. It had been a lovely surprise. We'd opened a chilled bottle of Chardonnay and I'd cooked steak. We'd had sex. I nodded and motioned for him to go on.

'The house was empty. Apart from Della, she was cleaning the downstairs lavatory. I went to get a coffee and what I thought was Della's phone was on the worktop. It made a sound. An alert of some kind, so thinking she had a message I took it through to her. Della explained that it wasn't her phone. She found it in the downstairs bathroom when she was cleaning.' He took another deep breath and ran his hand over his face. 'Shall I get us a brandy?' he asked. 'Whisky?'

I shook my head.

'I need a drink,' he went to stand up and I grabbed his hand.

'Please,' I said. 'Just tell me.'

He took a deep breath before continuing. 'It was an old Samsung. Galaxy something or other.' He shook his head. 'I opened it up to see whose phone it was and suddenly I'm on Twitter. I'm in an account, looking at a small profile picture of Katie.'

'Katie?' I leaned forward.

Phil nodded. 'It was Katie's phone.'

'Impossible,' I interrupted. 'Katie's phone isn't a smart-phone. We made it that way so she can only do emergency calls and nothing else, cyber-bullying, you remember? She knows…'

Phil held up his hand. 'It was Katie's phone. I was on her Twitter page. I didn't realise at first, it took me a while to figure that out. I should've just closed it down, told you, got ready to confront her, but…' he shook his head. 'To be honest, it seemed harmless at the time. A few messages on Twitter, some texts to her friends, nothing that any teenager wouldn't have.' I went to interrupt, but he stopped me. 'Of course she shouldn't have had another phone,' he said. 'She knows she's not allowed, and I meant to tell you immediately but…' he stopped then. Swallowed.

'So why didn't you?' I asked. 'Why didn't you tell me?'

'Work,' he said. 'I intended to deal with it that night, but then work called and I put Katie's phone in my pocket. Forgot about it. Forgot to tell you, forgot to tell Katie. You came back, full of your meeting with Suzie and the night got away from me. The deal with the drug for Alzheimer's was on the cards, we were negotiating that massive order and I was back in London the next day. I forgot I had the phone at all. It wasn't until I was back in London and I hear this alarm. This sound and I realise it's coming from my pocket, it's coming from Katie's phone.

He took a deep breath. 'It's a message from someone called Rob,' Phil went on, and I could see that he was struggling. 'A photographer at a modelling agency.'

I gritted my teeth, bracing myself.

'So, I go to her messages and I see a whole heap of them. From him.' He ran a hand over his face, looked up to the ceiling.

'Phil?' I prompted.

'They went back months. The messages from him, Rob, they started back in August.'

I took a sharp intake of breath.

'He'd met her somewhere, talked of how it was nice to make contact. They were all innocent at first, just chatting about TV shows. About what she's doing at school, what options she's taken and what she wants to do when she leaves.'

I closed my eyes. Hadn't I warned Katie of this often enough? Talked about it with her, explained that this was why we'd banned phones, banned the Internet?

'I read them all,' he said, 'and it was easy to see why she liked him. He flattered her, at first about her taste in music and books and then on her looks. They'd been messaging about four weeks before he tells her how pretty she is, how she could be a model. He tells her how he works for modelling agencies. He's a scout. Tells her about the jobs he's doing with other girls, fashion stuff, how they'll be in magazines. He made it sound very glamorous.'

I put my hands to my face as he talked.

'And at first, Katie's replies are all thankful and full of those smiley faces. She says that she can't, that we won't allow her. That she'd love to be a model but how she's not pretty enough.'

My head started to pound. It was so clichéd, what Phil was telling me was something I'd see on the news. A report I'd shake my head at and then congratulate myself on having my own daughters upstairs in their rooms. Safe in the house when all the time they hadn't been safe at all.

'But then she asks about his website, Remote Models, and Katie's messages are all about what a great photographer he is. How his site is really good. He tells her about jobs he's doing, what fashion models he's signing up. He talks a good deal, Rach, I even went on his site and took a look. A few alluring pictures but nothing too bad, it would easily fool a fourteen-year-old girl. Hell, it might even have fooled me.'

'So those pictures,' I pointed to the envelope, 'this man, this Rob took those pictures? He got Katie to meet him?'

'Katie asked to meet him,' Phil shook his head. 'All his talk about what jobs he was getting for his other models, it worked. Katie wanted to do it. *She asked him.*'

I squeezed my eyes tight. 'Stupid girl,' I hissed and Phil reached out to me. Put his hand on mine.

'Haven't we told her?' I asked him. 'Haven't we said all this to her? Warned her.'

'The last message,' Phil said. 'The one that he'd sent that night, that made the sound? The one that reminded me I had Katie's phone? That message said that the photographs he'd taken were fantastic but he needed more before he could sign her up. So I searched through the Remote Models site, I looked but couldn't find anything of Katie, so I replied to him. As if I was Katie.'

'You sent a message back as if you were Katie?'

He was silent a moment. Then nodded. 'I asked where the pictures were, if I could see them and he sends a link. A link to a part of the website that isn't published. And that's where I found those,' he pointed to the envelope.

'You found those pictures,' I looked at the envelope. 'When was this? Last week, last Friday? Why didn't you tell me? Call me?'

A door slams from downstairs and we're both quiet for a moment, listening. The toilet flushes and heavy footsteps run back toward the lounge. We stay still for a second, and then hear the drone of the television.

'It was late, past midnight,' Phil said. 'What was I going to do? Wake you in the middle of the night and tell you that Katie had been meeting strange men? A strange man I was talking to via Twitter?' he shook his head. 'And what would you have done? Gone hysterical, woken up Katie and Jessica, and done God knows what whilst I'm in London. You'd try to sort it all out yourself, in your usual hyper way, you'd go on overdrive.' I went to protest but he sighed heavily. 'I'd just seen those pictures of her, Rach. I realised that he'd already met Katie, already seen her. What I was seeing was after the event and I wanted to deal with it. Me.'

'We have to inform the police,' I said. 'We need to tell them. Tell them right now.'

'Of course,' Phil said, he was still holding my hand and I pulled it free to wipe my face. I was suddenly hot.

'I should've gone to the police immediately. Reported him and spoken to Katie and you. I should've dealt with it rationally.' He reached for the envelope. 'But it was Friday night, what police station is open to deal with this kind of stuff at that hour? And, I couldn't help thinking; what if the police didn't deal with it effectively? What did I have to give them, a few photographs and some messages on Twitter?' Phil shook his head. 'You hear about people getting away with this kind of stuff all the time and I was still speaking to this monster. He thought I was Katie and he wanted to meet up.' He looked at me, his eyes heavy, 'I should've gone straight to the police, I know that now, but I was so angry, Rachel. I was *furious*. I thought I was doing the right thing.'

He paused and I realised I was holding my breath. Imagining Phil seeing our daughter dressed like that, in those poses whilst he was away from home, late at night, drinking to console himself. I heard myself whimper.

'What did you do?' I asked quietly.

He looked at me. 'I just wanted to make sure, Rachel, that was all. I wanted his name. His car registration. I wanted to record him admitting it. Take his photo. Make sure the little bastard couldn't get away once I'd reported him.' Phil looked off toward the wall, his face hard. 'So I arranged to meet him on Tuesday. I just wanted a word with him before I went to the police. At first I thought I had the wrong person, he was all dressed up. Full works, smart suit and all this professional camera equipment. And he was our age. Maybe a little older. He shook my hand when I approached him, didn't flinch.' He paused for a second. 'I showed him the pictures of Katie. Explained I was her father.'

I waited. My breath stuck in my chest.

'You know what he does? He laughs like he didn't know how young she was. Tells me it was her idea. That Katie told him she was eighteen, that she had ID, that she must be a tearaway and if he'd known her real age he'd have never have taken the photographs.' Phil gritted his teeth. 'So I told him I was going straight to the police and that's when the wheels came off.'

I saw a muscle work at the side of Phil's jaw, tight and pulsing.

'He threatens me. Tells me that I've entrapped him, that me and Katie have been working together. That Katie knew what she was doing and he can prove it. He tells me that if I go to the police, he'll ruin Katie's life, says he's got other pictures of her and he'll put them out there. I had to walk away,' he shook his head. 'Because I knew if I'd started on him then I wouldn't be able to stop. I was so angry. I meant to drive straight to the police. You have to believe me. I really intended to go to them. I sat in my car and tried to calm down. And then I saw him. Buying some food. As if he'd done nothing wrong. My God, Rachel, I didn't know what he did to her. I didn't know if he touched Katie or what he'd done with her, and I realised I didn't have any proof. I had nothing, I hadn't taken a picture of him, got his car reg. I'd done nothing. I was sat there, watching him, wondering if Katie had lied to him, if she had told him she was eighteen. I was thinking how to put the case to the police, how to make sure he was arrested.'

I saw the torture in Phil's face and for a second I was there. I could see how it was for him. Watching this man who'd taken our precious girl and made her into something else, perhaps even abused her. Made her into something for other people to leer at, stood, casually choosing from the menu whilst Phil was crippled with anger. The hopeless feeling, the belief that the police might not get it right. That justice might not prevail and you have the opportunity of revenge right in front of you.

'Then I get a message on Twitter whilst I'm sat in the car,' Phil said, his voice quiet and low. 'He thought I'd left, didn't know I was watching him. He's on his phone and I get a notification, a private message to Katie's phone again but it was addressed to me. Her dad.'

I waited for him to go on, my breath caught in my throat.

Phil stared at me. 'It says, "Here's the proof about Katie. Here's the proof that she was willing, that she knew what she was doing." It was a video clip, Rachel.'

I went cold. As if the blood was freezing in my veins.

'An attachment. He sends me a video clip and says that if I go to the police, he'll put the video up everywhere. And everyone will know exactly what Katie is like.'

I'd stopped breathing, had become paralysed with fear. A video clip. A film of my daughter. I'd thought the pictures were the worst of it, but looking at Phil's face I realised there was more.

'What was it?' I whispered and Phil shook his head.

'You have to tell me,' I insisted, my voice quiet. 'Tell me what was in the video.'

Phil looked away from me.

'Was it of him taking pictures of her?' I asked. 'Was it a film of the photo shoot, was Katie posing for the camera, was it of him and her together?'

Phil slowly nodded.

'What were they doing? Talking? Was she kissing him? Phil!' My voice had become high as I imagined the worst. His silence was terrifying. 'Phil, please! Tell me what she was doing?'

'I didn't watch it all,' he said quietly. 'Just a few seconds until I realised...' he trailed off and then took a deep breath, 'it was Katie. You couldn't see him.

Couldn't see his face. He was filming her, filming Katie from above and she was...' he faltered for a second. 'She was on her knees. He was naked, had his hand on her head, pushing her. Katie was... he was pushing her head, forcing her to touch him, to... and she was,' he stopped. 'Fucking hell Rachel, do you need me to spell it out? She was on her knees and he was filming her, forcing her to give him a...'

I put my hand to my mouth. I was going to be sick. I went forward, as if to go to the toilet but my cast made it impossible. I couldn't understand, couldn't believe what he was telling me. Couldn't marry up what he was saying with Katie, our Katie, my little girl who was downstairs watching some Disney film. It just wasn't possible.

'All I had to do was drive, Rachel,' Phil said gripping my hand. 'Drive and not stop.' His eyes were wet, his face crumpled. 'He was right in front of me, smiling at his phone, at this film he'd just sent of my daughter he'd forced into giving him oral sex.' He was breathing hard, we both were. 'At that moment, I wanted to kill him,' he said quietly and I was silent, unable to respond.

'I was passing the roundabout, turning onto the side streets toward Crewe before I thought about what I'd done, and how badly I'd done it. Before I realised what this would mean for our family, for you, Katie and Jessica. The window screen was smashed, but only in the left corner and I made it to the train station. I parked it over near the back of the football ground, there's no CCTV there and I put money in to last the week. I wiped the car down at the front, got rid of the blood and went to the station. I'd come up with a plan of sorts, a way that I could protect you all from how stupid I'd been. I was going to join my train to London and report my car stolen when I got to the office. But then, before I got on the train, I get this call from Della,' he looked up at me, 'and I realised you'd been there.'

22

Suzie

There was no change. The nurse repeated that they had her landline and should there be anything, anything at all different in Adam's condition, then she'd be the first to know. Even so, Suzie rang the hospital to check once she got home. She'd stayed at the hospital for the entire day and most of the night.

It had been just past nine in the evening when a consultant had finally popped his head around the door in Adam's hospital room, he walked in with a breeziness about him, not even looking at Suzie, just reading things off machines and charts. When he did finally turn to face her, he gave a brief smile before repeating what the nurse had been saying, using clichés and empty words and stressing that Adam should make a full recovery in time.

'But how did it happen?' Suzie had asked before he left the room, she'd stood up, her handbag dropping from her lap and landing with a soft thud on the floor and the consultant had looked at the nurse.

'What did he do to be like this?' Suzie looked at Adam. 'What happened to him?'

The consultant had walked back over to the notes by Adam and studied them for a moment.

'Collision,' he'd said and looked up. 'His injuries were caused by a car.'

Suzie had stared at him, stunned. Car accident. Adam had been in a car accident. She'd thought Adam's condition was the result of something else, something more unique. That he'd slipped on the icy roads and banged his head as he fell, or been attacked and hit with something, but to hear that a car accident was responsible, that *bad driving* and nothing more was to account for his state, it seemed to trivialise it somehow. Make it normal. As if it was something that could happen to anyone.

The consultant and nurse had both stressed that she needed to speak with the police, that they only had the briefest of answers as to how Adam came to be with them, they could only tell her how they were going to get him out of hospital, not how he got in and Suzie had nodded, suddenly exhausted. What difference did it make how he got to be lying in that bed after all? He was there, and knowing what put him there would make no difference to his recovery.

Something scratched at the back of her mind as the consultant gave her the contact name at the police department, something trying to come into focus, a question she should ask or a note she should make, but at that time she didn't have the energy. Adam was unconscious, he would wake up, but no one could give her a date and in the meantime, she had things to do so that when he did recover, everything could go on as planned.

'I've got your laptop,' she'd said earlier as she'd held Adam's hand. 'I'm going to go home now and work out how to get to the safety deposit box. I'll get there first thing in the morning, get the cash and take it to the bank. And then I'll pay back that horrid man Mark, you silly thing, taking money off him.' She stroked his hand. 'I don't need to go on a fancy honeymoon if it means you dealing with people like that,' she told him. 'So I'll sort this all out. I'll find the money in the safety deposit box, pay everyone back and when you're better we can do things properly. One bank account. A joint bank account.' She stared at him but there was only the sound of the small electrical hum of the machines that he was wired to, the soft footsteps of nurses and visitors and their muffled voices.

Suzie smiled brightly at him, as if he could see her. 'So!' she said, 'I'm going to get off home now and give you some rest. I'll be back tomorrow as soon as I've been to the bank.'

Later, back at her flat, as Suzie was closing the curtains against the night and switching on the central heating, she thought she would take her small speaker in to Adam the next day, or perhaps her headphones. She'd play their wedding song to him, the one they'd picked together. He'd feel something when he heard that, she was certain.

The night had turned into a vicious thing, after sleety snow all day, the wind had picked up and she could hear it rattle against the windows as she took a glass of wine and Adam's laptop into her small lounge to be by the fire. The lamplights did nothing to make the room cosy, it was cold with a thin carpet and hard sofa that had been in when she arrived. Adam had talked big about redecorating before selling it. 'Character,' was the word he'd used. Said it needed 'bucketfuls of character' and if he got rid of the gas fire and put in a log burner type thing, it would bring something of a cottage feel to it and sell quicker.

Suzie wasn't sure how a second floor flat in central Chester could have a 'cottage feel' but she went along with it and this time last month, she'd been toying with the idea of storing logs in a decorative basket to add to the deception. Now she fiddled to switch on the gas and wondered how long she had before the bank would start proceedings to evict her.

Picking up Adam's laptop, she took another gulp and opened it up to be greeted with a password screen. No matter, she'd be able to guess it. She was his fiancée. Of course she'd be able to work it out.

Smiling, she typed in her own name. The screen shuddered, and the password prompt reappeared. She typed in her full name, Suzie Marie McFadden, again it shuddered and she was back to the same page. She frowned, it would be something personal, that's the way Adam worked things, something like the name of his first pet or school. She bit her lip, trying to remember things about him and went into the kitchen to collect the wine bottle, the landline phone rang and she snatched it up.

'Suzie?'

Her stomach plummeted. In her haste, she had forgotten to check caller ID.

'Hi, Mum,' she said, and walked back into the warmth of the lounge. 'Everything alright?'

'Well...' her mother began and Suzie filled her glass to the brim. Her mum lived twenty-five minutes away in Frodsham. For ten years, Suzie had lived on a neighbouring street to her mother. She'd been able to walk to her house. Back when she was living with Carl, they'd all had ideas of pushing a pram through the streets that connected them. She still felt guilty that it never transpired, that the lack of grandchildren and her moving away was somehow her fault and not because of Carl's fixation with Tina's tits.

'Your dad's not so good,' her mother went on and Suzie closed her eyes whilst she listened to the catalogue of horrors that her mother brought out and added to her guilt. Finally, after hearing about her father's angina, the closure of a corner shop and the dog's stiff back leg, her mother began to get to the real reason for her call.

'So, everything on schedule with the wedding?'

Suzie opened her mouth to answer but no words came.

'And your business?' her mother cut in, thinking Suzie's silence was an affirmative answer. 'That new thing you're doing with Rachel, how's that going? How is she, by the way, I often think about her mum down in Devon. Some kind of hippy, now isn't she?'

'I don't know, Mum,' Suzie said quickly. 'We don't really talk about that kind of stuff.'

Her mum gave a laugh. 'Of course you girls don't. I'm just so pleased it's going so well for you both. Who'd have thought, you two working together after all this time? And how is the lovely Rachel, still plotting world domination?' she laughed again and Suzie cut in.

'Mum, listen, I hate to cut you off but I'm really busy, we've a massive job on this weekend and I'm snowed under.'

'Right, yes,' her mother said and Suzie went to say goodbye when her mother interrupted. 'It's your brother I'm calling about actually,' she said and Suzie closed her eyes. 'It looks like he didn't get the job.'

Suzie swallowed. Of course Dave didn't get the job, of course he couldn't find any work, of course he was still looking for handouts.

'He could do with a loan, just until he gets some work,' her mother said. 'His redundancy won't last long, and with the kids starting secondary school, it's all cost more than he thought.'

Suzie held her breath. *Here it comes.*

'So I told him you were paying us back next week and he could have some of that.'

Suzie was quiet.

'Shall I give you his account details?' asked her mother. 'He needs about five thousand and then you can transfer the rest to us.'

'The thing is, Mum,' Suzie began and she could feel the words slide back down her throat before she'd started to say them. She could hear her mother's breath on the other end of the line, see her expectant expression, know without question that if she told her the truth, right now, her mother would understand. Would do everything she could to help. 'The thing is,' she started again, 'is that, I...' she took a deep breath. 'I might not be able to get to the bank next week after all, y'know with this big job we've got, it's all hands on deck!' she gave a tense little laugh.

'Of course, of course,' her mother said and Suzie felt sick at the kindness in her voice. 'Whenever you get the chance, love, I know you're busy with work and your wedding plans. Did I tell you that Auntie Sarah can make it now? But she's vegan, don't forget, not even fish.' Her mother paused and Suzie felt a lump in her throat, tight and constricting. 'I won't pester, love, I only called because of your brother and well, we would give it to you towards the wedding, you know we would, but as you're doing so well and now you're working with Rachel and your business is growing...'

'It's fine!' Suzie said and then took a breath in. 'Sorry, I mean, it's okay. I'll transfer it as soon as I can, the week after next. I'll have the money to you then.'

She finished the call as quickly as possible and slumped on the sofa. Her wine glass was almost empty. She'd drunk more than half the bottle whilst speaking to her mother and her stomach churned in protest.

Suzie had borrowed seven thousand pounds from her parents when she first started working with Adam. He'd said she needed it for the new photography equipment he was selling to her, that she needed something to put toward the cost of the studio and that seven thousand, along with the loan she got from the bank, would be enough to make her his business partner. She was meant to pay them back this week, with the money she got from the Gatsby job and the rest from Adam, but now... Suzie swallowed. Now that wasn't going to happen.

She thought about her parents in their small terrace, all their savings gone, her idiotic brother asking for money and how she could possibly tell them that Adam was in a coma in hospital and if she didn't work out how he ran the business, she'd lose everything.

Snatching the laptop, she opened it back up and the password screen greeted her. His face appeared in her mind, the first time they'd met. She had been wandering around Chester racecourse, the sun in her eyes, her new camera heavy in her hands. Adam had come over and asked her who she worked for. Asked what camera she used. Told her she should ditch Nikon and start using Canon. 'Canon', she typed in and the screen refreshed itself to the blue backdrop and the password prompt. Wrong answer.

After she'd visited his studio for the first time, he'd asked her out to dinner. She thought it was an interview, but when he put his hand on hers she realised that he wanted more. After three bottles of wine between them,

Suzie had told him all about Carl and what he had done to her. She remembered Adam saying it was outrageous the way she'd been treated, to string her along like that. He talked about how he wanted a family, how he'd like to have children of his own someday, a family home somewhere out of the centre. He'd been so honest about it the conversation had made Suzie melt.

'Family,' Suzie typed in and again the screen refreshed itself to the prompt.

Squeezing her eyes shut, she pictured Adam's face, tried to hear his voice talking to her. There was something he liked to be called when they were having sex. What was the term he used? What did he like her to say to him? Something stupid, embarrassing. Something she thought was a bit odd when she was on her hands and knees with Adam going at it from behind, but she'd called him it because he wanted her to. She'd called him it because it turned him on and now she remembered.

She opened her eyes and typed in the words.

Sugar Daddy.

The screen jumped into action. She was in.

23

Rachel

I was numb. A chill swept the length of me and I could taste bile at the back of my mouth. I didn't want to think of it, but could think of nothing else.

'You okay?' Phil was rubbing my back. He had hold of the bin from the bedroom, a decorative little thing that I never used. He thought I was going to throw up and couldn't make it to the bathroom because of my cast. He was holding it in front of me as if I was drunk, as if I'd overindulged and was paying for it. I looked up at him, his face a mass of emotion and then I heaved, dry retching into the empty bin one more time.

'I didn't want to tell you,' he said as I wiped my mouth. 'I wanted to protect you, to take care of it myself, take the bastard to the police and then let you know when I'd dealt with it. When we could speak to Katie together, form a plan of how to look after her. I wanted this to be different. You have to believe me, Rachel. I didn't plan to run him over.'

'Oh God,' I looked up to the ceiling, my eyes flooding. 'What he did to her, our little girl? The film of her...' I grabbed the bin and heaved over it again, Phil rubbing my back as I did so. 'Katie,' I said. 'We need to get her up here. If he did anything else to her, oh Phil...'

He grabbed my hand. 'Rachel. We can't. Listen to me, if we talk to Katie about this, if we let her know that I've seen that film, those pictures, and then she hears that the man who took them has been run over. Run over by my stolen car? She's not daft. She'll piece it together and then we'll be asking her to lie. To keep quiet. Not tell the police. The same with Jessica. We can't tell either of them. Ever.'

I stared up at him; his face was pale. He looked ill.

'But Phil,' I said. 'I can't not talk to Katie about this. She's been abused. She's been through something awful. We can't just...'

'We can talk to her about it later,' he said stopping me. 'When this has all died down. I've thought about it, and we'll get her some counselling, some therapy. Hope it comes out that way, get her the help then.'

I shook my head, it was swimming. It was too much. I looked at him stunned, unable to respond. We sat in silence, the low drone from the television that the girls were watching downstairs the only sound.

'You ran him over,' I said finally. 'Left the car in Crewe and that's where you were last night. To burn it out? Your clothes in the machine this morning, you were washing them because of the smoke?'

He nodded slowly and I squeezed my eyes shut.

'What would you have done?' he asked. 'Rachel, if you saw that film of her, if the person who'd taken it was in front of you and you had a gun in your hand...'

'The parking ticket, that was for the car park at Crewe?'

'Didn't even know I had it,' Phil said. 'You must've found the receipt. I never meant to, but Rachel, how could I *not* drive at him? When he'd just shown me that?'

I was quiet for a moment.

'But your train ticket, the one you gave to the police?'

'No time stamp,' he said. 'I printed out the tickets at Crewe station and wiped the ink on the time stamp as soon as they were printed. Smudged it.'

I remembered Sergeant Bailey running his finger along the top of the train ticket, the look he gave to his colleague and whimpered.

'What were you thinking?' I whispered and Phil grabbed my hands.

'I wasn't thinking,' he said. 'I was reacting. I wanted to kill that bastard after what he'd shown me of Katie. After what he'd done to her.' He gritted his teeth. 'That morning I should've been on the train to London, I'd told the office I might be in late...'

'Felix...?'

'Telling the truth, although he does have a gambling addiction. But he was right, I'd cancelled the presentation but I hadn't yet cancelled my train tickets. I think part of me thought the meeting wouldn't happen, that he wouldn't turn up.' He went to the window. 'And then, afterwards, I thought I could use it as a sort of alibi. Tell the police that's where I was.'

'But Phil,' I shook my head. 'There'll be CCTV in those stations, you'll be on camera. They'll find out that you weren't on that train...'

'They haven't yet have they?' he asked quickly. 'Otherwise I'd have been arrested. At the police station, they asked me questions but they didn't arrest me. Didn't even say I was a suspect. And why would I be? They don't know what he did to Katie. As far as the police are concerned I have no motive. No reason at all to run that man over. We are strangers. It's not a film, Rachel, this isn't television where the detectives are super sleuths. I dare say that

Sergeant Bailey has got numerous other cases that he's working on. Other, more serious crimes that are taking his attention.'

'More serious than running someone over?' I asked. 'Than a hit and run?'

'You'd have done the same,' he said quietly, and I was silent for a moment as I thought over the enormity of what had happened.

'You ran him over,' I said after a while. 'You left him for dead. You wanted to *kill him*. And I understand, you're right, I would've wanted to do the same. I would've wanted to murder him, drive a knife into his chest after seeing what he made Katie do, but you shouldn't have done it.' I shook my head. 'You should've just taken it all to the police! Right then. Immediately. You should have driven to the police station.'

He grabbed my hand again tightly. 'Don't you think it's easy to say that now? To look back and know what I should've done? I'm trying to make it right, I'm trying my best, Rachel, I'm fixing it. Yes, I made a mistake but now I'm sorting it so it won't be yours, won't be Katie's.' He stared at me intently. 'I've an alibi of sorts and I've got rid of the car. If you hadn't have been so interfering, if you'd not gone on Twitter, if you'd just stayed asleep last night instead of...'

'Phil!' I yanked my hand out of his. 'Listen to yourself.'

He stood. Went back to the window, his shoulders tense. We stayed in silence for an age. My mind wasn't capable of processing it all: the images of Katie, the fact that she'd posed for those pictures, had undressed for them to be taken, that she'd been abused.

He came towards the bed, sitting on the edge. 'You think Katie is the only girl he's done this to?' he asked me.

'You think she was the first? The last? Rachel, there was a website full of girls like her. He's a master of his game.' Phil leaned forward and wiped my cheeks that were wet with tears. He blinked a few times, trying to push back his own tears then took a sigh.

'I could go to the police,' he said quietly.

'Police?'

Phil nodded. 'Perhaps if I confess I won't get long, five, six years...'

'I don't want you to go to jail!' I was startled by the force of my words.

We stared at each other, my heart thumping. 'That man who did that to Katie. He hurt our daughter and I don't want you to go to prison for hurting him.'

Phil opened his mouth to say something but I shook my head. 'Just wait a minute,' I told him. 'Just stop talking a moment. Just give me a minute to *think*.'

I imagined a life where Phil went to jail, his crime public knowledge. A life where Katie was the subject of gossip, where we all were.

Walking through the city centre and people pausing to watch us as we did: the family of the man who ran someone over. We'd be judged. I'd be the reckless mother who wasn't keeping her daughters safe, I'd be the woman on the news that I'd previously shaken my head at. I was the one who wasn't watching the ball, who had let this happen and who would want that kind of person catering and planning their event? My business would fail. I wouldn't get work anymore. I'd have to take up some other, menial job to pay the bills.

Katie would be forever known as the girl who was taken in by the paedophile. Everyone would know what had happened to her. Jessica would have to deal with the fact that her little sister had been the victim of abuse, that as a family, we'd let her down. As a mother, *I'd let them down*. People would know *that* about us before they knew anything else. My scalp prickled, my body hot and sweating.

'Fuck!' I put my hands to my face.

Phil pulled them away.

'I might not get that long, I could be out—'

'Phil, I don't know if I can do it,' I said and the thought of losing him, of losing everything, was suddenly terrifying.

He stared at me a moment. 'If I don't confess, we can't talk about any of this to Katie,' he said. 'We have to keep quiet. Until we can perhaps get her into some kind of therapy, make up some reason. And we have to pray there's nothing on CCTV of me at that station. We have to pray that the police won't find out what I did.'

I swallowed, my mind running, I could hear the sound of Sergeant Bailey saying he'd need to speak with us again, the way he paused on the answer machine.

'And we have to pray he doesn't wake up,' Phil said. 'Because if he comes out of his coma, if he tells the police that he saw me...'

'Could he do that?' I asked quickly. 'Did he see you? See it was you driving the car?'

'He'll remember meeting me,' Phil said slowly. 'He'll remember I was there.'

'Fuck!' I hissed again and we were quiet for a moment.

'It'll be my word against his,' Phil said. 'I'll deny it. Say I was never there, but then...'

I thought about the photographs. If he should come out of his coma and accuse Phil what course of action would the police take? They'd find the photographs of Katie and begin to unravel everything.

'Can we stop it?' I asked him. 'Is there time for us to get rid of these,' I pointed to the photographs, 'to get rid of the association?'

Phil shrugged and I felt like screaming. I couldn't see a way out. I didn't know what to do.

'What's best?' I asked quickly. 'Think of Katie. Nothing else. Think of Jessica, what's best for our daughters?' I grabbed his hands. 'Would it be better for them if we talked about this? Confessed what you did, tell Katie we know and make sure she's okay? But then she'd have to watch you go to prison as a consequence, or is it best for the girls if we keep quiet? Say nothing and pray he doesn't wake up, or if he does, that he doesn't remember? Katie would have her father at home, but she'd have to deal with what happened to her alone and we'd have to deal with the uncertainty of him accusing you and what that could bring.'

'In time,' Phil said slowly, 'Katie might come to us. She might want to talk to us about it.'

'But she might not,' I said. 'And anything could have happened to her. Anything. We're only seeing the photographs. We're only seeing the one film he sent you.' My hands went to my throat. 'We might never know what he did to her. Phil, what if he did more? What if he did other things to her?'

Phil took in a deep breath, 'I don't know,' he said. 'Rachel, I don't know what to do.'

I closed my eyes, trying to stop the panic.

What if he'd done more?

24

Suzie

It took a moment for Suzie to work out what she was looking at. It was fleshy and wet with a dark interior. She shifted uncomfortably for a moment and peered closer. It was only when she spotted the outline of a tooth, that she realised she was looking at an open mouth. A female mouth, it looked like, taken from the side, fleshy lips parted, tongue resting provocatively on the bottom lip. The picture was so close it was almost abstract and she frowned, not sure why Adam would have such a thing as his screen saver. He took so many impressive pictures, colourful landscapes, black and white atmospheric urban shots and numerous portraits so why he should have this gaping mouth as his screen saver was puzzling.

She tilted her head and the image became more apparent, perhaps he was experimenting. Blowing up a macro image until it became some kind of artwork. When he regained consciousness, amongst the things they had to urgently talk about, she'd tell him he was wasting his time with this. No one would want close-ups of open mouths on their walls. She swallowed to try and get rid of the taste of stale wine; it was getting late. She took her glasses off, gave them a quick rub with the hem of her jumper and then started to investigate his desktop.

There were several applications, many of them things that she didn't recognise. Games, music players and other icons littered the left-hand side of the screen. Suzie ignored them all. She was only interested in where he kept the record of accounts, where the money could be. Adjusting the blanket so it was a little tighter around her shoulders, she navigated to the computer itself, looking at the hard drive. She went to documents and opened up the files, but there was nothing, just an empty screen. Adam had never used the office documents and had saved nothing to his hard drive. It was unused, completely blank.

'Shit,' Suzie hissed.

Forgetting about how sweet and sickly the wine had been, she picked up her empty glass and held it to her lips, throwing her head back to get the very last drop. Her stomach was swirling, empty except for the alcohol. She needed some food, something to soak it all up. Walking into the kitchen, she aimlessly opened up a cupboard and stared inside. She'd so wanted this to be easy, to see exactly what Adam had been doing and for it to be fully explainable. His laptop was meant to give up all the answers, it was not meant to be practically unused.

Reaching up, she got a well-used pint glass that had been robbed from a pub many, many years earlier and filled it with water. After she had drunk greedily, she looked around at what there was to eat. She found a box of crackers and a tub of soft cheese just past the sell by date. It would have to do under the circumstances, she didn't have the money to order a takeout and she didn't want to venture out into the night on foot to go to the corner shop.

She took it back into the lounge where Adam's laptop was, the desktop image of the open mouth gaping at her and the conversation with her mother still on her mind. Dave, her useless brother asking for money and her parents thinking that Suzie had thousands to play with and a new exciting venture that was beginning to be profitable. A wedding coming up and a whole new life to start. A self-pitying sob caught at the back of her throat.

'That's how it should be,' she said aloud to herself. 'That's what should be happening, and it will happen.'

She shoved three crackers into her mouth, then, when the initial hunger had started to subside, she opened the soft cheese and dipped a cracker in, using it as a makeshift shovel before sitting back down with the laptop on her knee.

'C'mon,' she said as she ran her fingers over the keypad, her mouth full, 'you wouldn't have this if you didn't use it. There's more than just photo editing software on here, there has to be.'

With sticky fingers, she searched several files, including 'pictures' and 'music' and all were empty. Perhaps he didn't even use the laptop to edit his photographs on, Suzie thought as she ate another cheese filled cracker, perhaps it was all done on the huge Apple iMac he had in the studio.

She clicked on the email icon but it wasn't activated either.

The gas fire hissed at her feet and the wind howled at the window. She'd have to move back in with her parents. At thirty-seven she would be crawling back there again. The last time had been mortifying and she had only been there for five months whilst she waited for the sale of the house she owned with Carl to come through and the purchase of her flat to be completed.

Her parents had converted her old bedroom into an office. She'd slept on an inflatable mattress, her head by the side of a paper shredder. The evenings spent listening to her mother's chatter about the neighbours. Trips to garden centres and small supermarkets at weekends. Endless talks about the dog's health.

'Not a fucking chance,' she suddenly spat out. 'I'm getting *married*.' She gripped the laptop and stared at it.

She looked at all the icons on the desktop again and then, she started to laugh. It was so obvious. She shook her head at her own stupidity. Double clicking the internet icon, she waited whilst it loaded.

'History,' Suzie breathed as she navigated to Adam's browsing history. 'Of course you'll have it all remote. In the cloud.'

The drop-down menu appeared and she took a sharp intake of breath. She thought she might see some porn, but didn't realise how hurt she'd be until she saw the triple x sign claiming what they were. She didn't read them. She didn't look at them, but scrolled past them quickly. All men looked at porn, she told herself as she quickly went down the list, it wasn't out of the ordinary.

Whatever Adam had been looking at that wasn't to do with accounts or transferring money could wait. Then she saw it, an email address and a balloon of hope lifted in her chest. Everything would be in his online email account, all his correspondence, if she wanted to find out Adam's movements with money, then it had to be in there. She felt a giddy quickening as she clicked it open.

It took her straight to Adam's inbox account, automatically logging her in, no password needed and a page full of his emails was suddenly in front of her. She giggled with relief, here would be everything she needed.

There were several junk emails that she didn't even open, the usual kind from online stores offering discounts and voucher codes.

She scrolled down, something from a magazine subscription, something from a phone company and then she saw it and a rush of adrenaline hit her.

'Bingo,' she breathed as she saw one titled, 'Manchester Safety Deposit Box.'

Opening it up, she felt a stab of disappointment as she read it was just a polite, impartial email explaining new packages they had available. Nothing else. Nothing to show that Adam had a safety deposit box; the email wasn't even addressed to him by name. She stared at it a moment. But if he didn't, why would they be emailing Adam about new packages? She grabbed the phone and quickly dialled the number. It was after hours but after a moment an answer machine kicked in.

'Thank you for calling, we are now closed. Our opening times are...'

Suzie hung up. Going back to his email account she went to the search box at the top of the screen and typed '*safety deposit box*' and waited. A page of emails loaded and the disappointment she'd felt earlier was magnified. There were emails from safety deposit boxes in London, Chester, Liverpool and Manchester. A page of them. All sales emails, all impersonal.

She opened up the second email from the top of the list, one from a vault in Liverpool and looked for the contact number. It was listed at the bottom of the email along with the line, '*Twenty-four-hour service*'.

Suzie held her breath as she dialled.

'Protecta Vaults,' a woman answered after the fourth ring. 'How can I help.'

Suzie's head swam. Her hand was sweating as she gripped the phone tight.

'Can you tell me,' she said, her words urgent, 'if an Adam Staple has a safety deposit box with you?'

There was a moment's silence.

'I'm afraid that information is confidential,' she said after a while. 'We can't give out any personal information about our clients.'

'But he's my fiancé,' Suzie sputtered. 'And he's been in an accident, and I think he's got a safety deposit box with you, and I need to get into it.'

'Do you have his account key?'

'Account key?' Suzie asked. 'What account key?'

'Without his key to the safety deposit box and his PIN, I'm afraid if you're not down on the account, which I presume you're not as you don't have a key, we can't access the box. That's if he has a safety deposit box with us at all.'

Suzie sat a moment, her mouth slightly open.

'But he's unconscious,' she said. 'You must have a procedure for this kind of thing. When a client is no longer able to function and they need someone to get the box on their behalf.'

'In those circumstances, without a key, there's not a lot we can do. If he should die…'

'Die!' Suzie's voice was high but the woman went on as if she hadn't spoken.

'We'd need a copy of the death certificate and the executor of the deceased estate would be granted access so long as they have the right papers.'

'But can you tell me if he has a box with you?' Suzie asked. 'Can you at least confirm that? Please?'

'Unless you have the key, we can't do anything.'

Suzie ended the call. Unless Adam died or woke up, she was no wiser to if he'd taken out a safety deposit box. She looked at the page of emails, with no idea if he'd picked any of these companies or none, and no way of finding out.

There was a loud bang outside the door and she jumped, the crackers falling to the floor and the tub of soft cheese falling face down on the carpet. Going to the window she pulled the curtain aside and looked out at the black night. Wind howled and threw rain against the glass, making her jump back a little. It was vicious out there. An empty bucket was being thrown about by the wind, banging against the pavement. She shuddered. Was there a shadow behind the tree? A figure watching her? Her thoughts went to Mark. Would he come here demanding a repayment? She would call him tomorrow. Tell him that Adam was in hospital. That he was in a coma and she needed more time.

Suzie shut the curtains and went back to the door. She checked it was locked, and then put the deadlock on. She thought of calling the police but after waiting a moment, when there was no knock at her door, she went back to the laptop. She'd think about Mark tomorrow, when she'd found where the money was.

Her heart was pounding with desperation. She ran a hand over her face and with her head a little clearer from the water and crackers, she had one more idea. She went to the search bar at the top of the email screen and typed in '*accounts*'. This brought several emails back and she nearly wept with disappointment. Each email subject line had the word 'account' in and they were pathetic, mostly new accounts opened for games, or joining up to photography sites. There were no emails with spreadsheets or other bank accounts he had, nothing to do with moving money, no emails to tell her what to do next.

And then she saw it.

It was halfway down the page and was two years old.

An email from a web hosting company. An email with Adam's name, his contact details, his address. It was his account details for a site called 'Remote Models'.

He'd never mentioned it, but Adam must have created a modelling business before he met her. Probably one of those businesses he opened up for a loan or credit but never actually ran. Regardless of what it was, if she could find out how he ran it, it might point to another bank account, which might point to something else. Or details of the safety deposit box. Something.

Feverishly, she went back to the top of the inbox page where the search box was and typed in the words 'Remote Models'. Twenty pages came back, full of emails. She opened the first two and shook her head, understanding nothing of what they referred to, but as she looked through more, it became clear that Adam was indeed running a model agency and running it recently. A model agency she knew nothing about.

She methodically went through the emails in date order, looking at the oldest first. Tracing the progress of Adam's model agency, confused as to why he'd never told her about it. There was correspondence about web design and numerous emails about hosting and domain names along with advertising invoices from companies specialising in web traffic. The cost of it was staggering, there were emails from search engine optimisation agencies and design companies promoting his site. The price they charged was unbelievable. It seemed Adam was paying for the services of several on a weekly basis to keep his website in top ranking.

'What the…?' she murmured as she opened one from a week ago, and found it was an email from the web hosting company. Adam had asked for more space, more bandwidth and the terms and conditions regarding uploading images of 'artistic nudes'. Reading it, it seemed Adam wanted to show body parts but was unclear if it would mean his site would be regarded as pornography and result in suspension.

She went back to the search bar, ready to go to the Remote Models website and see exactly what type of photographs Adam was taking, when she noticed a small notification at the side of the search bar, next to the icon of the magnifying glass.

It had a small blue tick against a red box and the words, '*All photographs up to date*' written alongside in a small typeface.

'Photographs?' Suzie asked and clicked on the tick.

A separate window sprang open. An online database. Adam's online database. His private storage area for his photographs, ones downloaded from his phone as well as from his camera disc.

She used something similar in the studio, it was the first thing Adam had taught her, once you've taken the photographs, back them up. Back them up on email, on cloud, on something that's outside of your computer and is private and safe should anything happen to your hard drive, but this wasn't the backup that she was used to. This was something different and as she waited for the screen to load, she saw it was in the name of Adam's password. *Sugar Daddy.*

A few thumbnail images loaded and Suzie frowned. They were blurred. One had clearly been taken from his phone, too low of an exposure, completely amateur. Why would Adam be taking shots like this? Then as the other image loaded Suzie realised they were taken on location. They were hand-held and looked like they'd been taken in a rush. They were shaky, blurred images. Others began to load and these were of a different quality. These were taken in a room, in dim light. There was a bed and Suzie leaned forward to see but it was too unclear. The thumbnail too small, only showing the outline of shadowy figures. Suzie clicked on an image that wasn't as dark as the rest.

She looked at the picture. Suzie leaned in and looked again, adjusting her glasses. Then she screamed.

The laptop fell from her knees as she jumped back. It landed on the floor, the screen facing up. She stood on the sofa in horror, looking down at the laptop.

After a moment, she went back to it.

It couldn't be, not possible, not him. Not that. *Not that.* But it was.

The shadowy outlines quite clear now she knew what she was looking at.

The photograph was of Adam, taken by Adam. A horrific selfie, taken with his hand outstretched so the viewer was looking down at the scene. He was naked. They both were, and he was holding her tight.

A horrid wretched sound escaped her, animal like. The face beside Adam's was semi in the light, her eyes were looking up at the camera, her mouth open. It wasn't anyone that Suzie recognised. Her small body was curled underneath her; she was completely naked. Small hands on Adam's bare thighs as they both looked up directly into the camera, his face one of pure delight. Suzie picked up the laptop, collapsing on the sofa with it. She clutched her sides and stared in complete shock.

The other person in the photograph with Adam wasn't a woman.

It was a girl. With small underdeveloped breasts, milky white skin and the chubby face of adolescence.

Friday

Snow showers expected.

25

Suzie

For a moment when she awoke, she felt nothing. She stretched out her legs and vaguely wondered why her tongue was stuck to the roof of her mouth, why her eyes felt like pingpong balls and why her stomach felt like she'd done a hundred sit-ups.

It hit her like a bowling ball falling on her chest.

Adam. Young girls. Website.

She sat up abruptly, head spinning, and made it to the bathroom just in time to retch into the toilet. Greenish bile hit the bowl and her stomach cramped in pain. She wiped her mouth and slumped on the floor. She didn't cry. She had cried for hours last night, on and off. Every time she remembered something, his voice or her hopes for the future, a fresh wave of tears would engulf her.

In parts the fear, the terror of the whole thing would momentarily paralyse her, she'd be motionless, heart rapid and limbs stiff. And then there were periods where a memory would strike her like a knife She would suddenly remember his touch, how he used to move the hair from her forehead. How he used to kiss the back of her neck, and then she'd look at the horror presenting itself and have to blot her mind to the Adam she thought she knew and it would hit her all afresh.

At first, she'd thought the extent of it was the four images of Adam and the girl. Each had been taken at the same place and Adam had taken all the pictures, an array of arrogant selfies. In each one his face wore a satisfied, proud expression. As if he were doing something very accomplished, undertaking some special achievement, not molesting a young girl in a dark hotel room.

She'd wailed, the kind where the weeping reverberated throughout her body. She'd thrown up, twice. She'd gone to ring her mother, her old friends, Rachel, but had cancelled all calls before she'd even made them.

Once the initial shock had passed she began to examine the images. She became an amateur detective, searching for clues and signs that might offer up some explanation. She brought them up on the screen, enlarged them and looked at the backgrounds. Was that a bottle of wine? What time did it say on the clock?

She studied the girl's face, the wide eyes and half smile. Could she be older? Was she one of those people who looked deceptively young for her age?

Was Adam drugged? High? Why was he doing this, why?

She'd gone back to his emails, to his secret model agency and the truth dawned like an unfolding torturous realisation.

She almost didn't.

It was tempting to close the laptop, go to bed and pretend the girl in the picture was older and Adam was high, off his face and unaware of how young she was. A one-night stand, a moment of madness. But that option was impossible. A quick internet search brought up the site.

Remote Models was basic. A straightforward portfolio of someone named 'Rob'. It seemed Adam was calling himself Rob and presenting himself as a photographer who specialised in supplying models to various agencies for work in the fashion and beauty industry.

There was no mention of what agencies, or what modelling work these girls got, only photographs of them posing. Location shots, carefully lit, carefully posed. Black and white images of them smiling, looking thoughtful or full-length pictures of them sitting in various positions. And all the models were girls. Young girls.

Suzie raced through page after page of them. She recognised Adam's photography, the way he framed the shots, the way he had them standing, and then she saw her. The girl from the photograph with Adam, the one who was naked with him. She was smiling at the camera in black and white. A variety of headshots done as though she were an actress. A young girl, a very young girl and Suzie's throat closed in at the sight of her, squeezed in on itself so it was almost choking her. She went to click on the small icon for more information about this young girl who Adam had got naked in a hotel room, when a pop up sprang open asking for a password.

It was addressed to '*admin*'. Adam used this laptop to upload his photographs to the website and it had remembered and stored his details. It was already filled in, eight small black dots in the password box.

'Please,' she whispered as she clicked on the box to take her to where Adam controlled everything. 'Please, please, please.'

When the next screen loaded it was clear that her pleas to the unknown had gone unanswered. A series of posts that Adam had uploaded lay on the right side of the screen and Suzie clicked on his most recent one. An image loaded.

UNPUBLISHED was written in large letters over the post and Suzie gagged as she saw it. This was no model. This was no artful black and white image of the like that she'd just seen, no full-length shot of someone standing beside a tree. This was a girl, twelve or thirteen at most with overdone make-up sitting on a barstool. She was wearing lacy knickers and nothing else. Her face, unsure and frightened stared at the camera. Her immature body on full display. Quickly, she pressed the 'back' button, needing to get the image off the screen and then she saw it; a long list of unpublished pages. Each with a name.

'Lucy, Rebecca, Leah, Phoebe…'

'ARGH!' she'd slapped herself hard across her face as she read the names, at how long this had been going on. Her cheek stung.

Each unpublished post was of a girl that Adam had got to pose naked. They were all done in full make-up with ridiculous props around them, all studio shots. And they were all young.

Just when she thought she'd seen the extent of it, she found a folder marked 'films'. Suzie only looked at one. It was labelled 'Becky' and it was in a hotel room. It had been filmed on a tripod, from a distance but it was enough for her to see Adam having sex with Becky. It was enough for her to see Becky's frightened face, to hear Adam's voice instructing her what to do, enough to understand.

And there was another folder. This one marked 'finished', but she dared not click on that, she didn't want to know. She wanted someone else to see it, someone other than her to decide what to do. And then, just when she thought she'd discovered it all, she saw the social media icons at the top of the screen. Clicking on one, she was logged in automatically and here she saw his private messages, his Remote Models Twitter account, Facebook, Instagram, as well as others she wasn't aware of, calling himself 'Rob' and telling girl after girl how 'photogenic' they were. How they had 'talent'.

She learned he'd been sending out presents to them, showering them with expensive things, perfume, watches, designer clothes, the kind of things that made young girls feel grown up and valued. She saw his texts about meeting up in hotels across the country, the meals and alcohol he'd bought them. The outfits he'd made them wear, the places he'd taken them to. Adam had given the impression that he was some kind of successful businessman, but as Suzie went through the messages, tracing Adam's movements and purchases, it became clear that Adam hadn't worked in a very long time, and she suddenly realised where all her money had gone. There was nothing hidden in a safety deposit box somewhere, there was no hidden stash waiting to be found, Adam had spent everything on creating his illusion of a wealthy businessman to fool these poor girls and when Suzie's money ran out, he'd taken loan after loan to keep up the pretence.

She then found his other social media accounts, the ones where Adam was pretending to be a teenage girl himself, luring them in as if they were finding a new friend and something about it seemed familiar. Something about the name he'd called himself, *Shutterbug*, and it bothered her. Had he called himself that when he was with her? Had Suzie used that name with him, like when he asked her to call him *Sugar Daddy* and she'd had to stop then, saliva had filled her mouth, making her retch and she felt faint.

Struggling, she'd dragged herself away at that point. She'd planned to take it to the police, hand the whole thing to them in the morning, but as she moved her hands away, the page of the website moved, she had hit the scroll bar and it was now showing the bottom of the site. She'd sat panting, a stale vomit taste in her mouth, her eyes stinging and her cheek sore from where she had slapped it, looking at a small thumbnail of a model that had just been uploaded to an unpublished part of the site. There was something about the small face, the brown eyes and long black hair that made Suzie catch her breath.

'No,' she breathed. 'For fuck's sake, no.' Suzie looked at the name below, *Katie*, and a splinter of ice pierced her stomach. She slowly clicked on the thumbnail to make the image bigger and a low moan escaped her.

It was Rachel's daughter.

Adam had got Katie, Rachel's daughter, her friend and business partner's daughter to pose naked for him. To sit on a barstool with a painted face and show him her bare body. She thought to his films, to his folders, and she began to shake then, violently shake and she'd had to close the laptop. Had to push it away from her as she curled herself up in a ball. She brought her knees up to her chest and squeezed her eyes shut and tried to make the horror of it disappear.

'Rachel,' she moaned as she cried into her hands. 'Rachel, I'm so sorry.'

—

Suzie dressed slowly that morning. She wore a black outfit consisting of a shirt and jacket with wide pants. She looked like she was going to a funeral.

On her dresser were two memory sticks.

One contained it all. Everything. She'd downloaded the full website, all his correspondence, the contact details, the pictures, films, everything. A small little thing ready to give to the police.

The other memory stick contained Katie. It was the last thing she did before going to bed. It was the one thing she could do for Rachel. She did a search of the site and two files came up marked '*Katie*', a folder with images, and a folder with a short film. A short film of Katie and Suzie had wept at the sight of it. It had taken fifteen minutes before she was able to transfer that video clip to the memory stick. Fifteen minutes whilst her hands shook and she retched. She didn't open it. Didn't want to see what Adam had made Katie do, what he'd filmed of her. She would give it to Rachel and tell her that she'd not watched, that she didn't know what it contained. That she wasn't, even at this stage, aware of the full extent of it. Whatever was on that film was for Rachel and Phil, not her.

Sitting heavily on the bed she looked up to the ceiling, tears fell and she blinked them away. Before she went to the police she would go to Rachel and a great dragging feeling swept through her entire body at the thought.

How do you tell someone that? How do you tell your oldest friend that your fiancé has been grooming their daughter? Give them a memory stick containing something vile. Tell them that their life is shattered?

For the last fourteen years, Rachel had been a mother to Katie but Suzie could only remember seeing her a handful of times until eighteen months ago when she'd become friendly with Rachel again.

When Rachel first became a mother, it had been a shock because they were young and it was the last thing that everyone thought Rachel would do. She'd seen her after Jessica was born, pushing a huge pink and white pram around the streets, her face set in a tired expression. Suzie had been walking home from Chester, she'd been shopping and her arms were full of carrier bags containing a new outfit, make-up and other nonsense. Rachel had moved back and was living with her odd mother and they'd stopped to chat, Suzie had peered into the pram and seen the most adorable face. Fat and sleeping, her chubby hands raised either side of her face. Jessica had seemed like something unreal at the time. Something that Rachel had borrowed. They talked briefly but it was clear that they no longer had anything in common. Rachel was going home to nappies and making up bottles whereas Suzie was going clubbing. Meeting a gaggle of girls for drinks and dancing.

The next time she could remember seeing Rachel it was years later and by then, Katie had been born. Suzie had heard that she'd got married, had another daughter. She had a vague recollection of sending a gift and card, but the clearest memory she had is when she drove past them one evening. She was with Carl then and they'd been on their way to a party or concert, somewhere that Suzie wasn't too happy about going and she'd seen them come out of a restaurant. It looked like they'd just had a family meal. Jessica had been running fast, holding a balloon with some restaurant name on it. Rachel and Phil were shouting for her to slow down as they walked each holding the hand of another child between them. It had been Katie, her dark hair swinging and she skipped along, and Suzie had gasped at the sight of her. There was Rachel, her family around her, Katie now old enough to be starting school and they'd all looked so happy. It had given Suzie a pang of envy.

Then, when Katie was about eight, Suzie had seen them coming out of the cinema. She was still with Carl and Katie had looked so grown up, so tall. It made her realise how old she was, and that she still wasn't a mother. Whenever Suzie saw Rachel over the years, whenever their lives crossed or they had a sporadic meeting for a 'catch up' Katie had always been talked about along with Jessica. But it was Katie that Suzie used as a kind of barometer against her own life, a measure that she used to mark time. Katie leaving primary school and she still wasn't pregnant, Katie in her second year at high school and Carl had left her. Katie getting excellent grades and she was still single.

Then, when she was at her lowest ebb, Rachel had invited Suzie around for coffee and Katie had answered the door. She must've been about twelve at the time and she was a different girl. Long hair down to her waist, her eyebrows plucked and shaped, her slim figure dressed in a tight fitting top and Suzie had joked about how old she made her feel. Said the clichés of how much she'd grown and Katie had laughed, she had the same laugh as Rachel and it moved Suzie.

She'd talked with her then, asked about her clothes and they both discovered a love for Zara and for a moment, it was like Suzie was chatting to Rachel from school again. Giddy and enthusiastic and smiley, and when Rachel came and Katie went, it left Suzie with an ache. A sadness that she didn't have a daughter of her own. The feeling was hard to shake off. It wouldn't leave her. As the months went on and Suzie became more involved with Rachel, the fullness at what Rachel had only served to show what Suzie didn't, and it left her with a longing. An emptiness.

She knew it was silly to compare herself to her friend, but she couldn't help it. Rachel had so much; she had everything. It was only when Suzie met Adam that the feeling lessened. Adam had shown her a way forward. He'd waltzed into her life and promised her everything she'd wanted in a few months: a brilliant career, a better home, a family, the promise to become a mother. For the first time, Suzie felt like she deserved a place at the table with Rachel, instead of watching from the sidelines. Meeting Adam had given her the confidence to suggest they work together, start up the events businesses. She'd been on her way, things were finally coming together for her. Adam was the solution, not the problem, he'd offered her everything she wanted.

She closed her eyes. She'd been such a fool.

That was the last time she'd seen Katie, just a few days ago. She'd been in her school uniform. Suzie remembered her face, the striking hair against her pale skin, her intelligence, her alertness. Had she spoken to Adam about Katie? She must have, she'd talked of introducing him to Rachel and Phil often enough, all those plans that he'd cancelled for one reason or another. She must have talked to him about their children, about the aloof Jessica and beautiful Katie.

'Oh God,' Suzie said putting her hands to her face as a fresh wave of despair swept over her. 'Oh God, what have I done?'

She stood up. Sleep and lack of food had made her mind foggy. She didn't quite know what she was going to say or how she was going to do this, only that it had to be done. Her legs were shaky and unstable and she saw his laptop as she'd left it. What would the police do with it all? She leaned against the door for support and then, before she lost her nerve, put both memory sticks into the side pocket of her handbag. She lifted the laptop and then put it back down. It was out of charge, useless to take with her. She'd have to put the memory stick into Rachel's laptop and show her on there as the Remote Models site wasn't live any longer, she'd taken the whole thing down.

A sob caught in her throat as she thought of Rachel, unknowing, innocently thinking that her family was intact, her problems consisting of a broken ankle and the catering for the Gatsby party. She was struggling to think if there was any other way to do this, another way to tell Rachel and Phil, to explain it all and then she remembered Phil. Phil who was having an affair and it stopped her for a moment.

With everything about Adam, she'd forgotten about Phil's affair.

How they'd seen the messages on Twitter and in that moment, it came back to her. *Shutterbug*.

The Twitter messages they'd seen that day had been from Shutterbug. That was the Twitter username that Adam used. Adam's car was found at the retail park. Those messages had been from *Adam*.

It was Adam arranging to meet Katie at the hotel, not Phil conducting an affair, and as she realised it she fell against the wall, her heart hammering. It took a moment for her mind to get around the idea.

Adam on Twitter. *Shutterbug. Champagne and a hotel room*.

Her legs almost went beneath her.

Rachel had gone to that retail park expecting to find Phil, but what did she see instead?

She put on her jacket panting, chills running along her spine. She felt like she'd run a marathon, her tired brain trying to work it out. Trying to put all the pieces together. Rachel said she hadn't seen Phil. Phil said his car was stolen. But Rachel had seen something. She'd been in a state at the hospital. Adam's car abandoned, his accident. Bleeding on the brain.

Suzie's phone ringing made her jump. It was the land-line, a loud ring echoing throughout her flat. She went to it quickly, thinking in her panic that it must be Rachel. That Rachel was calling to tell her, to explain what she saw that day.

'Ms McFadden?' the voice was soft, Suzie recognised it but couldn't place it. 'It's Janine here from the hospital? We've been trying to get hold of you.'

'I think my mobile's broken,' Suzie said. 'It's smashed.'

'I've some news regarding your fiancé, Adam Staple?' Janine went on and Suzie held her breath.

'I'm pleased to tell you that he's regained consciousness. Although it's still very early, Mr Staple had made clear signs of response. He's awake Ms McFadden.'

He was awake.

26

Rachel

The Christmas light switch-on is a big deal in Chester. There's a parade where community groups and local artists get involved, with floats, banners, dancers, people in costume, all led by a brass band playing Christmas songs.

It usually starts somewhere near the town hall and worms its way through the city, along the main drag of Eastgate street, and through the gateway arch of the Eastgate clock, the original entrance to the Roman fortress, all singing and whooping and being cheered on by the crowds. It's stunning and spectacular and chaotic.

Katie's school was involved this year. The PTA had sent many a letter fundraising for something or other and a theatre group that Jessica had previously been a member of were performing. It marked the start of late night Christmas shopping and the opening of the Christmas market.

Apart from the really miserable, everybody seemed to go, and Phil was usually amongst the really miserable so each year I had to argue my case for him to attend. He hated it. Couldn't stand the crowds, the forceful commercialism but the girls loved it. And so did I.

Katie and Jessica met their friends there, I inevitably joined up with a few of the other mothers from school and Phil, despite his grumbling, was fine after a few paper cups of mulled wine. It was a key date in my calendar, a mark when Christmas was starting, and I'd get that old familiar buzz when I knew that both my work and social life were about to go up a gear. It was usually a date I loved, one I anticipated but on that morning, where normally I would have been filled with plans and instructions, I had practically forgotten it.

'So?' Katie demanded and I couldn't remember what she'd been saying.

I was sat in the kitchen, coffee in front of me, crutches by my side. I'd washed, sent a message to Della telling her to go straight to the Gatsby house. I'd dressed, made it downstairs and was now involved in an argument with Katie, but I had no clear recollection of doing any of it.

'Mum?' she prompted, and began to brush her hair. Her lovely, long, thick black hair that seemed to shimmer in the weak winter sunshine and I watched her, entranced.

When she'd first been born, she'd arrived with that hair. A full head of black hair and the midwife had laughed, we all did. I'd been shopping with her a few weeks later, she was still very much a newborn, and a couple of women had stopped me to peer into the pram. They'd seen my beautiful daughter and both cooed and made the usual noises, and then one of them said, 'Just look at the little beauty, straight out of the wrapper and a full head of hair to boot. She's not messing about, is she?'

I'd never forgotten that expression. '*Straight out of the wrapper and a full head of hair to boot,*' she'd said it like Katie had arrived prepared, ready for anything and it was true, she proved to be resilient in ways that surprised me. She gripped life, took hold of it and shook it. Unlike Jessica who struggled with insecurity and her sense of self, Katie had never doubted who she was. She was so independent, right from the start. I never felt the need to worry over her as I had Jessica. I always thought Katie so capable. She was like me, able to take anything on without it phasing her in the slightest. I'm not saying there aren't periods when she drives me to distraction, when I can scream at her stubbornness, and there was a long time when she was around ten that we fought like cat and dog, but on the whole, she's a good kid. A brilliant kid. A wonderful daughter. Her grades are good. She studies hard and has ambitions of working in fashion.

I watched her that morning and could not marry up the girl in front of me with the girl we had talked about last night. She was so young, how could she have undressed and posed like that? Done those things? With a stranger? It was impossible. I couldn't believe it. Not my daughter, not her, not *Katie*.

'Are you even listening to me?' Katie rolled her eyes. 'Mum? Are you listening? What's wrong with you this morning?'

'Sorry, what?'

'Mum! Tonight! Is it okay if I meet Olivia and Eve? I'll have my phone and we'll be back by nine. They want to meet up outside the Disney store. To get a good view. You can go to where we usually do, near the bank, but I want to…'

I had no idea what she was talking about. I could only see her hair, the way she was brushing it. Her small fingers checking for snags with each stroke. She stopped and gathered it up, looking at her reflection in the window, pulling it into a high ponytail, so tight I could see the skin around her eyes taut and suddenly it was there, the photograph of her. Hair piled up on top of her head, heavy eye make-up and I was drenched in cold sweat.

'No,' I said suddenly. 'No, you can't. You're not going.'

Katie spun around dramatically, hair falling about her shoulders.

'What?'

'We're staying in tonight. All of us. None of us are going to the switch-on. It's too much with my leg, and your dad hates it anyway.'

Tears of complete injustice and anger welled in her eyes, her small hands went into fists and she was close to stamping her foot, just as she had done as a toddler. Having just witnessed a glimpse of the different version of Katie, to see her act in this way and to look this way, with her hair loose and her cheeks red was intense. Just like that, she was back to being a child again.

The swing of personas was fiercely dramatic and I thought of her friends, were they the same? Did they sit on the cusp of maturity, with the ability to fluctuate so suddenly between child and woman? And what of their mothers? How did they handle this breathtaking change?

'What's this?' Phil was buttoning up his blazer, coffee cup in hand, getting ready to visit the regional office. He flashed me a warning look, a glare that told me, *'It's just another day. Act normal. Nothing is wrong.'*

'Mum says we're not going to the parade!' Katie practically screamed. 'But I've had these plans for weeks. She knows I'm meeting the girls there, she knows it!'

Phil stared at me, he was already holding out his hands, palms tilted upwards in an effort to calm the air about us. 'Of course we're going to the parade,' he said. 'Go. Get your shoes on, get your bag. It's time to leave for school.'

'Dad, I mean it,' Katie was saying as Phil ushered her out. 'There is no way I'm not going. I've made plans.'

I heard Jessica smirk, heard her goad Katie in the other room and an argument begin. Phil marched in and quickly stopped it, I heard him give them both instructions to get ready to leave. He came back into the kitchen, came straight over to me and stooped so his face was level to mine.

'I can't do this,' I whispered, shaking my head. 'I can't look at her. Talk to her, I can't do any of it without imagining...'

He gripped me, his hand on my shoulder.

'Stop,' he said. 'Think about it. Think about *her*. Think about them both, our daughters, think about what we agreed last night.'

I shook my head.

'I don't want her to go to school even,' I said, wiping my face. 'I don't want to let them out of my sight. Either of them. I want to lock the door. They should stay home, we all should.'

Phil took a deep breath, he took hold of my hand, ran his thumb along my palm.

'I'm doing the school drop off. Calling in at the office. As soon as Suzie arrives, you're going to the house, to meet Della and do that Gatsby party. You'll meet the people from the marquee, talk with the clients, organise the food. You'll see how Suzie has styled the house and compliment her. You'll be in control, organising stuff, doing it all, doing everything like you always do. Then tonight, we are going to the Christmas parade and you'll laugh. You'll drink mulled wine and you'll let me push you about on that wheelchair and make light of your broken ankle and it will all be normal.'

Katie bounded back in then, her eyebrows rose in question and I held my arms out to her. It was a reflex action; I couldn't help myself. Phil took a step toward me but Katie, knowing how to manipulate situations to her favour, surrendered to a hug.

I squeezed her tight, breathed in the scent of her, felt her small frame in my arms and didn't want to let go. I wanted to tell her I knew, to ask her if she was okay, what had happened, how it had happened. I wanted to sit her down and talk for hours about the string of events that had led to her baring her young body. I wanted to ask her about him, what he'd made her do, if her friends had got involved, if any of her friends knew, but then, I remembered the conversations from the previous night. The never ending discussions about what would be best for Katie, what would be best for Jessica, our daughters. Their welfare was the only cornerstone we had to work around.

In the end, we both agreed that we would wait. Think about it a while. For as long as that monster was in a coma, we had time. Time to make the decision. Blurting out what I knew, unprepared on a busy school morning, was not the answer.

She went to pull away and I swallowed hard. I shut myself up.

'Love you,' were the only words I let out of my mouth.

'Yeah, yeah,' she pulled away, looking at me suspiciously. 'So?'

'So get your coat on, or we'll be late,' Phil said and he looked at me, I gave him a small nod and he went to the door. For now, this was the path that we'd decided on. Normality. Ordinariness. Routine.

I heard the door slam with Phil still reassuring the girls that we'd be going to the Christmas parade and collapsed on the table with my head in my hands. The thought of what was in front of me was beyond daunting. I went for my phone, then realised that Phil must have taken it with him. He'd confiscated both my phone and laptop at about three in the morning when he caught me trying to hobble downstairs to view the website of Remote Models.

When I needed to Google what state people were in after they came out of a coma, if they could be classed as a reliable witness. I had an urge to call the hospital where he was, to speak to a nurse or a doctor there and ask what were the chances? What were the chances of him waking up? How long did we have to come up with a plan?

It had been quarter to four when we'd finally stopped talking, we'd been over and over it and for lack of a decision we'd decided to do nothing. One more day to think, to take time to consider what was best for our daughters. But now, sat alone in the kitchen waiting for Della to arrive, knowing I'd have to act normal with her whilst I churned inside, I didn't know if I was capable.

The chime of the doorbell made me jump and pain shot through my leg. I waited, and then, remembering I was in the house alone, went for my crutches. It rang again, insistently.

'Coming!' I shouted, wondering why Suzie was so early, I'd sent her a message to come at nine, to give myself some time to collect myself. I hobbled forward, I could see the outline of a figure behind the glass door, two figures, one was in the background and the silhouette registered some recognition but by then I had opened the door and it was too late.

Detective Sergeant Bailey stood before me, his younger partner hovering in the background and I was glad of my crutches. The expression people use of their legs buckling from under them I'd thought a dramatic exaggeration, but without the support of my crutches, I felt that's exactly what would've happened to me.

'Steady,' Sergeant Bailey held out his hand to catch me but I straightened myself within time. I gripped my crutches, sweat prickling on the back of my neck and I tried a smile, I felt my face move but was certain it was unconvincing.

'See you've not yet got the hang of those crutches,' he said and smiled. I nodded, neither in agreement nor disagreement but for lack of anything to say. My mind was a blank, I didn't know my lines. The cold air washed over me, it was starting to snow, delicate little flurries were floating down and I thought of Jessica and Katie, squealing with excitement at the sight. I shouldn't have let them go, Phil should be here. I didn't know what to say to the police whilst I was alone. Now that I knew everything, I needed him here, I didn't know how to act.

'Are you okay, Mrs Farrell?' he asked and I nodded. 'Is Mr Farrell in at all?'

'Taken the girls to school,' I said and my voice was breathy, like I'd just jogged up the path.

'Well,' he straightened himself a little, looked behind me into the house. 'Can you tell me what time he'll be back?'

'He's going to the office,' I said, my voice tumbling over my words. 'He's going straight to the office after the school drop off.'

Sergeant Bailey shared a look with his partner.

'Shall I tell him to call you when he's back?' I asked and he shook his head.

'I think we might make a trip there, we've got the address.'

My heart started to gallop. 'He might be on the road,' I said, 'calling on clients, so if there's anything…'

'We've got a bit of good news,' Sergeant Bailey said and I held my breath. 'We might be able to find the person who stole his car quicker than we thought.'

I waited for him to go on, a sick feeling building in the base of my stomach.

'The person who was hit,' Sergeant Bailey grinned. 'The victim. He's out of the coma and on the mend. Can't be interviewed yet of course, but we think we'll have something from him in the coming weeks. If we're lucky he might've seen the person driving the car at him. Just wanted to keep Mr Farrell updated, and ask him a few more questions. Clarify some things. He told you we found his car? Burnt out in Crewe.'

I sagged against the wall. I felt as if I'd been punched, I was winded. *He was awake.*

'You should sit down!' he said laughing. 'You're not safe on those things.' He held out his hand to offer support whilst I leaned against the doorframe and got myself as steady as I could. He turned to his partner and smiled. 'She needs a learner sticker on those crutches.'

It was all I could do not to slide to the floor.

'He's awake?' I asked and my voice was barely above a whisper.

'He's awake,' confirmed Sergeant Bailey. 'We'll try to catch Mr Farrell at the office, but if we miss him and he comes back here, make sure he calls us.' They went to leave and then he turned back. 'And we'll need to interview you, officially. So,' he looked at my cast, 'don't leave the country.' He let out a laugh but I couldn't respond. 'Good news,' he said and studied my face. I couldn't respond. I didn't have it in me.

'I'll see you later,' Sergeant Bailey's words were a promise and as I watched them leave, I felt myself tremble.

He was awake.

27

Suzie

'Can he talk?' Suzie asked. 'Can he speak? Is he speaking?' Her breathing was shallow, she felt dizzy. As if she'd slipped into another dimension, an alternative reality where everything was nightmarish.

The nurse who had introduced herself as Janine took a short intake of breath. 'Adam's not quite there yet,' she said. 'He's opened his eyes and is responding which are excellent signs of recovery.'

'But he hasn't said anything?' Suzie asked and Janine made a sound like she was choosing her words, a soft click of the tongue against the roof of her mouth.

'I'm afraid not, Ms McFadden,' she said. 'Adam is making significant steps to recovery but it's a process. The specialist will be available later this morning to talk to you in more detail, he'll be able to tell you what to expect.'

'I'll be there as soon as I can,' she told Janine and ended the conversation. She sat for a moment, gripping the phone, her breath short and quick.

Adam was awake.

Suzie tried unsuccessfully to force her brain to concentrate, to remember what they'd told her about the stages of recovery, the different states Adam was likely to go through before he was fully back with them. But for now, he was awake. His eyes were open.

She made her way out into the cold morning, wrapping her thin jacket around her. The van windscreen and windows were iced over. She climbed inside, her breath a white fog in front of her face. The engine started after the second turn, a choking, deep rumbling sound. She turned on the heaters that immediately blew out icy air and waited for the van to warm up. She pressed her foot down hard a couple of times on the accelerator and revved the engine, curtains of the surrounding terraces moved at the sound. People were leaving for work, bundling children into cars and she watched as a man tried to scrape bits of ice from his windscreen with what looked like a credit card.

She shivered and waited, cupping her hands in front of her face and blowing into them. He was awake but couldn't talk. She wondered if he could nod, if he would be able to understand questions and nod in response. She looked at her bag on the passenger seat beside her and thought about the memory stick in the side pocket and all it contained. If she told him, would he understand? And the money? She wondered if Adam would be able to nod his head about how he'd used all of her money before she ripped it off his neck.

The van slowly began to warm up, two small patches in the windscreen started to clear and although it wasn't quite enough, Suzie took off.

As she reached the end of the street, her indicator clicking loudly, it began to snow again. Blobs of white floated lazily down against the black sky, the windscreen wipers taking them out as they hit and as Suzie gained speed it was as if the snow was attacking her, flying directly into her path, and she had trouble keeping her focus on the road.

She headed out of the side streets and toward the centre of Chester. The windscreen wipers scraped against the glass as she crept forward. Christmas music was playing loudly from somewhere and Suzie couldn't work out if it was from a nearby car, and then, as she looked in the direction of the centre, she remembered. Tonight, the Christmas markets opened and the lights were switched on.

A horn cut loudly through the air and Suzie jumped. She changed gears and lurched forward. Stalled and then jerked ahead, going through the traffic lights just before they turned back to red leaving a trail of angry cars behind her.

By the time she got to Rachel's house, the snow was heavy and she was jittery.

As she got out of the van, Suzie realised she was wearing her Ugg boots. Fake Ugg boots, with the sides collapsed and the heel turning in on itself. They were the ones she used as slippers, she'd had her wedged boots out ready but must have left them in the hall. She stared at her feet for a moment, amazed that she'd come out of the house in her slippers and, for the first time since she was fifteen, had forgotten to put on a pair of heels. She felt small.

She put her hand out to the side of her and took tiny, even steps toward Rachel's front door, afraid of slipping and not being able to say what she needed to. Her bag was over her shoulder, held tightly against her rib cage, the memory sticks inside. Suzie felt like she could see them through the imitation leather, feel them and everything they held.

The front door was slightly open as she reached it and she gently pushed it.

'Rachel?'

The house was silent. She walked into the hallway, stamping her boots on the mat and looked around. She held her breath for a moment and listened.

'Rachel?'

Nothing. There was no one home, and then, from the kitchen was a faint sniffing noise. Pulling off her wet boots, she went through the French doors in her socks. She felt like a child, like an intruder, the smallest she had ever felt in her entire life.

'Rachel?'

The dining room was empty and then, in the kitchen, she saw her, leaning over. Slumped against the sink for support, her cast sticking out at the side. Rachel was crying, messily. She was dabbing at her eyes with a piece of kitchen towel that was already black with mascara.

'Oh,' she said as Suzie came to the side of her. 'Is it that time already? I heard you shout, but...' she took a sniff, looked at her tissue that was full of tears and make-up. 'I'm just tired,' she said as if it were an explanation. 'Just really, really tired.'

'The door was open,' Suzie said and took in the messy kitchen that was usually spotless. The discarded bowls and cups, the crumbs on the floor, the empty wrappers from what looked like the previous evening's meal and the state of Rachel. She put her hand around her shoulders. 'Rachel...' she began but Rachel shook her head at the tone of her voice.

'I'm fine,' she said stopping Suzie from continuing. She gave a false smile. 'Just tired.'

Suzie took a moment. 'Where are the girls?' she asked. 'Where's Katie?'

'Phil.' Rachel nodded at his name, she was folding the sodden tissue, folding and refolding it. 'He's taken them both.' She looked at Suzie, tears brimming at the edges of her eyes. 'The police have just left,' she said. 'And I've tried to ring him, but he's not picking up.'

Suzie took a deep breath. 'The police?' she asked slowly, it sounded ominous, it was the next port of call on her list.

Rachel nodded. 'They wanted Phil,' and her mouth made an ugly expression that she quickly tried to stop. 'About his car, just routine questions.'

Suzie stared at her friend, it was almost as if she could see the pep talk going on in Rachel's mind, the rallying 'get yourself together' type words. Suzie watched her swallow, put her hand over her face and shake her head a little. She decided to come out with it, to tell her straight away what she knew, to tell her everything immediately.

'I know who the messages were from,' she said and Rachel looked up at her. 'The Twitter messages,' Suzie said. 'The ones we found the other day? The ones we thought were from Phil? I know who they're from. I know all of it, I came here to tell you. I know what happened, Rachel.'

They sat at the kitchen table. It was a replay of how they'd been three days earlier and if Suzie's sense of humour hadn't abandoned her, she would've found it somewhat comical. To be sitting in exactly the same place with Rachel, trying to explain what her fiancé had done.

On the journey to Rachel's, Suzie had told herself she would do this without emotion, she would try and detach herself and just tell Rachel. Just present it to her without anything else, without any of her own pain added, put forward what Adam had done and wait to be told the rest of it, but that was beyond her. She couldn't spare her friend her own agony, and as she took out the memory sticks, one clearly labelled '*Katie*', she had to take a moment.

Rachel was shaking slightly, her face red and puffy, the sodden tissue still in her hand, even though there was a fresh box between them. Suzie thought they should perhaps make coffee first, or something a little stronger, but it was like putting off a firing squad. A sip of alcohol wouldn't make it go away.

Suzie pushed the memory stick toward Rachel, and as she did so, she saw that she was also shaking. There was a tremor to her fingers that she couldn't control.

'Rachel, I don't know how to start.'

Rachel closed her eyes and tears fell onto her cheek.

'I found this last night,' Suzie began. 'I was going through Adam's laptop and I found,' she looked at the stick, 'pictures. Pictures of…' she looked up at the ceiling, praying for a way to articulate it all. 'Katie,' she finished and Rachel made a painful sound.

'The pictures, they're photographs of Katie, and well, they're not ordinary photographs. Not ones that you'd want to see. She's… well, she's posing in the pictures… and she isn't wearing any clothes, you see the pictures…'

'Pictures?' Rachel interrupted and Suzie stopped talking. Rachel's voice was alarming. It made Suzie's heart clench. 'You've got the pictures of Katie?' She looked at it, looked at Katie's name written in Suzie's handwriting.

'They're not pictures I took,' Suzie said. 'They're not ones you'd want to see. Katie, she's...' Suzie took a moment, 'naked. She's almost naked on some. And there's a film, I think, I've not watched it, not looked at it, I don't know what...'

Rachel began to weep. Suzie couldn't continue. She watched as Rachel curled in on herself, and Suzie had to put her hand out in case she came too far forward.

'Rachel, I didn't know,' Suzie found herself saying, desperate to state her innocence, 'I had no idea, I didn't know any of it. I came here as soon as I found them. As soon as I saw them on his laptop, I knew I had to come here first. Tell you about them. About him. About what he did, before I went to the police, to anyone. I came here. I came straight to you because I get it. I think I know what happened, what you saw on Tuesday. On the retail park and this is the reason,' she pushed the memory stick toward her friend. 'This is the reason why you saw Katie there, why you saw her at the hotel. Why she wasn't at school.'

Rachel wiped at her face. She said nothing. Suzie was sweating, despite the cold, she was clammy.

'Where did you see the pictures?' Rachel's voice was quiet. 'Phil said they weren't on the website. They weren't on the internet. Those pictures hadn't been published. He said he had to get a special link,' she looked up at Suzie, her eyes puffy and red. 'Are they on the internet? Is Katie on the internet?'

'No, no!' Suzie shook her head. 'She's not on the internet. The pictures aren't published, they're hidden.'

Rachel closed her eyes in gratitude then nodded. 'Phil said he had to ask to see them,' she almost whispered. 'Said he had to ask for a link.' She looked up. 'So where did you…?'

'That's why I'm here,' Suzie swallowed. Her throat was dry. 'To tell you how I found them. To tell you what I found.'

Suzie took a deep breath, then, as what Rachel had said penetrated, stopped.

'Phil had to ask?' Suzie leaned forward. 'Rachel, you said Phil had to ask to see these pictures, so you know? You've seen them?'

Rachel was staring at the memory stick. She was biting her lower lip and it had become bloody, dotted with spots of red that she licked away before beginning to bite again.

'Phil knew Katie was doing this?' Suzie asked carefully. 'Phil knew? He had to ask for a link?'

Rachel closed her eyes.

'Rachel?' Suzie prompted. 'Phil knew Katie was modelling? Is that it? You're telling me that Phil let her…'

'He didn't let her!' Rachel almost shouted, her face blotchy and red. 'He just found them last week. She has a smartphone, Katie, she has a smartphone we didn't know about and Phil found her messages. On Twitter.'

Suzie nodded, 'It was Katie arranging to meet Adam…'

'Katie wasn't arranging to meet anyone,' Rachel let out a wail. 'That was Phil. He was pretending to be Katie. What we saw was Phil on Twitter. He was the one arranging to meet…' she took a moment. 'What did you say? Adam? His name is Rob.'

Suzie stared at her, then realised, she'd yet to confess what she'd found last night but first she had to get it straight.

Had to fully understand what Rachel was telling her.

'It was Phil?' she asked again slowly. 'Those messages on Twitter? Arranging to meet at the hotel on Tuesday. That was Phil? Not Katie?'

Rachel nodded.

'But Phil was in London. The other day, when I thought he'd been having an affair, you told me he was in London. That you hadn't seen Phil.'

Rachel looked away and Suzie felt it begin to slowly unlock. Felt her mind begin to put the pieces in place and they slotted together perfectly.

She dipped her head. Swallowed. Took a deep breath.

'It was Phil,' she said quietly. 'It was Phil pretending to be Katie on Twitter. He found out about what Adam had done to Katie, and got Adam to meet him at the retail park. It wasn't Katie, it was Phil. He wasn't having an affair, he was finding Adam.'

'Why do you keep saying Adam?' Rachel asked and Suzie blinked at her.

'They said at hospital it was a car accident,' Suzie said and Rachel's face trembled, she looked away from her and down at her hands. She was shredding a tissue. Little bits of it fell on the wooden floor at the side of her cast.

'And you saw it didn't you?' asked Suzie. 'You were trying to tell me yesterday. What Phil did to put Adam in a coma.' Suzie thought back to Tuesday, when Phil had arrived at the hospital, not a scratch on him. 'It was a car accident, but Adam wasn't in his car, was he?' she asked. 'I assumed it had been a crash, a great big smash between two vehicles, but I've been stupid, haven't I? They called me about his abandoned car, not his *damaged* car.'

'Adam?' Rachel asked and Suzie put her hands up to her face. For a moment she couldn't talk, couldn't look at Rachel.

'You saw him do it?' she asked from behind her hands. 'You saw Phil run Adam over.'

'Adam?' Rachel asked again.

'And then Phil makes up the story that his car was stolen, when it was him all along.'

'Suzie, who is Adam?'

'You see Phil do that to Adam and you say nothing.'

'It was Rob. Phil was meeting Rob, not Adam.'

'*It was my Adam*,' Suzie said pulling her hands away. 'That's who Phil was arranging to meet. Adam did this.'

She pointed to the memory stick that was on the table between them.

'He was calling himself Rob. He took those pictures of Katie, the film. He set up the modelling website.' She took another breath, filling her lungs as much as she could. She looked up and kept her eyes heavenward. 'I was looking for money,' she said. 'For his account. I'm broke, completely broke. I'm bankrupt. He took all my money, Rachel. He's taken everything I had and used it all for this. To charm young girls, to look rich, to give the impression that he's some kind of jet setter,' she gave a hollow laugh. 'I was looking for the details of his bank accounts, and so I went on his laptop. And then I find this site, this modelling site that he's set up. Full of young girls, doing all kinds of things,' a sob caught in her throat and she pushed herself to go on. 'And then, oh Rachel, I find Katie,' tears fell as she said her name. 'He did it to Katie and oh, Rachel. The stuff on there,' she closed her eyes. 'He must have been doing it the whole time, the whole time we were together. Before we were together. He must have seen me as a money tree, he must have seen me with Katie, he must have met me to...' her words trailed off and Suzie hung her head. She'd lost control. She grabbed a tissue, knocking over the box as she did so and pushed it into her face to block the tears.

'Adam?' Rachel's voice was not much louder than a whisper. 'Your *fiancé*? That Adam?'

Suzie nodded.

They stared at each other.

'And Phil ran him over didn't he?' Suzie closed her eyes, 'Phil found out what he'd done to Katie and ran him over. And you saw him do it.'

Suzie was about to say how there was a part of her that could understand what Phil had done, why he'd done it. That if she'd been sat behind a wheel with Adam in front of her when she found out last night, she might very well have ploughed her car into him. But instead, she was knocked on the side of her face. Rachel had slapped her. Hard.

Suzie's head reeled. She felt where Rachel's hand had been, the stinging sensation, the prickling hurt. It wasn't nearly as hard a slap as Suzie had given herself the night before, but it added to her already smarting cheek, and the shock of it jolted her.

She turned back to Rachel, who was staring at her with wide, fearful eyes and breathing hard. 'We said he might not have been working alone,' she said. 'When we talked last night, we both agreed there could be others involved. How long have you known? How long?' Rachel asked and raised her arm to hit Suzie again but she caught it, her hand gripping Rachel's wrist. They were still seated and Rachel tried to move but Suzie increased her grip and twisted it slightly, forcing Rachel to stay still.

Rachel was about five inches taller than Suzie and had a bigger build, but she was no match, unable to move, her leg in the cast keeping her fixed. And Suzie worked out, she lifted weights twice a week at the gym and she was strong, if she wanted to, she could snap Rachel's arm and they both knew it.

'She's fourteen,' Rachel hissed. '*Fourteen!* Do you do it together? Is that how it works? We knew it had to be someone Katie trusts, she wouldn't just do something like that on her own and all the time it was you. You introduced her to him.'

'*Me?*' Suzie almost screamed the word. 'You think I'd be involved in this perverse filth?'

Suzie turned her hand a little and Rachel winced, she gave another pull, and then let go. Rachel snatched her hand back and rubbed at her wrist, a red mark already visible.

'Do you think I'd have been with him if I knew he was into this stuff?' she asked and Rachel blinked. 'If I knew he was into photographing young girls, filming them, photographing Katie? If I knew he'd even spoken to Katie, you think I wouldn't have told you? You think I wouldn't have taken him to the police? I thought he was away photographing cars,' an angry sob escaped her. 'He told me he was working on location, I didn't know he was doing…' she couldn't finish the sentence. 'I thought he loved me,' she said and her voice cracked, it had a pitiful moan to it. 'I didn't know. I didn't know a thing about it. I just found this when I was looking for the money.' She roughly wiped her face, 'I've been nothing more than a cash cow for him. A meal ticket. He never loved me at all. I've sent out eighty invites for the wedding, booked the room,' her face contorted with the words, a great shuddering sob building at the back of her throat. 'And all the time, he's doing this.' She took a moment. 'So no, Rachel, I did not know. I did not know that the man I planned to spend the rest of my life with was into abusing kids.'

She was panting, as was Rachel.

They were staring at each other, unsure how to navigate the situation before them and then, after a moment, Rachel's face crumpled. Her body began to shake. Suzie heard her take huge gasps and put her hand out in comfort, although she didn't actually touch her.

The snow was still falling outside. It covered the garden and buildings providing a surreal glow, the kind of light that instilled delight in children and sentimental adults. Suzie looked at it as Rachel cried and thought she'd never find joy in anything again.

She waited for Rachel's sobs to subside, and eventually, they did.

'I'm right aren't I?' Suzie asked. 'Phil ran Adam over and put him in a coma.' Rachel's jaw clenched. 'And you saw it. You saw it happen.'

Rachel was silent and Suzie took a deep breath. She looked away. It was suddenly all so obvious. Rachel's accident, the way she had been behaving, the way Phil was at the hospital. Adam's abandoned car, and she felt a fool for not working it out sooner. Suzie realised she must have very little perceptiveness. She'd been so willing to believe in her own fairy-tale that she hadn't noticed the nightmare happening all around her. She wasn't clever or smart; she was a stupid, stupid idiot.

She couldn't seem to catch her breath. She looked out at the snow to take a moment, hoping that the air would travel to her lungs as she inhaled. That it would stop her feeling so dizzy and helpless.

'Adam's awake,' she said and Rachel's eyes flickered. 'The hospital rang just before I set off. He's not talking, but he will be, soon.' She paused. 'I'm going to the police. Now. To tell them about him. Show them what he's been doing. I've got it all on another memory stick, his website, his emails, the messages on social media.' She waited for Rachel to respond, she stayed silent. 'Come with me.'

Rachel looked up at her.

'We'll tell them together,' she said. 'Explain what Adam was doing, show them it all and then you can tell them what you saw Phil do.'

Rachel closed her eyes.

'I understand why you kept quiet,' Suzie said. 'But you can't anymore, you see that now don't you? You have to tell the police. They'll understand,' Suzie wiped at her cheeks. 'It was provocation. Phil did it because of what Adam did to Katie, they'll understand that and we'll get through it. Together. We'll get through it. You can't keep quiet about this, Rachel; it's too much. Katie needs to know. Come with me. Now. Let's go to the police.'

Rachel shook her head. She opened her eyes and gave a kind of half smile, a pitiful, lopsided thing that made Suzie's stomach clench.

'I'm not going anywhere,' Rachel said, stopping Suzie from continuing.

'Rachel, you're not thinking straight,' she took both of Rachel's hands in hers, changed her position. 'Did you hear me? Adam's awake. He's out of the coma. I'm not waiting until he's better, I'm telling the police now so that he goes straight from hospital into prison. And it's only a matter of time before he's talking. He'll tell the police it was Phil, but you need to do that. You need to tell them first.' She swallowed, trying and failing to stop herself from crying. 'Come with me. We can do it together. Together.'

Rachel shook her head. Pulled her hands slowly away from Suzie's.

'You think it's worse, what Phil did?' a cry caught in the back of Suzie's throat. 'Rachel, my fiancé has abused young girls. I'm telling the police that. The man I loved has been abusing young girls. He stole all my money. I've lost everything.'

'But you don't have kids to lose,' Rachel said quietly and they stared at each other. 'And me and Phil do. So I'm not going to any police station and I'm not telling anybody anything. I need to think about my girls, my family and what to do next now that he's awake.'

28

Rachel

The van made a terrible sound as Suzie took off. The exhaust was blowing, it rumbled and choked and I could hear the gears grind as she forced them to engage. I hadn't moved; just let her go whilst I stayed in the kitchen, clinging onto the table as if it were a life raft. The snow had stopped for a moment and left everything in a white blanket, covered up all the moulding, rotting leaves and muck in the garden. Outside the window, everything looked clean. It glowed, making the light different and surreal. In the silence, I opened up my fist and looked at the memory stick she'd given me. *Katie.*

It was everything. Suzie had promised, this was the lot. She'd removed Katie from Remote Models, and all of that was on another memory stick that she was taking to the police. No one else would see Katie, she was safe again.

I curled my fingers back around it; they were slick with sweat. I looked out at the white garden. I didn't trust myself to move. My skin crawled with the thought of it, of how he's there, this man I've never met, in every facet of my life. He's been everywhere except right in front of me, and now he was lying in a hospital bed, recovering, ready to start speaking and accusing Phil. To send him to prison, and that in itself was laughable. Phil had acted out of love, out of protection for our daughter. Yet in a court what would that matter after what he'd done? It felt unjust. I looked out on the white garden and searched for a middle ground, an alternative between the black and white of right and wrong, but there was nothing. Phil was guilty, as was Adam, but their crimes were worlds apart.

In the kitchen, everything seemed in high definition suddenly, the shape of the scatter cushions around the chairs, the hand carved wooden bowl filled with apples. I could see every knot and grain in the bowl, all the dents and bruises on the skin of each apple.

The phone rang but I didn't move, I sat still and listened to the answer machine kick in. My cheerful stupid voice filled the air, my recorded message that was done a lifetime ago.

'I'm trying to get hold of Mrs Farrell. Mrs Rachel Farrell of Farrell McFadden Events,' the voice said after the answer machine message had finished and I recognised it as Mrs Laydon, the mother of the girl from the Gatsby party we were meant to be doing the next day. 'The marquee staff have arrived and are in the process of putting up the marquee, and Della is here, but they need some direction and Mrs Farrell or Ms McFadden should really be here now. I'll try her mobile again but please ask her to call me as soon as possible.'

My head began to bang and I raised my hand to my temple. I should've called Della, told her to go home. I should've returned Mrs Laydon's call, explained that we wouldn't be doing the party, that she'd better call Tailor Made Events because Rachel Farrell of Farrell McFadden Events was having a breakdown. Farrell McFadden Events was no longer functioning. Nothing was.

How would everything have played out if I'd gone to the police three days ago, without talking to Phil, without letting him explain and hearing about what had happened to Katie? How would it have been if I'd told Detective Sergeant Bailey when he asked me that night if I'd seen the accident, if I'd told the truth? Told them that yes, I was at the retail park because I thought my husband was having an affair, and yes, I did see him there and yes, I did see him run someone over and drive away. What would have been the run of events then? In a parallel universe somewhere, that course of action had taken place and I wondered if that version of me was any happier with the outcome.

Katie would be at school, oblivious to all of this. She'd be in her lesson, chewing on her pen and making notes unaware of how she was at the centre of a storm. Phil had explained last night how we had to keep quiet, that if she knew we knew about the photographs that it would implicate her in things. That once she learned the photographer had been run over by Phil's stolen car, she'd easily put it all together. Just as Suzie had.

I gripped the memory stick. Last night, between us we'd argued the case that in staying quiet we were protecting Katie, her father would be at home, she wouldn't see him go to prison for her actions. She wouldn't see her world collapse around her. But she would have to deal with what had happened alone. I felt the hard edges of it in my hand and feared that by staying quiet we weren't protecting her at all.

I stood, reached for my crutch and winced as my leg reminded me that a bone was actually broken in there. That I should've been resting and recuperating these past few days, I ignored it and with effort, slowly made it to the hallway table where the phone was. I didn't expect him to answer, I'd called him five times after Sergeant Bailey had left and each time it had gone to voicemail. I knew that he'd be busy at the school gates, driving to the office, hurriedly going into meetings. Blocking his mind to the events of the past days in a way that I'd seen him do before. Compartmentalise, he'd told me. He shut things in boxes until he needed to bring them out and look at them.

'Rachel?' He answered on the fourth ring, and I flinched at his voice. 'Everything okay? You off to the Gatsby house?'

His voice was overly cheery, a charade. Enthusiastic questions masking his concern. I took a moment and knew he could hear it in the silence.

'Suzie knows,' I said quietly and I heard him take a sharp intake of breath.

'Sorry?' he asked. 'What did you say?' The background noise changed as he moved, his voice had an echo and I imagined him in a stairwell. The first place he could find that offered some privacy.

'She was just here,' my voice sounded flat. 'She guessed it, she put it together because she saw the pictures of Katie. And the police,' I told him, 'they're looking for you. They said they may come to your office.'

Phil swore. 'What? Suzie knows, what? And the police, did they...?'

'He's her fiancé,' I interrupted. 'The man you ran over, is Suzie's fiancé. His name is Adam.'

There was a moment's silence.

'She isn't involved,' I said quickly. 'She told me and I believe her. She came here to tell us what her fiancé has been doing to Katie, but then she put two and two together.'

'Her fiancé,' I heard Phil murmur.

'And I don't think we should keep quiet to Katie anymore.' My voice broke as I said her name. 'She needs to know, Phil. She needs to talk to us and we need to talk to her. She's involved, Phil, and I can't keep quiet about it. My daughter needs me. She needs us.'

'Rachel,' he began. 'Rachel, hang on, what you're saying there, you're saying I should…'

'And he's awake,' I said. 'The police were here. That's why they're looking for you. He's out of the coma and awake.'

'Rachel,' his voice was urgent. 'Don't do anything. Don't talk to anyone, don't open the door. I'm on my way home.'

I watched the snowfall in the garden with the dazed expression of a crash victim and called Della, told her in few words to take the day off. Told her that the Gatsby party was cancelled. I didn't have it in me to call anyone else, all I could think about were my daughters.

They say that when you have a traumatic event, there is the 'before' and the 'after', that all things fall under those two categories, but no one talks about the precipice. When you're looking down on the sheer drop below and can feel yourself tipping, there're no clichés or wise quotes for that and I wondered if it's because no one gets that moment. Was my sitting in the kitchen, watching the snowfall and feeling my life slide away a rare thing or did people avoid it, like diving? Once they knew what had to be done, did they jump straight off or, like me, did they sit on the edge and contemplate?

By the time Phil arrived I was calm almost, as if detached from myself. I told him everything and he sat and nodded throughout.

'And this is everything?' he asked.

'She promised that's all of it,' I told him. 'She went straight to the station from here. She separated Katie's pictures and film from what she's about to give the police as she thought we should have them.'

He was silent for a moment, staring at the stick.

'Do you think she'll keep quiet?'

I took a second. Suzie was loyal, I knew that much about her, but I remembered the way she'd ordered me to join her at the police station. To tell them what I knew about Phil.

'I'm not sure,' I told him and he was quiet. 'Phil?' I asked.

He was silent for a moment and then he looked up. There was a resigned smile on his face and his eyes were full of sadness and regret. I burst into fresh tears.

'Hey,' he came over, put his arms around me and I wept into his shoulder. Clung onto him and sobbed heavily as he held me tightly.

'I'm so sorry,' he said as I gripped him. 'I'm sorry for getting you involved, for putting you through this. For not coming straight to you once I'd found out, for thinking I could sort this alone.'

I didn't think there were any more tears to fall, I thought the crying part was over, but I was wrong. I didn't think I'd be able to stop.

He leaned his head against mine, went to stroke my cheek as I took shuddering breaths. We stayed like that for a while, our faces close, looking at each other and then, he moved away.

'I'll call a solicitor,' Phil said and I put my hand out, stopping him from taking the phone.

'There's someone else you need to speak to first.'

29

Rachel

I don't know what Phil said to the school, what he said to Katie, how he got her home or what they discussed in the car but when she walked in, her face a mass of confusion, I felt the ball of tension I'd been carrying burst.

'What is it?' she dropped her school bag and came over to me. 'What's happened? Has someone died? Is it Grandma? Nana?' She looked to Phil who was stood in the doorway, the car keys still in his hand. 'Dad?'

'Sit down, Katie,' he said slowly, and then, she saw the envelope on the table in front of me. I pushed it toward her.

'We know, sweetheart,' I told her. 'We know all about it.'

'He said you'd be like this,' Katie said and wiped her face. We were in the lounge, moved there after Katie had seen the photographs and became hysterical. She'd screamed at us, accused us of spying on her and then, become fiercely defensive before breaking down and succumbing to talking rationally.

'He said you'd overreact and get it all out of proportion,' Katie swallowed, she looked so small, so young, but there was an edge to her. A rebellion that I'd not noticed before, something in the way that she continued to defend her actions and the photographs.

I'd presumed that this would be easy, that she'd be glad to tell us how she'd been taken advantage of, but that's not what appeared to be happening. Katie appeared to be defending him.

'That's why I never said anything.' Katie looked up, her eyes red. 'He's not what you think, Mum. I know what those photographs might look like, but it's not. It's not what you're both thinking. He took those as samples, just to try some stuff out. No one else will ever see them, it was just for my portfolio. Did he send them? Is that what happened?' she pulled at the tissue in her hand. 'Did you open my post? He said he'd send me the proofs but I didn't hear from him. It's really not what you're both thinking.' She looked up then, her eyes pleading.

Phil went to pick up the envelope, to pull out the photographs again but Katie snatched them off him.

'Dad! Don't look at them!'

She clutched the envelope to her chest and I looked to Phil for help. He matched my gaze. Neither of us were prepared for Katie acting this way. For her *protecting* him.

'Tell us what happened,' Phil said gently. 'Just tell us how you met him and what happened. We're not angry, Katie,' I nodded in agreement. 'We just want to know how these pictures came to be taken.'

'I met him at the school prom.'

So that was it. The end of year prom. The end of the school year, a formal dance for those that were leaving but the younger year, Katie's year, were also invited. I remembered it vividly. The dress, the hair, the make-up. Katie had talked of nothing else for months: how to compete with the older girls, how to measure up. She'd spent an age practising her make-up and hairstyle. Some girls' parents had ordered limousines to take them to the hotel where it was being held. We'd allowed Katie to have a small glass of champagne before she left, we'd taken pictures. Talked about how it would be her turn next year, when she would be leaving high school and getting ready for college and I'd gotten quite tearful.

'He was the official photographer,' Katie said, 'and he's brilliant. You can't really tell from those photographs he did of me, but he's a fantastic photographer.'

We stayed silent. Waiting for her to continue.

'He only did that gig, the school prom, because his mate had asked him. He was helping out his friend otherwise he'd never do something so,' Katie shook her head, 'y'know, beneath him. He's a fashion photographer. For magazines. And model agencies. He's a scout. He finds models, that's his real job.'

My heart picked up pace and started to hammer in my chest.

'Anyway, he was leaving. Just packing up and me and Olivia were going to the toilet when he calls me over.'

'He called you over?' Phil's voice was urgent.

Katie nodded. 'He knew me. Knew my name. He knew you, knew that you and Suzie were friends.'

I felt my mouth drop open. He'd known I was friends with Suzie.

'But I never met him,' I said. 'How did he know who I was when we never met?'

'He said he was meant to meet you, but something came up, so he never got to. He came over or something, to apologise and was waiting in the car when Suzie came to the door and you weren't in, but he'd seen me. He'd

283

noticed me, he said…' she paused, debating whether to continue.

'Katie,' I prompted. 'You have to tell us everything. *Everything.*'

She took a moment, picked off another bit of tissue. 'He's leaving Suzie,' she blurted out, finally. 'He made me promise I wouldn't tell anyone. He doesn't love her. He's only with her because he feels sorry for her.'

I closed my eyes.

'They've only been together a few months and she's got all serious with him. Wanting to marry him and have kids! It's sad. She's so sad, Mum.' Katie looked up at me, 'You know she is. She's so clingy and needy. You even said so, I heard you, telling Dad that she must be on the rebound to be getting engaged so quick.'

I took a deep breath, unable to comprehend what she was telling me.

'And Adam, he's so kind. He doesn't know how to get rid of her. He's too nice. And well, we just got talking that night,' Katie shifted in her position. 'He told me he's a scout for a model agency, he'd thought I'd be a good model and stuff. He took a few more pictures of me that night at the prom and he gave me his business card and his Twitter name. He asked me what mine was,' she smiled then, at her own intelligence. 'I'm not stupid, and I know you said you didn't like me going on Twitter but…' she let out a breath. 'And I wouldn't just tell any old stranger what my Twitter name is but he had a proper card. He told me he knows this model agency and they're looking for new models. He's a scout.'

'Why didn't you tell us?' I asked, my voice coming out in a moan. 'That night, when you got back from the prom, why didn't you tell us that you'd met him, sweetheart? Suzie's fiancé? That he wanted you to pose for him?'

'Because he asked me not to!' Katie said as if it were the most logical explanation in the world. 'He said that if I told you, you'd tell Suzie and it wasn't fair on her. He's too nice, he said he didn't want to hurt her. He wanted to tell her himself.'

'But the photographs,' Phil said. 'Katie, you're a bright girl. Why didn't you tell us, ask us, before doing the photographs?'

She looked down, was quiet.

'Because I knew you'd say no. That you wouldn't let me do it. And he said I have a real chance at being a model. He said that you've got to get in quick, that you can't really wait until you're sixteen because then all the slots for young models have gone.' She looked up, the defiance back in her eyes. 'Do you know how old Kate Moss was when she was discovered?'

We were both silent, stunned by her sudden questioning.

'Fourteen! Fourteen, Mum. My age. She was my age when she was modelling and what am I doing?' She looked at me and huffed. 'I'm not even allowed on the internet.' Katie wiped her face; the crying had stopped for a moment. 'You let Jessica go out, you let Jessica...'

'Jessica is two years older than you...'

'He didn't even want to do it,' Katie went on. 'I had to persuade him.'

'You?' Phil asked. 'Persuaded him?'

She nodded. 'He said he couldn't, not unless I asked you and I couldn't ask you because then you'd say no. And then he asked Eva if she wanted to do it, and Eva's not even as pretty as me and she was going to be this famous model whereas I wasn't, so I begged him to take some pictures of me. And by that time, we'd become good friends.'

'Become friends?' I asked and Katie looked away.

'We texted,' she said. 'He was giving me tips on how to be a model, that kind of stuff, and in fact,' she lifted her chin, 'he's kind of my boyfriend now.'

The world tilted. I felt like I might slide to the floor. This wasn't what I thought, this involved trust and loyalty. This was him constantly grooming my daughter.

'Kind of your boyfriend?' My voice was barely audible. 'This man is more than twice your age, he's…'

'Age doesn't matter when you fall in love!' she blurted out and she was so young. So very young and naive and I looked to Phil for help. But I only saw my disbelief reflected back in his face, disbelief and anger.

'And that's what models do, Mum!' Katie went on. 'He explained it all to me. It's what everyone does now. If you want to get noticed by the big names, Chanel, Burberry, all the top fashion brands then they need to see you without clothes. They don't want to see you sitting there in your school uniform. They need to see your figure, how you'd model *their* clothes and they can't do that if you're wearing some stupid dress or something.' She shook her head, a flash of something back in her eyes. 'You see them at the New York fashion shows and they're all naked. He showed me a film. The models are all running off the catwalk and stripping to get the next costume on. If I want to have a career as a model, I've got to get used to taking my clothes off in front of people. And besides, he loves me.' Katie nodded to herself. 'He told me. We love each other. So it's not like I was doing it with some stranger.'

Phil's hands were in fists, his jaw clenched.

'Sweetheart,' I reached forward and took her hand. 'What he said to you, it wasn't true, he said those things so you would...'

'No!' she sat back. 'Mum, I've already told you, Adam's not like that. He's not weird, he's not a pervert. It's not as if he's some *paedophile*.'

I looked at Phil.

'Katie,' I began, and started the conversation that I never thought I'd have with my own child.

30

Suzie

The ICU ward was hushed and quiet. No one marvelled at the early morning snow, no one looked out of the window and talked of plans for Christmas. In here, the only time was *now*, and if it happened to be day or night, that was irrelevant. The nurse, Janine, was at reception. Her face came alive when she saw Suzie.

'It's such brilliant news,' she said in a hushed voice, 'but like I said on the phone, he's not yet fully with us. Don't expect too much, these are early days and the process of recovery is long. You need to have patience and...'

Suzie shook her head, her face and eyes hurt. She couldn't listen to any more from Janine, look at her animated expression. When she'd left Rachel's, she'd got in the van ready to go straight to the police, to hand it all over to them and wait for the outcome, but it suddenly occurred to her that she needed to see Adam first. That she needed to tell him she knew, that she'd worked it all out. She wanted to hiss it in his face, that he was going to prison for a very long time and she was going to be the one to put him there. She needed that. Suzie very much needed to tell him, face to face, that she wasn't being stupid anymore. That she didn't believe in his fairy-tales, or happy endings anymore.

'Can I see him?' she asked and Janine stopped talking and nodded.

'Of course, of course.'

Suzie kept walking and Janine fell into step beside her telling her of the checks they'd already done, what medication Adam had been given and how responsive he'd be, when the consultant was next available and what he'd like to discuss. Suzie heard none of it; her mind was still full of Rachel. The way she'd said no, she wasn't going anywhere, the way she'd sat in her kitchen, her face blotchy and puffy and talked about her children. About her girls and how they made everything different. She'd been almost sanctimonious, using her kids as a reason for not doing the right thing and Suzie wasn't sure how she felt about that, because Adam had not only ripped her life into shreds, he'd also slashed any hopes of her becoming a mother. And Suzie wanted children. Very much. She wanted to see the swell of her belly, to experience the unconditional, overwhelming love for another human being that motherhood brought. Suzie had thought it would happen with Carl, but had been forced to say goodbye to that idea and then, when she met Adam, she'd thought that *this* was it. This was when it would happen.

She wasn't yet forty, she still had time. He'd talked of buying a family home with extra room, of moving out of the city, moving somewhere near the open fields, some-where Suzie had harboured romantic notions of raising children. He'd walked through the baby section of depart-ment stores with her and smiled secretly so she'd given him a playful shove. He'd even spoken of how he'd have liked a son and as she walked along that ward, Janine's hushed whispers at the side of her, she realised he'd manipulated even that small slice of her as well.

He'd been aware of Suzie's maternal longing and toyed with it to cement their relationship that much quicker, to get her money and her trust that much more easily. A new grief descended upon her as they reached his room, Adam had destroyed it all, stolen it. Everything that made her *her*, her very essence, he'd taken all of her hopes and dreams and contrived to use them against her in his manipulation. It felt like there was nothing left.

'Not too long I'm afraid,' Janine said. 'It sounds odd, I know, but we mustn't tire him out. He can't overdo it,' she smiled. 'I'll leave you alone for a few minutes.'

She put her hand on Suzie's shoulder for a moment, mistaking her tears as ones of joy and left. Suzie walked into the room slowly. There were still just as many machines around Adam, for some reason she'd expected them all to be gone now that he was out of his coma.

He was still lying down, the only difference was that Adam's face was now clear, the small mask that had been over his mouth had disappeared and although his face was swollen, Suzie was glad she could see him properly. She wanted to do this to his face, as it were, as much as she could.

Walking up to his bedside she looked down at him, his eyes were closed.

'Adam?'

There was movement, behind the lids and he rolled his head. Janine had said that he was sedated, on medication so they could manage his condition, his pain, and Suzie wished it were something she could undo. Rip out any drugs he had in him, she wanted him to feel everything, every bruise, every cut, every slight alteration to his condition. Being cocooned from his pain was too kind.

'Adam, it's Suzie.'

He turned his head toward her, his eyes opened and for a second, they registered her. There was a moment of kindness in those eyes, of blessed identification. Acknowledgement that she was here, with him.

'I know,' she hissed and walked toward him. 'I found your laptop.' She leaned over so her face was inches from his, looking down at his swollen features. Her body was shaking, but she waited, waited until his eyes found hers.

'Remote Models,' she told him.

His eyes gained clarity.

'Remote Models,' she said again. 'I found it all.'

He blinked.

'I'm taking it all to the police,' her voice trembled with the force of what she was saying. 'I'm giving it all to them and you are never getting out of prison again.'

She stared at him.

His arm moved, waved on the bed, his hand searching out hers.

'You filthy bastard,' she said and then, she did something that she had never done in her entire life. She spat at him.

Her spittle landed on his cheek, it seemed feeble. She expected to feel different. She'd expected to feel vindicated, absolved. But as she looked at him, her pathetic effort of defiance a few drops of her spit on his cheek, the feeling didn't come.

He made a sound, tried to form a word and she stepped back. She watched as he moved his arm, his hand waving about from his elbow. He was trying to find her, to get her hand, even now, he was searching her out. Trying to make it right. She watched his hand reach to her and the gesture made her want to vomit.

She put her hand to her mouth. Took another step away from the bed. Where was the feeling of justification? Why didn't she feel different? An overwhelming urge to run came over her, to sprint out of the room and along the ward. To go as fast as she could and get as far away as she could.

His arm was still looking for hers, dangling around from the elbow searching for something, trying to get at some comfort and his head lolled from side to side. The action was repulsive. Hideous. She stared at him like people stare at motorway accidents, horrified but unable to look away. How could she have loved this man? Planned a life with him? A future? He was searching for her, still. His hand reaching for her comfort, as if he could explain it all away, pick up where they left off.

She'd been to bed with him. Had sex with him. She'd held him, kissed him, shared her dreams and hopes with him. Loved him. Been seduced by the version he presented of himself to her with no question. She had been so trusting, so gullible. What kind of woman did that make her? To not know, to have no idea? What did that say about her version of love, about what she expected from a relationship?

Her heart started to pound and her stomach clenched. She had expected to feel some kind of closure. She wanted to feel vindicated. She wanted to call him a pervert to his face, a filthy bastard and be done with it. Leave full of rage and anger and go to the police to turn him in, but that wasn't happening. Instead, the foul feelings she had toward him were now turning in on herself and she stumbled back, horrified. Watching his head turn, his hand run along the bed sheets trying to find hers.

No, she would have to leave, and quickly. She couldn't be here.

Go to the police, go to her parents, her friends and beg for mercy. Plead for forgiveness at her ignorance, at her complete and utter blindness as to what kind of monster she'd fallen in love with.

She took a step back, her hand at her mouth and left the room in a rush, only to collide with someone else.

'Rachel?'

Rachel was leaning heavily on her crutches, panting. Her face a sheen of sweat. She was without a jacket and there was a bluish tint to her skin.

'Rachel, what are you...?'

'I got a taxi,' she said not looking at Suzie. 'They don't know I'm here. I left as Phil was calling the police, Katie in her room. Crying.'

She was staring at the room, the doorway to where Adam was, her eyes fixed. Unblinking.

'I realised that once the police knew,' she said quietly, 'that this couldn't happen.'

Suzie shook her head, not understanding.

'And I'd never get to see him. The man who did all this. Who abused my daughter, who turned my husband into a man who wanted to kill. I'd never get to talk to him.'

Rachel was breathing hard at the side of her. Suzie should take her into the family suite, sit her down, get her a coffee. She looked manic, unstable. Rachel needed to calm down. Suzie should call Phil, tell him to come and collect her. Rachel was not herself, her cast must be painful, she needed to rest. She clearly wasn't thinking straight, running to the hospital like this, alone. To the place where the man who'd ruined everything was. Who knew what Rachel was thinking as she stood there, staring into the room where Adam lay? She looked deranged, exhausted and unhinged. Suzie should call her family, tell them where she was, take Rachel away. Instead, she took a deep breath.

'He's in there, Rachel,' she said pointing to the room she'd just come out of. 'Adam is in there.'

31

Rachel

Phil had been trying to get hold of Jessica when I left. Katie had gone to her room, she was confused, upset and couldn't stop crying. She ran upstairs as Phil went to make the calls. He'd rung a solicitor, and was trying to get a message to Jessica, who was at college, oblivious to it all.

We needed to tell her, to talk together as a family. To get legal advice and make some kind of plan before we called the police. And as I sat there, listening to Phil's low tones from the other room, it occurred to me that once we did tell the police the truth, once Phil had confessed, and solicitors and lawyers and whoever else was involved, then I'd never have an opportunity like this again.

He was lying in a hospital bed, not very far from where my family was imploding and he was conscious. Once I had the idea, it wouldn't leave me. I knew I had limited time and I had my mobile phone.

The taxi arrived in ten minutes. By that time Phil had spoken to a solicitor and was trying to get hold of Jessica. I saw it pull up and I didn't even get my jacket, just grabbed my handbag and left. I figured I had a good fifteen minutes before they realised I was gone, Katie would stay in her bedroom and Phil had a long list of calls to make whilst he still could: his parents, people at work, so I didn't panic.

I wasn't surprised to see Suzie there, coming out of that room, her hand over her mouth like she might throw up. She looked like I felt, raw. And then I was in the room. With him. Alone. A body in a bed. Me and him. The man who'd ruined it all.

Monitors and equipment surrounded us and I wanted to take up my crutch and use it as a weapon. I could slice through all the equipment that was keeping this man alive, knock them over, send them flying. The rubber handle would serve me well as I lifted the crutch and brought it down sharply across his body. I could smash it down on him. Again and again. I'd get quite a bit of damage done before they stopped me.

'Ughmmmm.'

It was a low sound, a slight gurgle at the end of it. I hadn't expected him to speak. I knew he was awake but I didn't think he'd be making noise. I went forward slowly.

'Sssssummmm…'

His hand looked as if it were waving. It was dangling around from the elbow.

'Sssssummmm…'

I stopped. He thought I was Suzie. Of course. She'd just left and he couldn't see my face. As far as he was concerned, I was her, come back in. I went forward and peered over him. Monitors were strapped to his chest, a clamp on his finger, drips attached to his arm, tubes going under the sheets, dressing covering the top half of his head and swollen features. His complexion was grey and he looked like a zombie, just coming back from the dead.

I studied his face, drank in every inch of him, and then, I laughed. Was that it? Was this him? Suzie had described him as handsome as Adonis himself, and Katie had said he was charming. She said he made her feel safe. And here he was. He looked so small. Feeble. Pathetic. He didn't even have that big of a build.

His face was swollen but now I studied him I could make out the high cheek bones, the curls of hair from under his bandage. I could begin to see what he may have looked like, how he could've been.

'Sssssmmmmmm…'

'Gone,' I told him. 'She's gone now. You won't be seeing her again.'

His eyes were bloodshot and rolling, but I could see he was desperately trying to control them. Slow blinks in between which he made short focus, a brief connection before they went again.

'Anyone there?' I asked. 'Can you hear what I'm saying?'

He looked at me.

'My name is Rachel,' I said, 'but you'll know me better as Katie's mum.'

Our eyes locked. That was enough. He knew. I was certain. He might be drugged and struggling to keep up, but he was there, he understood. But that was fine. I had time. I could do this slowly, wait until he understood everything I was about to do.

'My husband ran you over,' I told him and waited whilst he did a very slow blink. His head rolled and I went to move it back. My crutch dropped to the floor as I moved my arm, I took a second to regain my balance and then I took my hand and got hold of his chin. His flesh was warm and clammy, there was something wet on his cheek. I turned his head so he was looking at me again.

'My husband ran you over,' I repeated, 'because you abused our daughter. You abused Katie.'

His eyes went wide for a moment and then I could see it, the trace of denial, the momentary defence.

'Don't you dare,' I told him. 'Don't you fucking dare. You abused her, made her pose for you, made that film of her. Made her do *that*. She's fourteen you bastard. *Fourteen*.'

He winced in pain and I realised my grip on his chin had got hard, my fingers were clamped around his swollen face like a vice. He was trying to roll his head away from me, his greasy hair sticking to the sides of his temples but I held fast.

'You know why I'm here, don't you?' I asked and my voice was calm, it was then that I realised it was the first time I hadn't felt in a state of panic for days. The first time since I'd been at the retail park that my heart was beating normally, that my stomach wasn't swirling in a storm of anxiety. It was the first time I could think clearly.

For a second, he seemed to focus. His eyes met mine and I nodded.

'That's right,' I told him. His mouth tried to form a word but it was lost as I still had hold of his jaw. 'I'm here to tell you that it's over, it's all over. You are over.' He'd started to drool a little, my fingers were getting wet but I couldn't move them. I needed him to see me, to understand.

I looked at the wires and machinery keeping him alive. All the technology surrounding him, all the money keeping him going. I thought of the professionals, the nurses, the consultants, all helping him get back to the monster he was before. The NHS was struggling enough, did we need to help people like him? Couldn't we save billions if we stopped trying to save the ones who really shouldn't be saved?

I looked at the monitor that was in charge of his heart. That small pulse. There were thick pillows behind his head. What if I took one of those pillows? How much pressure would I have to apply?

The room was dark and apart from the hum of machinery, it was quiet. I had time. There would be syringes in here somewhere. I'd heard that if you injected air into someone, it would enter the bloodstream and cause an embolism. Or what if I pinched the drip, or the long thin tube that was taped to his arm? What if I dislodged that, removed it from the IV filter, would that mean air was entering him rather than the lifesaving medicine he was getting? Would the monitors alert the staff before it was finished?

'Rachel?'

It was Sergeant Bailey. I blinked rapidly at him as he came beside me and got hold of my arm. It was fixed, I couldn't move it.

'You can let go now,' he said and I shook my head. 'Rachel, we know. We're here, you can let go of him.'

He went to my fingers that were still clamped around Adam's jaw and began to peel them off, one by one.

'Your family is worried about you,' he said as he removed my hand from Adam's face, 'no one knew where you were. He alerted us, your husband. He's told us it all, Rachel, and we've had a call from Ms McFadden. Some new evidence.' He looked to the bed, to Adam who was now trying to say something, a low sound coming from him, 'but you know all about that, don't you?'

'Nummmmbffff.'

We both stared at him for a moment.

Sergeant Bailey picked up my crutch that had fallen to the floor.

'You've two girls who need you,' he told me as he handed me my crutch. 'Who are going to need their mum very much indeed, Rachel, so let's not be stupid here, alright?'

I took it from him, regained my balance.

'Come with me now, you shouldn't be in here. Let's go get a nice cup of tea.'

I looked back to him, to Adam, the monster lying in the bed.

'I know,' Sergeant Bailey said before I could argue my case. 'If it had been my daughter I'd have wanted to do the same, but let us do our job, Rachel. We'll deal with him now, let's you and me go...'

'Sergeant?' It was his partner, the younger one with the overbite. 'Suspect has arrived at the station, he's in with his solicitor. The new evidence has been verified and we need...' He went on to list the state of play whilst I turned back to Adam. The man who was responsible for destroying everything. It would only take me a second. A pinch or pull of something while Sergeant Bailey was distracted, if I reached...

Then the alarm went off.

It was a flashing thing, loud and intruding. Adam was rolling his head, his large swollen head, swinging from side to side. The drool from his mouth was collecting under his chin and he was making a terrible sound. A low, formless moan. He tried to raise his head and it was then I saw his mouth had dropped heavily on one side, his whole face had dropped on one side. It was sagging down as if being pulled by invisible weights.

'Good God,' Sergeant Bailey said as staff ran into the room. There were suddenly nurses everywhere, shouting, moving. I was swept aside, ushered out along with

Sergeant Bailey who helped me get to the family suite. He left me there with his partner at the door whilst he went off to seek out a consultant, a doctor, to use his position to gain information.

I sat in that family suite and thought about my girls. My two beautiful girls. My husband who was sat in the police station, my best friend who was handing in evidence against her fiancé and I prayed.

I was never one to be religious, but I sat there and prayed as hard as I could. I made silent pleas with a deity I didn't fully believe in and begged that he should die. Prayed with everything I had that Adam Staple would go away. That he would never wake again.

One Year Later

Christmas Eve

Mild frost. No snow or rain forecast.

Epilogue

Rachel

Adam Staple did not die.

He suffered a massive stroke after regaining consciousness that left him in an immobile state. It was never determined what caused the stroke, or why it happened, only that it had.

'Locked-in syndrome' is how Sergeant Bailey describes it. 'He can understand everything, is conscious but completely paralysed. He can only communicate by blinking.'

I don't quite know the rules on sentencing a paralysed man, or how they'll determine his time in jail. It's a big police investigation. Everything Suzie gave them and then, new evidence emerged. Adam Staple has a criminal history. He'd been in jail before for similar crimes and as the police investigated further, it transpired that he was working with others, so the case is still ongoing, but for now, his condition is enough. It's enough for all of us to know that he'll never walk again, never talk again, never *move* again.

I was taken back to my family whilst Adam Staple struggled with his life. They were at the station, along with the solicitor and Suzie, and when they saw me, my girls and my husband, they ran forward. We all clung to each other as if in the centre of a tornado, everything rushing erratically around us. It was one of the most difficult days of my life. Explaining what had happened and why. I wanted to be angry with Katie, to shout at her for being so stupid, for lying to us, for knowing all along that this man was everywhere and for trusting him and not us and yet, how could I be cross with her?

He was an expert. Skilled and experienced in deception. Grooming and exploiting young girls was his speciality, he played on all of the things she wanted, used her childish vanity and naivety to his advantage. The woman they got to see us at the police station explained it better than any of us. She made us all see how Adam had targeted Katie, he'd used classic predatory behaviour, and, he'd done it many, many times before.

She's still suffering, even now, each time we visit Phil, each time we go through the gates, go through the checks, the burden of it lies heavy on her shoulders no matter how much we try to take it away. We insist it wasn't her fault, we've explained that no one blames her. We've enrolled her in more counselling and we're in family therapy but the damage will be there for some time. It's going to take a while for her to heal, but I'm so grateful. So bloody thankful that we found out when we did, because when I hear the stories of what happened to the others, it could've been so much worse.

Phil was charged and then out on bail after his confession, but his arrest was imminent anyway. Sergeant Bailey had worked out that his alibi was false. Phil's smudged train ticket, his hopeful thoughts that the CCTV cameras wouldn't have caught him were absurdly optimistic. The only thing that helped his case was that he confessed before they got the chance to arrest him. We had time before he went to court and we spent every second we could in that time together, as a family. We consoled Katie, explained it to Jessica and my daughters grew up in those days as I would never have wanted. But, they did. It happened.

'How much longer, Mum?'

I checked my watch. 'They'll be here in fifteen minutes,' I told Katie. 'Now get upstairs and check the guest room again will you? Put those clean towels on the bed.'

I looked about my kitchen. Bizarre to think that before this past year, I'd hardly cooked a family meal in it. I used to let Della do everything. Even though my job was as a caterer, I would let Della feed the girls and then eat alone or make something for me and Phil afterwards. It was only when I let Della go that I realised I'd not sat down and eaten with my daughters in over five years.

I was making a Christmas Eve curry for nine and it smelt delicious. It was hard to believe that my mother, her partner, and Phil's parents were staying with us over Christmas but that's what was happening. It was funny really, I'd always thought of Phil's parents as estranged, always thought my mother the same, but when they heard the news, they surprised me. Everyone surprises me actually, the level of support and concern from our friends and family overwhelms me. It still does. No one is as ever as judgemental as you fear.

'All set for Nana, Mum!' Katie called down and I nodded.

Her resilience and determination to get on with life is humbling. It could be the fact that her grandparents have rallied round, or that I'm no longer working so much and I'm at home for her, but Katie has made me so very proud.

Each time we visit Phil, she cries, we all do. But Phil makes it as good as he can for us. He's upbeat, I don't know if he's making it all up for our benefit, but he says prison isn't so bad. Apparently, he's a bit of a hero in there. Once they all learned what he'd gone inside for, their attitude to him changed. I don't buy it. Prison is prison no matter how respectful the inmates are, but I'm grateful to him for painting a nice picture for me and the girls. With good behaviour he could be out in a few years. We hoped for less, the solicitor made a strong case but the fact was Phil had intentionally tried to hide his crime.

He'd run someone over, provocation or not, and then left the scene. On top of that, he also lied to the police, tried to get rid of the evidence and so the result was prison. I want to scream at how unfair it is, how unjust, but I know that it isn't. What Phil did was wrong, it may have been done for the right reasons, but it was still wrong whichever way you dress it up.

I checked the curry one last time and then opened the wine, letting it breathe before they all arrived. I'd downloaded some Christmas music and went to set it up, wondering at the kind of woman I used to be before it all happened. I used to tell people that I didn't have time for music. Didn't have the time to sit and listen. I'd boast how busy I was to people, enjoyed listing off my commitments as if they were badges. 'Look how brilliant I am!' I'd be implying as I told them of how little free time I had. 'See how in demand I am! How indispensable, what a vital person I am!' If I could walk back in time I'd give myself a good shake. I'd slap myself about the face and shout, 'Wake up, you foolish woman, no one cares.'

I've still not quite got my response right for when people talk about it. Yesterday, a woman who'd read about

Phil's arrest in the *Chronicle* asked, 'That your husband then? The vigilante?' and I didn't know what to say. So I said nothing. I need to work on that.

The investigation into Suzie's role was brief, and once it became clear she wasn't involved she got an insurance pay-out. Business partnership insurance. It was the bank that told her, because although Suzie had let Adam sort out her finances, and steal all of her money, it seemed the loan she'd taken out involved free insurance. It paid out a lump sum should either of them die or have a critical illness. She was able to pay off what she owed and still have her flat but understandably she sold that as soon as she could. She wanted nothing that reminds her of Adam, or of her life with him, and besides, there were loan sharks involved. Names and numbers she handed over to the police, so she didn't want to be around should they call on her again.

I'd invited her to spend Christmas with us, but she was in Hawaii and couldn't get back. In the past year she'd set herself up as a travel photographer, working for some government tourism organisation out there or something. We wrote to each other, sent cards, that kind of thing, but as she explained at the time, she couldn't stay. After what the men in our lives had done, we couldn't run a business together. And besides, I wanted to close my businesses up. I just did consultation work now, nothing more. The girls were my priority and if it meant cutting back and penny-pinching then so be it.

'All set, Mum?'

Katie walked into the room. She'd had her hair cut, a short bob, and she looked lovely. It swung around her face and I went to her, kissed her cheek as we heard the rumble of a car engine outside.

'They're here!' Katie shouted, and there they were. My mother and her partner. Phil's parents. All arrived together, tanned, smiling and chatting. The most unlikely of friendships had blossomed in their communal concern over us.

'Is Della coming?' Jessica asked as she came downstairs and I nodded. 'Says she'll be a little late as she's some college assignment to finish.' Jessica grinned, we still kept in touch with Della. I'd helped her apply for a grant, was helping with her finances, how to manage her money and she was now studying to become a teacher.

'Hello, love.' It was my mother, ridiculously dressed in a long purple skirt and red velvet shawl. She came over and kissed me on the cheek, she'd got dreadlocks and they tickled my chin as she leaned in. 'How're you doing?'

I hugged her, smiled and bit back any urge I had to comment on her attire or hairstyle.

'Good,' I told her. 'I'm glad you're here.'

'Rachel, are we in the downstairs room again?' Phil's mother asked. 'Did you manage to switch off that radiator, it was so warm in there last time?'

'I did,' I told Phil's mother. 'And it's all ready for you.'

I helped Phil's parents in with their cases and watched Jessica and Katie chatter with them all as they went inside.

Tonight we'd eat together, and tomorrow, Christmas Day, we'd speak to Phil in jail. Tell him about the ridiculous presents we'd got each other, passing the phone around and later, I'd write him a letter detailing how irritating his parents and my mother could be, hoping it would amuse him. We'd share presents, overeat, drink and generally have a nice time. It was something that I'd have thought unthinkable a few years ago. Something

I would've hated, protested against, but now I was so pleased they were here.

They were family. They were here for the girls. For me. And as I watched them all pile into our house, I thanked my lucky stars for them and vowed to enjoy every second I could.

To take things at the slowest pace I could. No running around, trying to make sure everyone was okay, no proving how indispensable I was and how efficient I could be. No showing off or playing the martyr. No getting annoyed and snapping.

I would do nothing but appreciate how precious each moment was, each second, because now I understood that tomorrow is never promised and anything can happen at any time. Anything at all.

Acknowledgements

I would like to thank everyone who gave me support and encouragement whilst writing this book. My wonderful agent, Jane Gregory and all of the team at Gregory & Co, Stephanie Glencross, Claire Morris, Mary Jones and Irene Baldoni. My brilliant editor Louise Cullen, and the team at Canelo for all their work and offering me such a great opportunity.

I am also very grateful to Patricia and Roland Young, Kirsty Brennan, Jill Pilkington, and Heather Peake for their unwavering support and for reading the early versions. Chris Whittaker for his legal advice and Debbie Leatherbarrow for her fantastic critiques. I also need to thank my fellow writers on the Curtis Brown Creative 2014 online course who saw this as an initial idea and helped me shape it.

A special thanks goes to Paula Daly for her unwavering encouragement, and above all my gratitude goes to Stephen, Aidan and Talia. Thank you for listening to every idea I have, for helping me come up with new ones, for the special writing pens and pads and for your never ending support and love. Thank you.